Adolf Alt

Lectures on the Human Eye

In its normal and pathological conditions

Adolf Alt

Lectures on the Human Eye
In its normal and pathological conditions

ISBN/EAN: 9783337369637

Printed in Europe, USA, Canada, Australia, Japan

Cover: Foto ©Andreas Hilbeck / pixelio.de

More available books at **www.hansebooks.com**

LECTURES

ON

THE HUMAN EYE

IN ITS

NORMAL AND PATHOLOGICAL CONDITIONS

BY

ADOLF ALT, M. D.

Lecturer on Ophthalmology and Otology in the Trinity Medical School
Toronto, Canada

WITH 95 ILLUSTRATIONS BY THE AUTHOR

DEDICATION.

PREFACE.

THE histological conditions of the human eye have of late received a good deal of attention, and their study has been opened to a wider circle by a number of atlases, which, like the one published conjointly by *Pagenstecher & Genth*, and another by *Becker*, can boast of an excellent execution.

A book treating systematically on this subject, and especially on the histological conditions of the pathological human eye, whose execution and price would allow it to be of usefulness to every one interested in this matter, has been to this day a want often felt.

For quite a number of years I have been engaged in collecting for my own instruction, microscopical specimens of normal and pathological eyes. This material for examination, especially its pathological part, has by the kindness of Dr. H. Knapp, of New York, and a great many other colleagues, to whom my sincerest thanks are due, become so large, that I think it in season to give the results of my researches to the medical public in systematic order. I have confined myself, however, in this book entirely to the eye-ball itself, and have left the accessory parts to be treated at a later period, when I shall be better able to do so than I can at present, on account of the scarcity of material which is at my disposal. Furthermore, I have given especial attention to the pathological conditions of the eye-ball. This I thought only natural, as with regard to the normal conditions I could bring forward but little that was new; and I could doubtlessly presume that all my readers would be more or less acquainted with these.

All of the illustrations are drawn from my own specimens, and I have anxiously tried to copy only what I really saw without being influenced by pre-conceived ideas.

I have thought it unnecessary to enlarge the book by an elaborate record of all the authors and articles I consulted, when studying up this subject, as a summary of them may be found in *Graefe & Saemisch's* cyclopedia. I have endeavored, however, to do justice to every author whose opinion I stated, confirmed, or disagreed with, by adding the name in brackets. If in consequence of having only my own comparatively small library at my disposal, I should have unconsciously omitted some, or been mistaken with regard to others, I beg herewith the pardon of the persons offended. Since the German manuscript, of which this book is a translation, was finished during November, 1878, of course I could not take into account the literature of this year.

This book is an elaboration of the notes written down while lecturing on the subject under consideration, at the New York Ophthalmic and Aural Institute in 1876 and 1877. Since these lectures were kindly and forbearingly received by my audience, I may, perhaps, venture to hope that they will also find readers who will peruse them in the same spirit. And if this book should be able to enlarge the interest already taken in the study of the histology of the finest human organ, and to act as a new stimulus to renewed strife to fill up the chasms yet unfilled in our knowledge, what labor I had to bestow on it will be amply repaid.

My sincerest thanks are due to Dr. T. R. Pooley, of New York, who has kindly undertaken the revision of the manuscript and proofs of my volume with a view to the correction, as far as practicable, of any errors of style or expression.

THE AUTHOR.

TORONTO, CANADA, *August*, 1879.

CONTENTS.

ILLUSTRATIONS.

THE HUMAN EYE.

I.

CORNEA.

1. NORMAL CONDITIONS.

THE tissue of the cornea consists of the following parts, viz., the epithelium, *Reichert's* or, as it is commonly styled, *Bowman's* layer, the parenchyma, *Descemet's* membrane and its endothelium, blood and lymphatic vessels and nerves.

The epithelial layer of the cornea viewed from the surface presents a delicate mosaic, formed of cells some of which angular, and others round. Each of these cells possesses a large, round or oval nucleus, in which usually several nucleoli may be seen. A small amount of cementing substance unites the cells with each other, and can be easily demonstrated by staining the cornea with nitrate of silver or chloride of gold.

In teased specimens of this superficial part of the corneal epithelium we frequently find such cells lying on their edge. They then appear considerably broader around the nucleus, not unlike the blood-corpuscles of the amphibia (*Waldeyer*).

These flattened cells form several layers.

Beneath them follow several layers of cells, characterized by being less flattened and bearing offsets. Of these we have again two distinct kinds. The one bear small offsets all over their surface—serrated cells—and the other have only one, two or three broader offsets on their inner surface. The small offsets of the former, which lie more superficially, interlace with each other. The large offsets of the latter, which lie nearer to *Bowman's* layer, dip into the interstitia between the cells of the underlying layer. Each of these cells again

has a large round or oval nucleus with several nucleoli.
I often also found in this layer cells with two nuclei and
smaller ones of apparently recent date. The same cementing
substance which unites the cells of the superficial layer, is
also found between these.

The innermost part of the epithelium is formed of one
single layer, called the basal layer. Its cells are long and
cylindric or club-shaped. Their form, however, varies greatly.
Sometimes they are broader in their outer and sometimes in
their inner part ; some are cone-shaped, while others have one
or two notches, in which the neighboring cells fit. They
all have a round or oval nucleus with nucleoli ; some of them
also have two nuclei (*Waldeyer*). These cells, too, are united
by the same cementing substance, and thus all the different
layers of the epithelium are united into one.

Waldeyer is of the opinion, that the new formation of
epithelial cells takes place in the basal and middle layers.
The corneal epithelium, however, consists altogether of living
cells, as even the most superficial ones have a nucleus, and I
therefore see no sufficient reason for denying to one of these
layers the ability of producing new cells. *J. Arnold's* experiments on the regeneration of epithelial defects of the cornea,
moreover, decidedly prove that the new formation takes
place in all the layers.

Under the epithelium of the cornea lies *Reichert's or
Bowman's layer*. This appears as a vitreous layer, which is,
however, not distinctly separated from the underlying parenchyma. A high magnifying power shows it to be somewhat
striated, and we may split it into fibrillæ by a number of
chemical agents (*Waldeyer*). I never found cells in this
layer in its normal condition. *Bowman's* layer cannot be
readily and evenly separated from the underlying parenchyma, as fibres springing from it pass into the latter, and
vice versa. They can be readily traced between the lamellæ of the parenchyma. They also were first described
by *Bowman*.

At the periphery of the cornea *Bowman's* layer is split
up into its fibrillæ, and these pass over into the conjunctival tissue.

Waldeyer's opinion that *Bowman's* layer is condensed parenchyma of the cornea, and not a separate membrane, is certainly correct. In the following we shall have to state additional reasons for this assertion.

Some few authors maintain that the outer surface of *Bowman's* layer bears small elevations in which the cells of the basal layer of the epithelium are said to fit.

The parenchyma proper of the cornea consists of the stroma, embedded in which lies a system of lymphatic canals, the cellular elements, blood vessels and nerves of the cornea.

The stroma of the corneal parenchyma is transparent and formed of exceedingly fine fibrillæ, which are united by a cementing substance. When isolated the fibrillæ appear wavy, but otherwise in no way different from connective tissue fibrillæ. I have never found elastic fibrillæ among them (*Henle*). The best agent to split the cornea into these fibrillæ, is a ten per cent. solution of common salt (*Schweigger-Seidel*). Sometimes I obtained a good view of them *in situ* by staining the cornea with logwood. It then became evident that the fibrillæ intersect each other at all possible angles, and not at right angles only, as *Waldeyer* and others maintain.

These finest fibrillæ of the corneal stroma are united into fascicles, and several of these fascicles together form a lamella. The lamellæ lie mostly parallel to the surface of the cornea, from which rule exceptions are rare.

Fibrillæ, fascicles and lamellæ are united with each other by a protaplasmatic cementing substance, which is seen as a fine homogeneous light streak between them, and has sometimes a granular appearance. We have thus an interfibrillar, an interfascicular and an interlamellar but always the same cementing substance.

Embedded in this substance, furthermore, are *von Recklinghausen's* corneal canals. It is well known that, by staining the living cornea with nitrate of silver or chloride of gold, these canals are easily demonstrated. Logwood and carmine do not answer this purpose very well. Berlin blue sometimes, but not constantly, yielded me as good pictures as gold or silver. In a plain view of the cornea thus stained, we see a system of fine canals which intersect each other at very varying angles, and which form here and there a larger cavity, which is called a lacuna. In transverse sections of the cornea we see that this system of canals (like the lamellæ) runs mostly in a direction parallel to the outer surface of the cornea, and that the lacunæ are arranged in rows lying, of course, in the same direction. The small canals, however, which unite the lacunæ of the larger canals with each other, pass through the corneal parenchyma at very different angles. In transverse sections taken from hardened specimens the lacunæ appear lens-shaped. From the plain views of a stained living cornea we know, however, that their shape varies considerably, according to the number of canals which are in connection with them.

The caliber of the canals and lacunæ is by no means uniform. As a rule, however, as pointed out by *von Reckling-hausen* and confirmed by *Waldeyer*, the canals and lacunæ which lie nearest to *Bowman's* layer are the narrowest, while those lying nearest to *Descemet's* membrane are the widest. The same rule holds good with regard to the thickness of the lamellæ in these parts of the cornea. *Waldeyer* and other authors before and with him have drawn the attention to these facts, and to the probability that the cornea consists of a conjunctival, a sclerotical and a choroideal part. We would thus find the widest canals and lacunæ in the choroideal and the smallest in the conjunctival part of the cornea.

Another means of demonstrating this system of canals and lacunæ, is to inject into them a colored fluid. *Bowman* while experimenting on the cornea of animals obtained by such injection a system of straight canals, which he called corneal tubes. As far as my experiments show, these corneal tubes do not belong to the human cornea. *Waldeyer* succeeded in injecting a colored fluid into the interlamellar and interfascicular canals. Since I could not procure *Waldeyer's* fluids in the proper condition, I made my injections with a saturated solution of Berlin blue. I thus not only obtained injections of the canals lying in the interlamellar and inter-fascicular cementing substance (as *Waldeyer*), but, moreover, a system of blue lines corresponding exactly with the arrangement of the fibrillæ, as I had sometimes occasion to see it after staining the cornea with logwood. These lines (See Fig. 1) were arranged in fascicles intersecting each other at various angles. I think, if I am not mistaken, that I have thus injected also the interfibrillæ canals, which, of course, were somewhat enlarged by the pressure exerted upon them during the injection. This system of interfibrillar canals is in direct connection with the interfascicular

Fig. 1. (1) The interfibrillar canals. (2) Interlamellar and lacunæ. N. Nerve-sheath filled with the injection-fluid.

and interlamellar canals, and all of them, as we shall see later on, are in direct communication with the canals enclosing the corneal nerves. (See Fig 1.)

Kuehne and others describe this system of canals as being filled with a continuous protoplasmatic substance. Most authors, however, resent this opinion. *Von Recklinghausen* and others after him, whose opinion I, too, share, maintain that these canals contain the nutritive (lympathic) fluid.

The canals have no walls of their own (*Waldeyer*). Contrary statements seem to be erroneous.

Besides the nutritive fluid, which fills the canals throughout, they contain three different kinds of cells, viz : fixed corneal cells, wandering (lymphatic) cells, and pigmented cells.

The fixed cells of the cornea, as they have been called by *Cohnheim*, lie in the lacunæ. Such a cell, however, never altogether fills the lacuna, in which it lies. They mostly adhere to one wall of the lacuna, and fill only about two-thirds of it. The cells appear as protoplasmatic bodies with an oval or round nucleus, usually containing several nucleoli. The protoplasma is very granular around the nucleus. *Waldeyer* succeeded in isolating these cells, and described them as very thin, completely flattened bodies, having a few short offsets. I have never been able to isolate them. I, however, frequently found their nucleus perfectly hidden by the granular protoplasma, which fact would prove that these cells are not always flat, but sometimes thicker around their nucleus.

Besides the agents recommended by *Waldeyer* and commonly used in studying these parts, I can recommend the staining of the cornea with eosine (*Dreschfeld*), an aniline color which is highly fluorescent. This fluorescence causes the outlines of the cells, etc., to be exceedingly well defined.

The offsets of a fixed corneal cell reach only a very small distance into the canals which communicate with the lacuna in which it lies.

A number of undoubted observations are on record which prove the contractility of the fixed corneal cells, and *Waldeyer* lately has seen them move about along the walls of the lacuna.

The pigmented cells which we sometimes find in the periphery of the cornea (especially in the eyes of negroes) are perfectly identical with these unpigmented fixed corneal cells. Their granular pigment is enclosed in the protoplasma, leaving the nucleus free.

Besides the fixed cells we always find in the cornea a number of wandering (lymphatic) cells. They differ in no way from those found in other organs, and they wander along the preformed corneal canals, and not promiscuously through the tissue. This is proven beyond doubt by *Genersich's* experiments, who brought living corneæ into the lymph-sacs of frogs. I have often repeated this experiment, and always with the same result, that is of finding the immigrated lymph-cells filling only the corneal canals. The same is seen in the earlier stages of inflammation of the cornea, when the structure of its parenchyma has not yet been destroyed.

The connection between fixed and wandering cells in the corneal parenchyma is not yet clearly defined. I can fully confirm the opinions of earlier authors, that fixed cells can become wandering ones. Whether, however, wandering cells can become fixed ones, is as yet an open question.

The parenchyma of the cornea is covered on its inner surface by *Descemet's* membrane. This membrane is a perfectly homogeneous, vitreous membrane, and is about two-thirds the thickness of *Bowman's* layer. I cannot agree with those authors who state it to have in transverse sections a striated appearance. No more can I concur in *Waldeyer's* opinion, who says that *Descemet's* membrane cannot readily be separated from the corneal parenchyma. Pathological specimens have taught me that a perfect detachment of this membrane is possible. *Walb* had also occasion to describe such a case.

Descemet's membrane is moreover an elastic membrane. In a previous paper I have stated its tendency to wind itself up in a spiral way from specimens of the animal eye. I can add now that I am in possession of specimens from the human eye in which *Descemet's* membrane is detached and shows three and four spiral windings. This detachment and the tendency to wind itself up spirally seem to me to prove that, unlike *Bowman's* layer, this membrane is really a separate structure, and not condensed corneal parenchyma, as *Waldeyer* seems to think. This similarity between *Descemet's* membrane and the vitreous membrane of the choroid, besides other similarities mentioned later, seems to confirm the opinion that the inner portion of the cornea is really its choroideal part.

The inner surface of *Descemet's* membrane is covered by a single layer of *endothelial cells.* These cells are not as regular and uniform in shape and size in the human eye as they usually are in the eyes of animals. They are five or six in number, angular, or round, and have a round or eliptical, sometimes bean-shaped nucleus, with one or more nucleoli. In transverse sections they often appear so flat that the thin layer is only recognized with difficulty, in other eyes they appear as large cuboid cells with a round nucleus. They are united by a cementing substance, not different from the one described in other parts of the cornea. In the angles between two or three neighboring cells, we frequently find stomata. Near the periphery of *Descemet's* membrane I nearly always find, like *Henle,* the "vitreous warts," which were first described by *Hassal.* I found them several times even in children's eyes, which proves that the opinion of *Waldeyer* and others who consider these "warts," to be a change caused by old age only is erroneous. They are round, vitreous bodies, sometimes granular, mostly perfectly homogeneous. Sometimes two or more of them coalesce, just as we shall describe later on of the vitreous (colloid) bodies of the lamina vitrea

of the choroid.   They generally push the adjacent endothelial cells aside, and alter their shape accordingly.   They are
seldom as large as the endothelial cells, are very hard, and
resist all chemical agents.

At the *corneo scleral-margin*, the region where cornea
and sclerotic pass over into each other, the tissues show certain characteristic alterations.

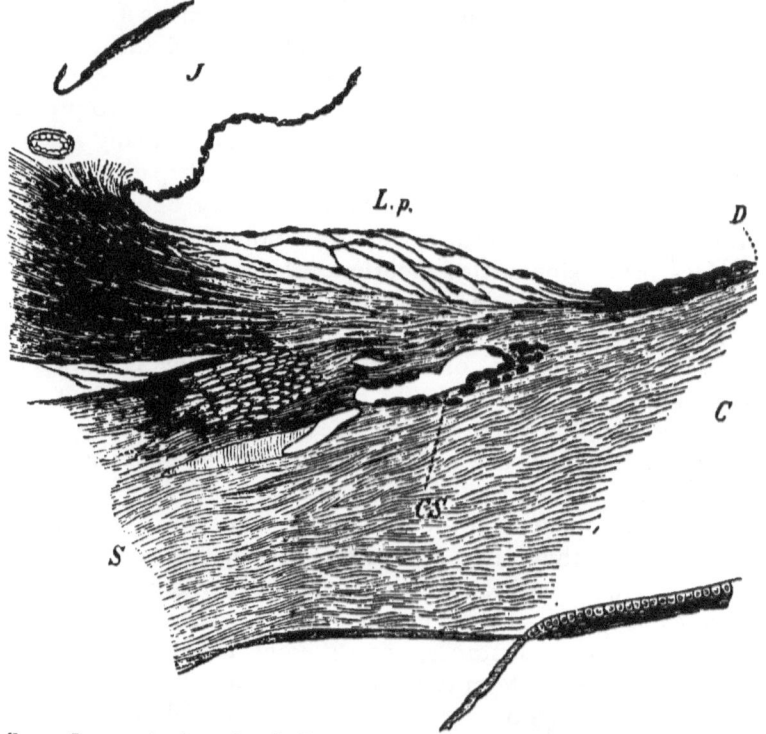

Fig. 2. Corneo-scleral margin. C. Cornea. S. Sclerotic. CS. Schlemm's canal. D. Descemet's membrane. I. Iris. Lp. The fibres of the ligamentum pectinatum with endothelial cells adhering to them.

The corneal epithelium passes directly over into the conjunctival epithelium.   The fibres into which *Bowman's* layer,
is, split up and the anterior lamellæ of the corneal parenchyma together enter the subconjunctival (episcleral) tissue
in such a way that these two parts cannot be separated without tearing the fibres.   (This is the so-called conjunctival
part of the cornea.)

The bulk of the corneal lamellæ terminate in the lamellæ and fibres of the sclerotic, from which they are not histologically, but chemically, different. The corneal canals also are continuous with those of the sclerotic (*Waldeyer*). (This is the scleral part of the cornea).

Descemet's membrane and the adjacent lamellæ undergo very important changes in this region. *Waldeyer*, when describing these parts, states that none of the previous illustrations gave an exact picture of these conditions, and I must add that his own does not do so either. The illustration herewith given (See Fig. 2) shows these conditions still better. It is drawn from a specimen taken from the myopic eye of an adult. We here plainly see that *Descemet's* membrane and the adjacent lamellæ are split up into fibres, which are partially lost in the tendon and connective tissue of the ciliary muscles and partially in the tissue of the iris. Adherent to these fibres are a number of endothelial cells which appear very similar to those covering the posterior surface of *Descemet's* membrane. Between the fibres are open cavities and canals which communicate on one side with the anterior chamber, on the other with *Schlemm's* canal. This system of cavities and canals is called *Fontana's* spaces. While in the animal eye these spaces are covered by what has been styled the "iris-trabeculæ" (Irisbalken), such trabeculæ

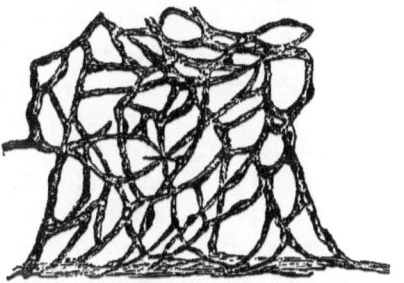

FIG. 3. Isolated fibres of the ligamentum pectinatum. The endothelial cells are shrunken and appear as darker swellings.

springing from the iris are not found in the human eye. The network of fibres formed in this region through the splitting up of *Descemet's* membrane, has been called the *ligamentum pectinatum*. In hardened specimens it can be detached with the periphery of *Descemet's* membrane, and we then find what Fig. 3 illustrates; a network of coarse connective-tissue fibres, which refract the light strongly, and have therefore a peculiar sclerotic appearance, to which a number of endothelial cells are adherent. This network passes over into *Descemet's* membrane on one side, on the other, as stated above, in the iris and ciliary body. Its outer part terminates in a fascicle of circular equatorial fibres, forming a ring which has received the name of the posterior terminal ring (*Grenzring*). Besides this there exists, but less constantly, an anterior terminal ring nearer the place where *Descemet's* membrane begins to be split up into fibres.

The *blood-vessels* of the cornea lie only in its most peripheral parts, and form a small border at the corneo-scleral margin which varies in breadth from one to two and a half mm. This difference in breadth is found in nearly every individual cornea.

These corneal blood-vessels come from the anterior ciliary arteries, and anastomose with the marginal blood-vessels of the conjunctiva, which have the same origin. The superficial arterial branches of the marginal blood-vessels very soon, after having entered the cornea, end in a capillary network which forms the so-called marginal loops of the cornea. *Leber*, in *Graefe* and *Saemisch's* cyclopedia, gives an excellent illustration of these blood-vessels. I frequently found, however, that these terminal loops when injected with a colored fluid have little cone or diverticle-like offsets, in the direction towards the centre of the cornea, which are, perhaps, remains of the fœtal præcorneal blood-vessels, and certainly must be of great importance for the pathological new-formation of blood-vessels in this membrane. In the inner layers of the cornea the capillary network passes over into comparatively broad veinous branches. The blood is carried by them to the episcleral and then into the anterior ciliary veins.

The blood-vessels of the cornea are histologically in no way different from others.

At the corneo-scleral margin from forty to forty-eight larger nerve-branches enter the posterior layers of the corneal tissue. They come partially from the anterior ciliary, and partially from the conjunctival nerves. Very soon after their entrance into the cornea they lose their double contour. They then branch off and form what is called the " narrow stroma-plexus." From this plexus smaller branches run forward, and just behind *Bowman's* layer split again into axis-cylinders and axis-fibrillæ, which pierce *Bowman's* layer and form the "sub-epithelial plexus" around the basis of the basal layer of the corneal epithelium. From this plexus again fibrillæ spring forward into the anterior parts of the epithelium and there form between the flattened cells the terminal, "intra-pithelial" plexus. Whether this is really the terminal plexus, and in what way the fibrillæ end, is as yet an open question. *Kuehne* and others say that they end in the cells. *Cohnheim* states that they have a special terminal nodule lying upon the external surface of the epithelium. Other authors maintain a free ending between the cells. My own specimens did not allow me a deciding opinion with regard to this point.

I can, however, confirm the statement of others that the larger nerve-branches lie in a system of canals which are sometimes lined with flat endothelial cells. Where the larger nerves are split up into their branches, an endothelial cell is often found lying on the nerve itself, these have been mistaken for ganglionic cells. There are, however, no ganglionic cells to be found in the cornea, in which opinion I agree with *Waldeyer*. In specimens which have been stained with chloride of gold, the axis-fibrillæ always appear varicose. *Waldeyer* is of the opinion that this varicosity is artificially produced, and does not exist during life, an opinion put forth before him by *Engelmann*.

It has been stated before that the system of canals in which the nervous fibres are embedded is in direct communication with the lympathic canals of the cornea, which is proven by injecting the latter with a colored fluid. (See Fig. 1.)

2. PATHOLOGICAL CONDITIONS.

A. Keratitis and its Results.

THE large majority of the facts collected in the following pages is derived from examinations of human eyes.

To whatever degree a cornea is inflamed, we find it to contain more cells than in the normal condition. These additional cells are chiefly round-cells and partially small spindle-shaped ones. They are the same formative cells which are called either wandering or lymphatic, and are identical with the emigrated white blood-corpuscles as we find them in the beginning in every inflamed tissue.

Cohnheim and his pupils maintain that these cells are all emigrated ones from the marginal blood-vessels of the cornea. According to *Bættcher* and others they are simply the products of the proliferating cells of the corneal parenchyma. My own examinations of the inflamed human cornea and experiments on the cornea of animals, force me to agree with those authors who believe that the additional cells, in such an inflamed cornea take their origin from both these points, viz., from the blood-vessels and the fixed (and wandering) cells. (*Stricker, Norris, Fuchs*, etc.)

I am, furthermore, convinced by my own experimental researches that the process of emigration of cells from the marginal blood-vessels precedes the process of proliferation of the cells of the corneal parenchyma. I once saw, for instance, a cornea perfectly filled with round-cells only three hours after a superficial injury. These cells could not possibly have been the result of proliferation of the corneal cells, and therefore could only be immigrated ones from the blood-vessels. These immigrated cells lie, as a rule, at first in the corneal canals, not in the lacunæ. Only when the process of proliferation begins in the fixed corneal cells, we find more than one cell in the lacunæ.

I have seen fixed corneal cells, which in this second stage contained three and four nuclei. If the process of inflammation does not stop here, the cells soon become so numerous that the tissue of the cornea suffers under the pressure and becomes gradually mortified. This necrosis of the corneal tissue may be confined to a small intraparenchymatous space (abscess) or may reach the surface (ulcer).

Whilst in the normal cornea, as we stated above, the wandering cells lie in the corneal canals only and not in the stroma, the latter cannot resist their vital power any longer in the later periods of inflammation, and we then see that the new-formed cells traverse the stroma of the cornea in all directions, totally disregarding the corneal canals.

We have in the following pages to speak of two different degrees of inflammation of the cornea, viz., infiltration-keratitis and purulent keratitis. These two kinds are, however, different only in degree; but they are histologically distinct enough from each other. Under these two heads we can, furthermore, place all the manifold kinds of keratitis which the clinicists can and must consider separately, and the histological conditions do not allow us to speak of more than these two kinds of inflammation of the cornea.

a. Infiltration of the Cornea.

The characteristic feature of infiltration of the cornea is the immigration (very rarely also the new formation) of round-cells into the parenchyma of the cornea. This immigration never leads to a perfect destruction of the latter, and only very rarely alters it at all.

The infiltration is usually confined to only a circumscribed part of the cornea, and never involves its entire thickness.

We find histologically, at first, only a number of round-cells filling the canals of the diseased part of the cornea. Later on we sometimes also see signs of proliferation in the fixed corneal cells. The round-cells lie chiefly in the inner layers of the cornea, and infiltration-keratitis but seldom affects the lamellæ which lie next to *Bowman's* layer. When the infiltration is confined, as is the rule, to the inner parts of the cornea, the epithelium remains unaltered; if it affects the lamellæ nearer the surface, the epithelium is always found in a pathological condition. It appears microscopically *in toto* irregular and lacks its normal lustre and smoothness; microscopically we find its cells very irregular in shape, granular and much enlarged, so that the whole of the epithelial layer covering the infiltrated portion of the parenchyma is somewhat thickened. This thickening may furthermore be due to serous imbibition or to proliferation and new formation of these cells. The corneal lamellæ surrounding the infiltrated part appear in no way altered.

Infiltration may heal by absorption of the immigrated cells which may or may not be preceded by the formation of new blood-vessels. These blood-vessels spring from the marginal vessels nearest the infiltrated part. *J. Arnold* has described the way in which this new-formation takes place, and I can fully endorse his views. At first we find small protoplasmatic offsets growing from the marginal blood-vessels, nearest the diseased part, which grow thicker as they grow farther into the corneal tissue. Gradually the central part of these solid offsets becomes hollow, and we find later on a protoplasmatic tube, with endothelium filled with a few blood-corpuscles. *Carmalt* and *Stricker* saw new blood-vessels being formed out of fixed corneal cells. They, however, stand alone in this experience.

This new formation of blood-vessels generally begins in the innermost layers of the cornea. Later on we sometimes find blood-vessels in the superficial layers too. The latter is the rule in cases of superficial infiltration. The new-formation of blood-vessels is sometimes accompanied by hypertrophy of the conjunctival tissue at the corneal margin, and the latter is then found to grow in between the epithelium and *Bowman's* layer, and to be filled with round-cells and new-formed blood-vessels. This interposed tissue has lately been styled pannous.

During the process of recovery, the new-formed blood-vessels either disappear or in rare cases, remain persistent. If the latter is the case, the larger ones generally have a well-defined adventitia.

Infiltration, as stated above, but very rarely alters the corneal parenchyma, and, as a rule, leaves no trace behind. In rare cases it leaves a scar. This is, however, always the case when infiltration results, goes in the purulent form of keratitis with partial destruction of the corneal tissue. If the infiltration concerns the corneo-scleral tissue, it sometimes produces sclerosis of the involved parts, which is then the result of the new-formation of translucent connective tissue between the normal, transparent lamellæ and subsequent obliteration of the involved corneal canals. This process is not to be confounded with that of the formation of a scar, since the new formation here does not replace destroyed tissue. Such a new formation of only translucent tissue takes place also around those blood-vessels which remain persistent, and is the cause of the grayish color of these parts.

We must enumerate under the type of infiltration-keratitis the following forms which clinicists consider as separate diseases, viz., corneal infiltration, parenchymatous keratitis (which does not, as a rule, show any alteration of the corneal parenchyma), pannous or vascular keratitis, phyctænular keratitis and some forms of traumatic keratitis (results of cuts inflicted by sharp or ragged-edged instruments.)

Among the forms of the clinically so-called parenchymatous keratitis there is one characterized by a network of systems of lines which are distinct from the grayish, infiltrated surrounding parts of the cornea, and cross each other at different angles. This network always lies in the superficial layers, and is seen when the narrow canals in the superficial layers are especially filled with round cells.

Phyctænula, according to *Iwanoff*, is a circumscribed infiltration of *Bowman's* layer, and always confined to the parts surrounding a nerve-branch, piercing into the epithelial layer. This simple local infiltration generally results in local purulent keratitis, with loss of substance and the formation of a scar.

Among the forms of traumatic keratitis one has always been of special interest to ophthalmologists. It has been called striped keratitis (Streifige keratitis). This form of infiltration-keratitis is found after injuries (mostly operative) on the corneo-scleral tissue. We find in such cases, besides the general dimness of the parts surrounding the wound, a number (generally from 10 to 12) grayish stripes, which start from the wound in a radiating direction towards the centre of the cornea, and after nearly reaching it are bent in the form of arches and disappear in the normal tissue. In order to find the real cause of this strange picture, I made a large number of parenchymatous injections at the corneo-scleral margin of animal and human eyes, and I came to the conclusion that these stripes are represented by the larger nerve-canals when they are in a state of infiltration. This explanation seems to be the more plausible, since, we know that at the corneo-scleral junction, from forty to forty-eight nerves enter the corneal tissue, and our operative wounds comprise, from one-fourth, to one-third of the corneal periphery. Moreover, we never see striped keratitis after wounds inflicted upon the centre of the cornea, where no large nerve-canals exist.

Infiltration-keratitis usually heals without leaving a trace, sometimes it causes sclerosis, of the involved parts, as above stated, and in rare cases (except in phlyctænula) it leads to purulent keratitis with its results. Infiltration-keratitis is furthermore constantly found accompanying purulent keratitis, and then involves the tissue surrounding the parts suffering from the purulent form of inflammation.

I have never found *Descemet's* membrane or its endothelium, altered in cases of infiltration-keratitis. This form also very rarely causes an inflammation of the tissue of the iris.

b. Purulent Keratitis.

The characteristic feature of the purulent form of keratitis is, that the increase of the cellular elements in the cornea is such, as to destroy the corneal tissue. This holds good whether the process involve only a superficial part of the corneal tissue or be deeper seated, whether only a part or the whole of the cornea be destroyed.

We can distinguish three forms of purulent keratitis, viz.: abscess, ulcer and kerato-malacia.

c. Abscess of the Cornea.

Abscess of the cornea is that form of purulent keratitis which always takes its origin, in the deeper layers of the cornea, and which may remain altogether confined to them, and never reach the surface of this membrane.

In this form of inflammation we always find a more or less roundish, flattened part of the corneal tissue filled with innumerable round-cells. The pressure exerted by these cells upon the stroma of the cornea leads to mortification and fatty degeneration of the involved parts, and thus a pus-cavity is formed. This cavity has generally the shape of a flattened globe, or is ovoid, with corroded walls. Sometimes trabeculæ may be found springing from one side of the cavity and reaching to the opposite wall. The cavity itself is perfectly filled with round-cells, which often surround a central nucleus of fatty (cheesy) detritus. The corneal tissue surrounding the abscess is in a state of infiltration, and generally most so on that side of the abscess which lies nearest the corneo-scleral margin.

In this stage the process may heal, without involving more than the parts originally attacked. The healing process always begins with the formation of blood-vessels, from the corneo-scleral margin in the way above mentioned. When the detritus and the cells are absorbed the walls of the abscess may simply heal together or the cavity may become partially or totally filled up with new-formed, (of course only translucent) connective-tissue. The blood-vessels may become atrophic and disappear or remain persistent.

As a rule, however, the process does not heal at this stage. More cells immigrate and are formed by proliferation of the old ones in the original cavity and the adjoining tissue, and thus more and more of the parenchyma, is destroyed. It may thus happen that the destruction of the tissue reaches to the outer surface—that is, a deep ulcer may be formed. In rare cases, when the abscess lies directly next to *Descemet's* membrane, this may also be destroyed, and the abscess thus opens into the anterior chamber, which may lead to the formation of an anterior synechia, when the abscess lies near the corneo-scleral margin. Moreover, the abscess can lead to a total perforation of the cornea and open at the same time upon the anterior and posterior surface of this membrane.

If the abscess does not perforate either *Bowman's* layer or *Descemet's* membrane, and its contents are not readily absorbed, the cavity may still be found after all the inflammatory symptoms have disappeared. It may then appear as a cystoid formation in the cornea. (See Fig. 4.)

Corneal abscess is very frequently accompanied by the formation of pus in the anterior chamber, which is called hypopyon. There are three ways in which the formation of hypopyon may take place. Since the corneal canals, as we have seen above, communicate directly in the ligamentum

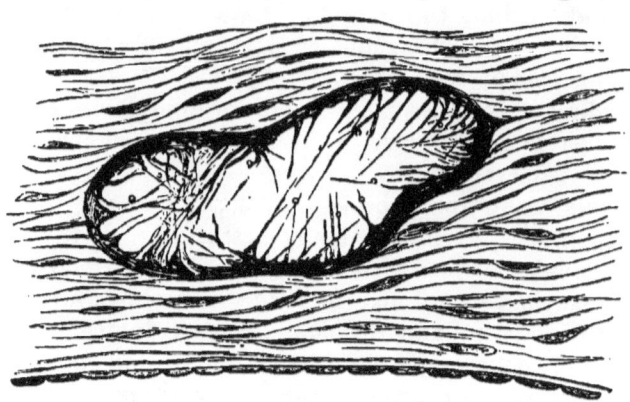

FIG. 4.—Cavity of an abscess in the cornea, after the contents have been perfectly absorbed.

pectinatum (through *Fontana's* canals) with the contents of the anterior chamber, the cells may wander into the latter through the former ; and this is probably the most common way in which, the formation of hypopyon occurs. Furthermore, if the abscess lies near *Descemet's* membrane the structure of this membrane, becomes pathologically changed. It becomes dim, and often two and three times thicker than in the normal condition. This change is soon followed by alterations in the endothelial layer. Its cells grow larger and

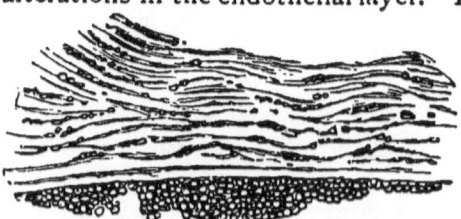

begin to proliferate, and the new-formed more or less roundish cells lie at first in little clusters on the posterior surface of *Descemet's* membrane.

FIG. 5.—Shows proliferation of the endothelium of *Descemet's* membrane, in a case of corneal abscess with hypopyon.

Later on they become detached and fall to the bottom of the anterior chamber. (See Fig. 5). If the abscess lies near the corneo-scleral margin, the iris and ciliary body frequently become inflamed also, and the inflammation of these parts is then the third means of the formation of pus in the anterior chamber. Hypopyon thus formed contains, as a rule, some fibrinous matter.

If the abscess leads to the formation of an ulcer or to total perforation of the cornea, it is the final cause of more serious results, of which we shall have to speak later on.

b. *Ulcer of the Cornea.*

Every loss of substance of the cornea, caused by purulent inflammation, and reaching to the surface, is an ulcer, whether the pathological process began originally on the surface itself, or involved at first the deeper layers only, and attacked the superficial ones at a later period.

The process of ulceration begins, as a rule, from the surface of the cornea, although, as just mentioned, it may also begin in the deeper layers. We mostly find at first an infil-

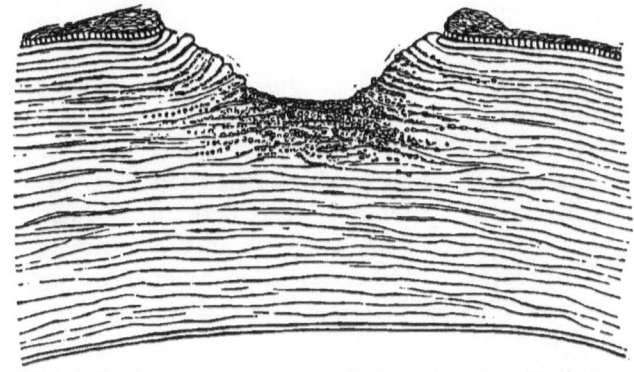

FIG. 6.—Ulcer of the cornea ; its ground and walls lined with round-cells, the surrounding epithelium proliferating.

tration of the lamellæ lying next to *Bowman's* layer. The number of cells is rapidly increased, and *Bowman's* layer as well as the epithelium are raised, and the latter begins to decay. The destruction is generally first noticed in its most superficial layers, and only gradually takes up the remaining ones. Meanwhile the attacked lamellæ and finally *Bowman's* layer also become destroyed, and thus an ulcer is formed. Its base is covered with pus, its walls are ragged, and the adjoining corneal tissue is filled with a large number of round cells, which decrease nearer the periphery of the cornea.

The epithelium surrounding the ulcer is also in a pathological condition. It becomes very much thickened in consequence of the proliferation of its cells, especially in its middle layers. The new-formed cells are nearly all serrated ones. In some specimens I found the proliferation going on also in the flattened (superficial) cells and in the basal layer. (See Fig. 6.)

The conditions are entirely the same when the ulcer is the result of a previous abscess of the cornea.

In this stage the process may stop and the ulcer heal. If it progresses, the parts surrounding it become more and more infiltrated and also destroyed, in the manner described above.

A strange change takes place in the direction of the lamellæ, which form the base and walls of the ulcer. They become bent towards the surface at an angle of about forty-five degrees. This is probably the result of mechanical influences.

If the ulcer no longer progresses, its bottom cleanses itself and its margins lose their ragged appearance. At the same time, if the ulcer is not entirely superficial, a new-formation of blood-vessels from the cornea-scleral margin takes place, as has been previously described. It seems that in these cases new vessels lie, as a rule, in the more superficial layers of the cornea. Otherwise they differ in no way from the new-formed blood-vessels we found during the healing process of an abscess.

The third stage of the disease, the reparation of the loss of substance, is ushered in by a marked proliferation of the epithelium, which sometimes very rapidly grows over the whole area of the ulcer. I am not certain whether one special layer of the epithelium is the active one in this process, but it seems to me that all the layers take an active part in it. The new-formed epithelial cells vary greatly in shape and size; they are mostly roundish, sometimes cylinder and spindle-shaped.

As soon as the epithelium begins to grow, a new and at first very delicate connective-tissue, which is filled with a great number of cells, is formed upon the ulcer. The epithelium, however, always covers the loss of substance before the new-formed tissue has reached the level of the surface of the cornea.

This new-formed tissue afterwards becomes much denser and tougher. Since *Bowman's* layer is never regenerated as such, the epithelium is no longer supported in the normal way, and grows into the new-formed connective-tissue in the shape of papillæ of different size. (See Fig. 7.) The margins of *Bowman's* layer around the original loss of substance are generally bent inward, and the new-formed tissue lies often on their outer surface, without, however, producing a thickening of the cornea. When the new-formed tissue is perfectly dense it appears somewhat lamellar, like the normal

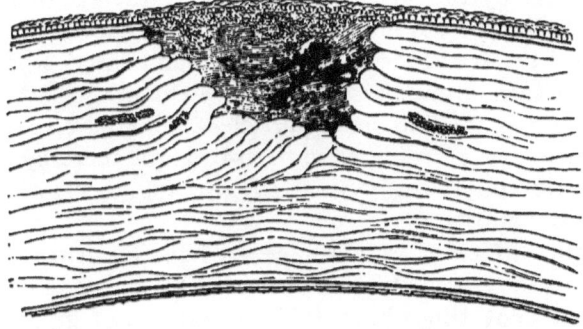

FIG. 7.—Healed corneal ulcer. The loss of substance filled with new-formed connective-tissue into which the epithelial layer sends papillary offsets.

corneal tissue. The lamellæ are, however, much smaller than the normal ones, and are not arranged as regularly as these, but intersect each other at obtuse angles. The fascicles which form the new lamellæ are also much smaller, and show, even a long time after the healing process has been completed, a much larger amount of cellular elements than the normal surrounding corneal tissue. The new-formed blood-vessels disappear, as a rule, or they may remain persistent.

The new-formed tissue is, as is well known, only translucent, and, although it generally clears up somewhat when the process of reparation is over, it never becomes transparent.

If the progress of the ulcer does not stop in the way we

just described, it destroys more and more of the corneal tissue, and finally leads to perforation of *Descemet's* membrane. Before this membrane is perforated, however, it is generally pressed forward and protrudes towards the surface of the cornea, a condition which has been called myocephalon or keratocele. This protrusion of *Descemet's* membrane may be caused by the normal intra-ocular pressure; but it is, however, usually increased.

If *Descemet's* membrane be thus perforated, the aqueous humor flows off, and the iris may become either simply attached to the cornea or prolapse into the wound-canal, which conditions we shall have to describe more fully later on.

With the microscope we are always able to detect a former ulcer by the following conditions: the irregular thickness of the epithelial layer, the partial absence of *Bowman's* layer, and the translucent, irregularly lamellated scar-tissue, with its abnormal number of cellular elements.

Sometimes we find small particles of metallic substances in this scar-tissue, which have been brought there by the use of metallic collyriums. *Saemisch* also found cavities filled with colloid substance.

All the different forms of ulcers, as distinguished by clinicists, show these same histological conditions. The parasites, which in recent times have been considered of great importance in the formation of every disease, have, of course, also been found in the cornea. I have never been able to consider them as the important agents they are thought to be by others, at least in diseases of the eye.

γ. *Keratomalacia.*

It is the characteristic feature of keratomalacia, that the deleterious new-formation of cells concerns and destroys the whole of the corneal tissue.

In all other points this process is the same as has just been described. The whole of the corneal tissue becomes mortified and is thrown off. The ensuing loss of substance is repaired through tissue growing from the surrounding conjunctiva and episclera. When the loss is thus perfectly repaired by the newly-formed connective-tissue, we find what has been styled by clinicists phthisis anterior, namely, a grayish, translucent connective-tissue in the place of the cornea, which is either flat or, as often happens in a later stage through morbid changes in the interior of the eyeball, drawn inward.

Although it is not out of place to consider abscess, ulcer and keratomalacia as three different and distinct types of inflammation of the corneal tissue, I will here again state that from an abscess an ulcer may originate, and that kerato-malacia may as well be the result of an abscess as of an ulcer.

In all of these inflammatory processes of the corneal tis-sue the conjunctiva and episclera are more or less altered. The purulent form of keratitis often cause inflammatory pro-cesses in the tissue of the iris sometimes of the whole uveal tract, and in a small number of cases causes panophthalmitis.

THE RESULTS OF KERATITIS.

a. *Formation of Scars and Pannus.*

Losses of substance, which concern only the epithelial layer, and leave the substantia propria of the cornea intact, usually heal, without leaving a trace. If, however, the smallest particle of the corneal tissue itself is destroyed, scar-tissue is formed to repair the loss. This newly-formed tissue is only translucent, and according to the degree in which it lacks transparency, we call it clinically *nebecula*, *macula* or *leucoma* of the cornea. It is evident from this that as a rule only the purulent forms of keratitis will pro-duce persistent alterations in the corneal tissue.

As above stated infiltration keratitis may lead to sclerosis of the cornea, and this is mostly the case when infiltra-tion lies near to or at the corneo-scleral margin. This sclerosis has erroneously been called interstitial keratitis. As already stated, the sclerosis is caused by the new-formation of connective-tissue between the *normal* lamellæ of the sub-stantia propria of the cornea, which obliterates the corneal canals, which by retracting reduces the quantity of fluid in the tissue of the lamellæ and produces atrophy. This new-formed tissue is formed from the fixed and wandering corneal cells, and the sclerosed tissue, furthermore, is distinguished from scar-tissue by its want of cellular elements.

Nebecula, macula and leucoma are clinical names for the same histological condition, namely, scar-formation in the tissue of the cornea. The way in which these scars are formed has been described above under the head of Purulent Keratitis. Besides the cavities filled with colloid and metallic deposits which were mentioned at the same place, deposits of lime are not infrequently found in such scars, and they consist of granules which are round or shell-like. (See Fig. 8.)

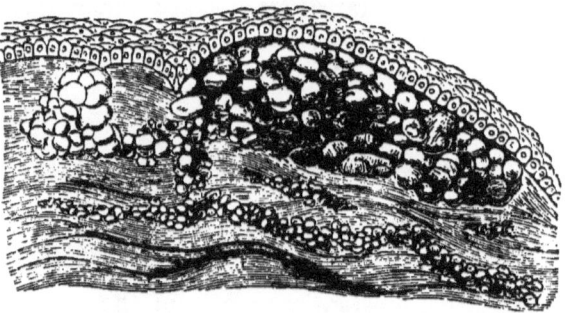

Fig. 8.—Deposits of lime in the cornea of a staphylomatous eye.

They lie mostly in the anterior parts of the cornea, directly under the epithelium, and I think they begin in the blood-vessels, whose ramifications are often beautifully shown by these deposits. It is not improbable that ossification of the cornea described by *Stellwag* was in reality nothing but such deposits of lime.

In phthisis anterior and large scars of the cornea the epithelium is often very much altered. It is found mostly horny or in a state of colloid metamorphosis.

Here we should mention, what is called a *facette*. Although I never had the occasion to examine a facette microscopically, it may be deduced from clinical observation that in such cases the loss of substance is covered by epithelium only, without the new-formation of connective-tissue. The peculiarity of a facette is therefore that the loss of substance is in reality never filled up again, although covered with epithelium, and this is why it hardly ever shows any dimness.

The formation of what is called pannus of the cornea has been spoken of before. I have here only to mention the conditions of persisting pannus. In pannous corneæ we find large blood-vessels with a well-developed adventitia and capillary blood-vessels. It is always easy to trace their origin back to the vessels of the corneo-scleral margin. Where they lie in normal corneal tissue they appear surrounded by a new-formed tissue, which when young is fine and cellular, and later on becomes tough and bare of cells. This tissue causes the dimness of the cornea which always accompanies the pannus. Small hemorrhages are not rare in this tissue, and máy be found also in vascular scar-tissue.

As has been stated above, *Bowman's* layer, when once destroyed, is never regenerated; the same holds good for *Descemet's* membrane. The latter is, however, never destroyed to the same extent as the former, and, if the cornea has been perforated upon its outer or inner surface, *Descemet's* membrane, is always found drawn into the canal of the perforation, and adhere it to its walls.

b. Anterior Synechiæ.

Anterior synechiæ are very frequently the result of purulent keratitis, when the latter has led to perforation. The name anterior synechiæ is usually applied only to the adhesions of the iris to the cornea; there are, however, as well anterior synechiæ of the crystalline lens, or, if the lens is wanting, of the vitreous body.

In anterior synechia of the iris, this membrane may simply adhere with its anterior surface to the posterior surface of the cornea, or the iris may have been drawn more or less far into the canal of the perforation, and having grown together with the corneal tissue may there be incarcerated. If the anterior surface of the iris only is adherent to the posterior surface of the cornea, this adhesion need not necessarily have taken place at the site of the perforation, but may

also lie in the neighborhood of the latter.   The endothelium
of *Descemet's* membrane and the anterior surface of the iris
are always wanting · in these places, and is replaced by a
small layer of tissue, consisting of long delicate spindle-
shaped cells, which are transformed endothelial cells.   That
this is really the case is readily proven in specimens where
the adhesion has only partly been accomplished.   The
endothelial cells then are seen to be partly enlarged, or to
have one or two offsets, while others are already spindle-

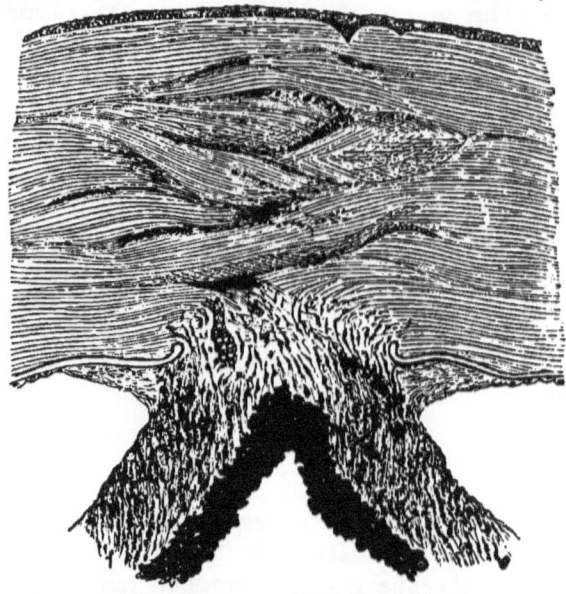

FIG. 9.—Anterior synechia between cornea and iris. The endothelium of Descemet's membrane forming a layer of spindle-shaped cells around the place where iris and cornea
are united.

shaped.   Sometimes these endothelial cells are also found to
undergo a regressive metamorphosis, and colloid degeneration is comparatively the most frequent one.

If the iris has been drawn into the canal of the perforation and there become adherent, it is after some time impossible to make out the exact line where the tissue of the iris
is united to that of the cornea, as they coalesce perfectly.
(See Fig. 9.)   The pigmented cells of the parenchyma of the
iris and the blood-vessels of the latter grow into the cornea,

and minute particles of pigment, freed by the destruction of the cells, are seen to be thrown some distance into the neighboring corneal tissue, and there remain stationary. In the beginning of this process cornea and iris are full of lymphatic cells, which later on disappear.

Descemet's membrane is in these cases generally drawn with the iris into the canal of the perforation, and sometimes its ends are bent inward upon the iris. In the first case the endothelial cells help in the formation of the scar-tissue, and can no longer be distinguished. In the second case the endothelial cells are found transformed into spindle-cells, as described above, and they form a small layer of delicate tissue in the angles, where *Descemet's* membrane is bent backward upon the iris and upon the latter.

The two different kinds of anterior synechia of the iris, viz., simple adhesion and incarceration, are found in all parts of the cornea. Their histological conditions are always the same.

Anterior synechiæ between the crystalline lens and cornea are very much rarer. They are generally combined with anterior synechia of the iris, or in rare cases seen without the former. They are furthermore mostly found in eyes suffering from staphyloma of the cornea. In all of the cases which I had occasion to examine, the crystalline lens was cataractous. Sometimes the anterior capsule of the crystalline lens was simply adherent to the inner orifice of the canal of a perforation, without being ruptured; sometimes the capsule was ruptured, and new-formed connective-tissue had grown into it. *O. Becker* states that in cases of anterior polar cataract, we have a right to diagnose an intra-uterine perforation of the cornea with anterior synechia of the crystalline lens.

Although it is probable that anterior synechiæ between the vitreous body and the cornea, especially in eyes from which the crystalline lens has been removed by an operation or an injury, are more frequent than we know of, I only once had an opportunity to examine such a specimen. (See Fig. 10.)

The specimen is taken from an eye enucleated on account of ciliary staphyloma. The following are the histoolgical conditions.

Nearly in the centre of the cornea the above described results of ulceration and perforation are to be seen. The crystalline lens is wanting. The vitreous body is healed in

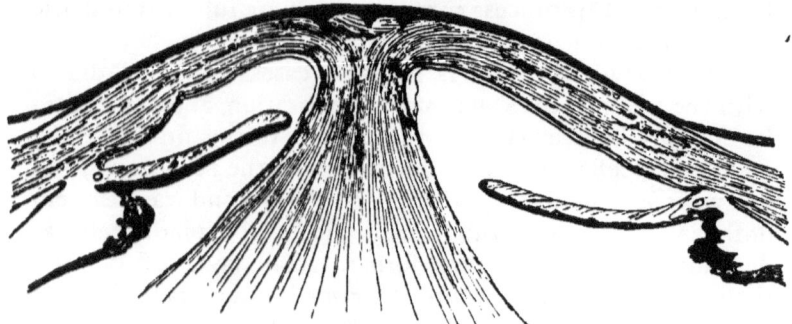

Fig. 10.—Anterior synechia between cornea and vitreous body.

the form of a cone into the scar-tissue of the cornea. It is here transformed into connective-tissue and perfectly coalesces with the corneal scar. The wound-lips of *Descemet's* membrane lie upon the iris, and can be traced farther backward than would be possible if they had simply been bent backward. A new-formation of vitreous substance must therefore have taken place. The surface of the conical prolapse of the vitreous body has a network of delicate fibrills, in the meshes of which a number of oval and bean-like cells with an oval and finely granulated nucleus are embedded. The cells of this network pass gradually over into the endothelial cells of *Descemet's* membrane, and are probably derived from them. The posterior part of the vitreous body is liquefied. (Similar pictures are drawn, for instance, in *Iwanoff's* experiments on the detachment of the vitreous body.)

Anterior synechiæ of the iris and vitreous body are of course very apt to cause chronic inflammation of the involved parts, which are continuously dragged upon in the act of accommodation. The anterior synechiæ of the crystalline lens can have the same effect by continuous pressure upon the iris. These conditions are therefore very frequently the origin of the perfect destruction of the so diseased eye, and of sympathetic affection of its fellow.

Anterior synechiæ of the iris are moreover sometimes the

origin of the so-called cysts of the iris, which will be treated of later on.

c. Prolapsus iridis and granuloma iridis traumaticum.

These will be spoken of in Chapter IV.

d. Keratoconus e cicatrice and staphyloma corneæ.

Since purulent keratitis, as has been above stated, mostly produces irritation or even inflammation of the uveal tract, it is often combined with an increase of intra-ocular pressure. The new-formed scar-tissue is therefore (the more so as the supporting layer of *Bowman* is wanting) frequently not strong enough to retain the normal curvature of the cornea.

If the scar lies in or very near the centre of the cornea, and there is no anterior synechia, the intra-ocular pressure may stretch the tissues more symmetrically, and thus produce a conical cornea (keratoconus.) (Keratoconus, which is sometimes seen as an humory malformation and without a scar of the cornea, does not belong here.) We find in these cases at a later period the radius of the whole cornea considerably shortened and the cornea, especially the central scar and *Descemet's* membrane, which is mostly unruptured, very much thinned. If the keratoconus is so large that the lids can no longer perfectly cover its apex, the epithelial layer upon it is often transformed into horny scales.

This conical stretching of the cornea may become stationary at any time; it can, however, also progress until it leads to a spontaneous rupture of the eye and subsequent phthisis, with its dangerous consequences.

If the cornea has been perforated and a partial or total anterior synechia of the iris or a synechia between iris, crystalline lens and cornea has been the result, the intra-ocular pressure frequently causes the formation of a partial or total staphyloma of the cornea. The name staphyloma of the cornea can therefore only be applied to those cases where the iris at least is adherent to the stretched and bulging scar-tissue of the cornea—that is, where an adherent leucoma yields to the intra-ocular pressure. We find, therefore, in these cases not only the corneal scar, but also the iris, unduly stretched. The latter membrane often becomes so atrophic that it is represented only by a thin layer of pigment upon the posterior surface of the cornea. The cornea is mostly attenuated in the same way as into keratoconus and atrophic; in rare cases, however, hypertrophic, and even sometimes to a high degree. (See Fig. 11.) *Manz* stated that he found

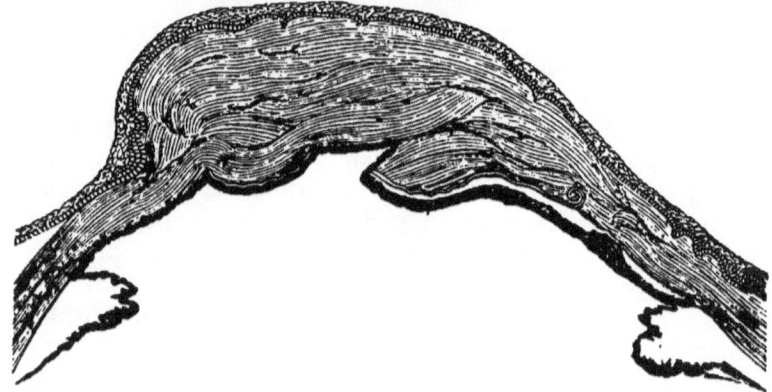

Fig. 11.—Staphyloma of the cornea, with hypertrophy of the latter.

in cases of staphyloma of the cornea an abnormally large number of serrated epithelial cells. From what has been stated above, it is evident that this condition is not peculiar to staphyloma only. If the staphyloma is so large that the lids can no longer cover it, its epithelial layer is often found horny or in colloid metamophosis. Deposits of phosphate of lime are not very rare in such staphylomatous corneæ.

e. Pterygium.

The formation of pterygium of the conjunctiva may be caused by a marginal ulcer of the cornea. This happens in the following way. The marginal ulcer causes infiltration and swelling of the adjacent parts of the conjunctiva, a fold of which comes into contact with the corneal ulcer, and gradually becomes adherent to its walls and bottom. That this may be really the case was proven in a case which I have described elsewhere, by the fact that *Bowman's* layer was severed from the periphery of the corneal tissue and bent backward upon itself. Furthermore, I found the conjunctival epithelium incarcerated between the conjunctival tissue of the pterygium and the ground of the corneal ulcer, and in a state of colloid degeneration. The whole of the tissue of the pterygium, which grows like a wedge into the corneal tissue, is merely unaltered conjunctiva, and we shall therefore have more to say upon this subject in the chapter treating on this membrane, the more so, since pterygium is not always caused by a marginal ulcer of the cornea. (See Figs. 12 and 13.)

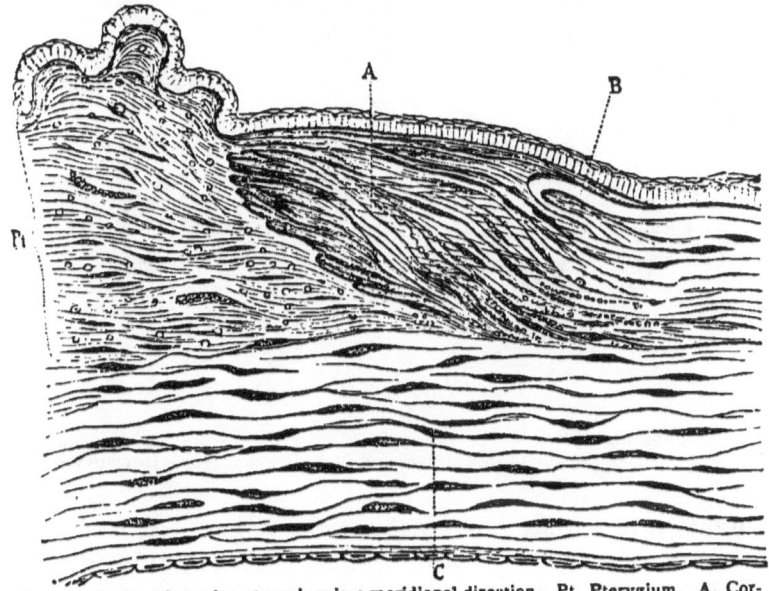

FIG. 12.—Section through a pterygium in a meridional direction. Pt. Pterygium. A. Corneal lamellæ raised by the pterygium. B. Bowman's layer. C. Normal corneal lamellæ.

B. INJURIES TO THE CORNEA, THEIR MODE OF HEALING AND THEIR RESULTS.

a. *Injuries without the retention of a foreign body.*

Injuries of the cornea which entail a loss of substance of this membrane, always lead to the formation of an ulcer, if ever so small, and heal in the same manner. They fall therefore under the head of purulent keratitis. They are rents or scratches, and such injuries by which a segment is cut off from the surface of the cornea. The conditions are different when

the cut is linear or an instrument has been thrust through
the cornea and only severed the continuity of the tissue,
without causing a loss of substance.

Let us first examine those conditions which are found when
an uncomplicated cut has been inflicted upon the cornea. This

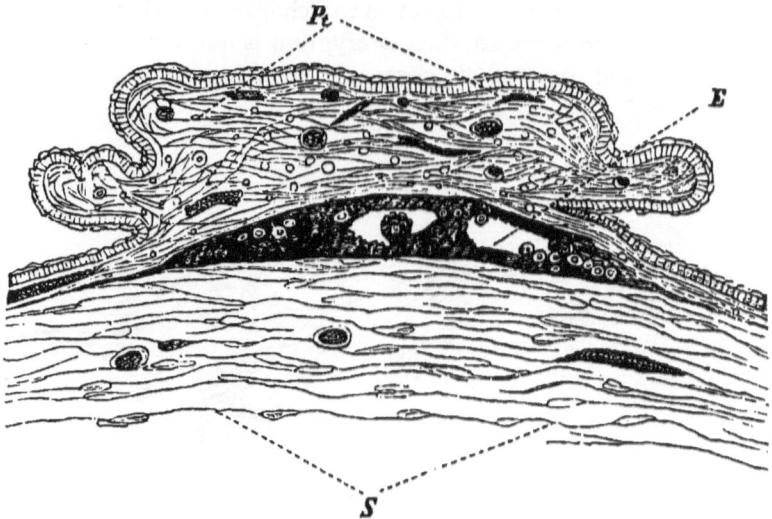

FIG. 13.—Equatorial section through a pterygium. Pt. Pterygium. S. Sclerotic (corneo-
scleral margin). E. Encapsuled conjunctival epithelium undergoing regressive metamorphoses.

cut may involve only a part of the cornea or perforate its whole
thickness, the healing process will be essentially the same.

As soon as three hours after the cornea has thus been cut,
the lips of the wound may be found infiltrated with round-
cells (cl. Infiltration of cornea.) These cells can only be immigrated ones, and cannot as yet be considered as resulting from
a proliferation of the fixed corneal cells. Very soon afterwards (in eight or ten hours) a fibrinous substance is exuded
into the canal of the wound, which is soon also invaded by
the round-cells. The epithelium margin of *Bowman's* layer
and they very soon after the injury has been inflicted, appear
bent inward, and two or three days afterward the epithelial
cells are seen to proliferate into the wound-canal. It seems
that the new epithelial cells take their origin from the
basal layer and the serrated cells; they lack, however, the

typical shape. (See Fig. 14.) While this proliferation of the epithelial cells takes place, the fibrinous exudation in the wound-canal is transformed into connective-tissue, which at first is very delicate and filled with Cells, and later on becomes denser and denser, and loses the numerous cells

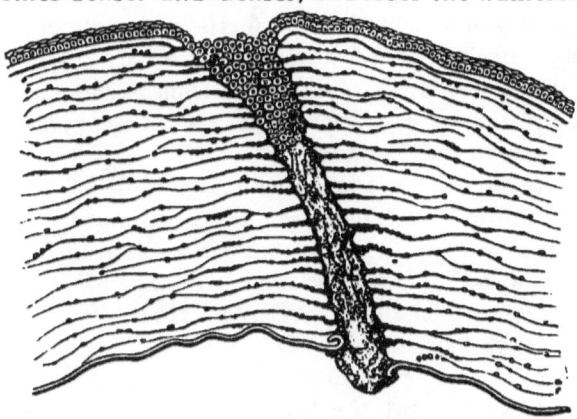

FIG. 14.—A healing corneal wound four days after it was inflicted.

accordingly. At this period of the healing process the epithelium generally fills the outer third of the wound-canal. If the wound has pierced the whole thickness of the cornea, the wound-lips of *Descemet's* membrane are, as a rule, at first projecting into the anterior chamber in consequence of the pressure exerted upon them by the fibrinous exudation. This condition, although declared to be final by *Becker*, is, however, not stationary. As soon as the new-formed scar-tissue begins to shrink, the lips of the wound of *Descemet's* membrane are dragged into the wound-canal. This condition remains stationary, and the wound-lips of this membrane are never reunited. The endothelial cells covering them begin also very frequently to proliferate, and then take part in the formation of the scar-tissue.

When the scar-tissue thus formed becomes dense and consolidated, the epithelial cells which had entered the wound-canal partly disappear again, and we then find only a small offset dipping through *Bowman's* membrane into the corneal parenchyma in the shape of an epithelial papilla. Sometimes the proliferation of epithelial cells is so considera-

ble that secondary cylinders are seen to start from this primary papilla and grow into the adjacent parts of the corneal
tissue, just as we shall later on find it when we treat of the
epitheliomatous growths of the cornea. These secondary
cylinders, however, never remain stationary, and have always
disappeared when the scar is perfectly consolidated.

Every uncomplicated wound of the cornea (which does
not cause the formation of an ulcer) heals in the way just described, and the histological conditions are so typical that we
can never err in the diagnosis.

From these facts, gleaned from the study of the healing
process of corneal wounds, it is quite possible to explain the
way in which a corneal fistula may be formed. I have never
had the occasion to examine such a fistula. But, if we assume that the epithelium may grow through the whole of
the wound-canal, or that the fibrinous exudation is by some
cause or other not transformed into connective-tissue, we
easily understand that the intra-ocular pressure, especially
if it is somewhat increased, can re-open the canal. Corneal
fistulæ are, as a rule, temporarily closed, until the anterior
chamber is refilled and the intra-ocular pressure reëstablished,
when the fistule is again opened. It is true, a corneal fistula
is very rarely, if ever, observed after a wound, but is generally
the result of an ulcer which has led to perforation of the cornea. The ulcers in these cases are, however, as a rule, so
small that their healing process is probably not greatly at
variance with the one after a perforating wound.

Wounds which lie in the corneo-scleral border heal somewhat differently, especially when accompanied by prolapse
of the iris. In the latter case the conditions greatly or altogether resemble those found after purulent keratitis with subsequent anterior synechia of the iris, and need not be dwelled
upon again here.

Corneo-scleral wounds generally gape more than those in
the centre do, and therefore the fibrinous exudation found
between the wound-lips is generally larger, and the healing
process is therefore more protracted. The fibrine, moreover, generally protudes over the outer surface of the cornea,
and the epithelium here rarely grows into the wound-canal.

The epithelial cover for the new-formed scar-tissue is two-thirds derived from the conjunctival epithelium. Since these wounds lie close to, or even sever the marginal blood-vessels of the cornea, new blood-vessels are, as a rule, formed during the healing process. Striped keratitis, which mostly accompanies the healing of such corneo-scleral wounds, has been more extensively treated of under the head of Infiltration-Keratitis.

Corneo-scleral wounds are most frequently caused by operations, especially iridectomy. When examining such eyes we find, nearly invariably, some part of the iris incarcerated in the wound. The cause of this fact is certainly that the stump of the iris is comparatively too long or the corneo-scleral wound lies too peripheric in comparison with the length of the iris-stump. (See Fig. 15.) If the stump of the iris, for instance, were as long as S in Fig. 15, and the corneo-scleral section lay in A, an incarceration of the former in the latter would be nearly impossible, while if the section lay in B, the stump could very easily be thrown between the inner lips of the section and there become retained.

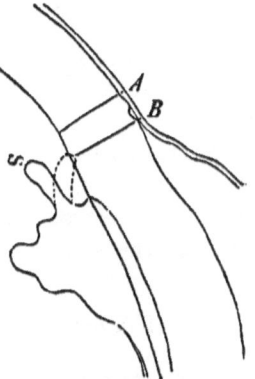

In other cases not the stump but neighboring parts of the iris become incarcerated. It will be hardly possible to evade this; but it might be rendered less frequent by making the corneal section no larger than the coloboma of the iris.

Fig. 15.—Stump of iris after iridectomy. Mode in which it becomes entangled in the corneal wound.

These incarcerations of the iris are frequently the cause of the formation of a kind of partial staphyloma, which is generally described as cystoid or ectatic scar.

In all of these cases we find pigment-molecules in the corneal canals adjoining the section. Sometimes also intact living pigmented cells from the iris wander into the cornea, and are there retained. These may, later on, proliferate and lead to the formation of a corneal cyst, which is lined by an irregular layer of pigmented endothelial cells and filled with a serum-like fluid. (Fig 16.)

It has been stated above that complicated corneal and corneo-scleral wounds may produce the same effects as pur-

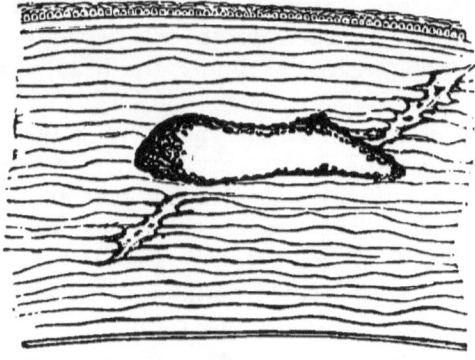

FIG. 16.—Pigmented cystoid formation in the cornea.

ulent keratitis. We must therefore also enumerate them among the factors which may lead to total destruction of the affected and sympathetic affections of the other eye.

In rare cases corneal wounds, instead of healing by simple infiltration, produce an excessive proliferation of cells, and finally necrosis of the lips of the wound. The conditions are then the same as in keratomalacia.

b. *Wounds with the Retention of a Foreign Body.*

A foreign body, if retained in the cornea after having wounded it, always produces, unless it be minutely small, a more or less circumscribed purulent keratitis, and is cast off with the pus.

Very small particles of metal only, and sometimes limesalts, are permanently retained in the cornea. They are, however, mostly brought there by the use of eye-washes after the infliction of injury, and do not cause it.

Besides these inorganic foreign bodies, organic ones are sometimes thrust into the cornea when the wound is inflicted (or during ulcerative processes), and it seems that they are retained without producing a lasting inflammatory

reaction. Among them are the particles of pigment and pigmented cells, as above mentioned, parts of *Descemet's* membrane, or the capsule of the crystalline lens and ciliæ. The
latter are always embedded in scar-tissue. The ciliæ are
generally found to be surrounded by a layer of epitheloid or
typical epithelial cells. (See Fig. 17.)

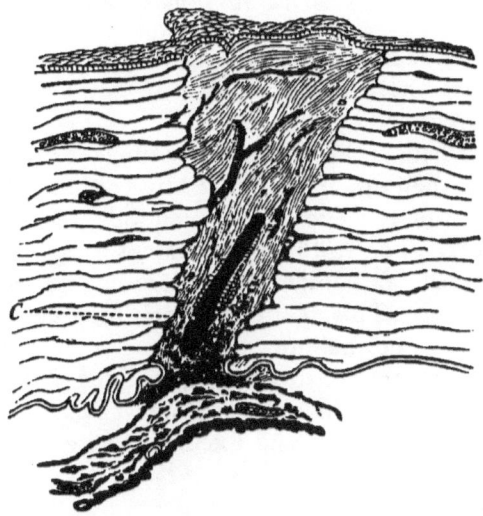

FIG. 17.—Eye-lash embedded in scar-tissue within the cornea, and surrounded by epitheli-
oid cells. C. Eye-lash.

c. Burns with Lime.

Among the injuries inflicted upon the cornea, burns with
lime are not very rare. *Gouvêa* made a number of experiments to study their exact conditions. According to his
statements, the epithelial cells and the adjoining lamellæ of
the cornea become perfectly infiltrated with lime, and thus
become necrotic. They are then thrown off by a circumscribed purulent keratitis, and the healing process is the same
as after this affection.

Such burns of the cornea are very frequently combined
with similar injuries to some part of the conjunctiva, especially
that of the lids. Since the conjunctival ulcer in such cases
generally lies just opposite to the corneal ulcer, the two
surfaces frequently heal together. This condition is called

symblepharon, if only a part of the conjunctiva and cornea are united. Extensive burns may cause the whole of the conjunctival surface of the eye-lids to become united with the eye-ball, which condition has received the name of an-chyloblepharon.

C. Regresssive Metamorphoses.

The regressive metamorphoses which are observed in the cornea (besides those found in scar-formations) are xerosis corneæ and arcus senilis.

Xerosis corneæ is the result of insufficient moistening of the corneal epithelium, and is caused by conjunctival diseases or a protrusion of the eye-ball of such a degree that the lids cannot cover it. The epithelium becomes irregular in appearance and grayish, and under the microscope is found to be horny and dying. This metamorphosis may even reach the basal layer of the epithelium.

Arcus senilis corneæ, the marginal dimness of the cornea which is found chiefly in old people, is caused by fatty degeneration of the lamellæ and fixed corneal cells, as *His* and *Canton* have described.

D. Tumors of the Cornea.

Although a large number of so-called tumors have been described in literature, I know of no real corneal tumors, and am forced to doubt the corneal origin of these tumors, the more, since hardly any of them involved the corneal tissue alone. So-called corneal tumors generally originate in the episcleral tissue, and will be described more at length under that head.

Among these tumors have been mentioned : papillomata, dermoid, sarcomatous and cancroid tumors, fibromata, and lately a granuloma of the cornea has been drawn by *Pagenstecher* and *Genth*, which I think must be considered as a granuloma of the iris.

II.

SCLEROTIC.

1. Normal Conditions.

THE tissue of the sclerotic is fibrillar, like that of the cornea. The fibrillæ, however, are not so transparent. They are united into fascicles, which interlace with each other without the regularity and parallelism so characteristic of the cornea. Here and there also elastic fibrillæ may be found enclosed in the fascicles. There are some more regularly arranged fascicles in the anterior part of the sclerotic near *Schlemm's* canal, and around the optic papilla, which run in an equatorial direction (circular fascicles).

The same cementing substance, we met with in the cornea, unites the fibrillæ of the sclerotic with each other into fascicles, and these again with each other into layers.

Furthermore, we find similar lymphatic canals embedded in the cementing substance of the sclerotic as we do in the cornea. In consequence of the irregular arrangement of the sclerotic fascicles it is, however, difficult to get as nice a view of these canals as in the cornea. It is, however, possible and my own researches support *Waldeyer's* statements on this point, that parts of these canals can be seen by staining the sclerotic carefully with nitrate of silver. The best specimens are obtained from the parts of the sclerotic adjoining the cornea. The sclerotic canals have, moreover, also lacunæ, containing fixed cells. The latter are identical with those of the cornea in shape and situation. They are flat oval bodies, with an oval nucleus, and have generally small offsets. By far the most of these sclerotic cells are unpigmented. There are, however, some pigmented ones to be found in every sclerotic around the entrance of the optic nerve. In the eyes of the white races they are but rarely found in the anterior portion of the sclerotic near the corneo-scleral margin, while they are never wanting in the eyes of the negroes.

Besides the unpigmented and pigmented fixed cells, the sclerotic also contains a comparatively small number of wandering (lymphatic) cells, which are in no way different from those found in other tissues.

The tendons of the external ocular muscles, and the external sheaths of the optic nerve insert themselves into the sclerotic. The former reach this membrane at very acute angles, and may be seen entering in the shape of a wedge, *Loewig* states that the tendons of the recti muscles, after having entered the sclerotic, form meridional (longitudinal) fibres, while the oblique muscles are said by the same author to form equatorial (circular) fibres.

The sheaths of the optic nerve, after coalescing with the sclerotic, form part of the equatorial fibres which are found nearly regularly around the entrance of the optic nerve in this membrane. The lymphatic space, which is enclosed between the sheaths of the optic nerve (intervaginal space), is sometimes, especially in myopic eyes (*Von Jaeger*), found to enter the sclerotic, severing it thus somewhat into two layers.

Earlier authors unanimously described a large round hole in the sclerotic, through which the optic nerve was said to enter the eye-ball. Such a hole, however, does not exist. The bundles of nerve fibres which constitute the optic nerve, do not pierce the sclerotic *in toto*, but more or less separately, so that, if the nerve-fibres could all be removed, the sclerotic in this place would have the appearance of a sieve, which has given to it the name of lamina cribrosa.

The inner surface of the sclerotic is covered with a layer of thin flat endothelial cells, which are quadrangular or polygonal. They may be easily brought to view by staining with nitrate of silver. This endothelial layer is, however, not perfectly continuous, since it is pierced by a considerable number of fibres, which unite the sclerotic with the choroid. Endothelial cells are also found lying upon these fibres.

The exterior surface of the sclerotic is covered with the loose episcleral tissue, the fibres of which enter and spring from the sclerotic. Where this tissue surrounds *Tennon's* space it is covered with a very thin layer of endothelial cells.

Anteriorly this episcleral tissue passes over into the conjunctiva bulbi.

At the corneo-scleral margin the fibres and lymphatic canals of the cornea go over into the fibres and canals of the sclerotic. In transverse sections of this part of the eye-ball we always find a number of vessels. *Leber* described them as a venous plexus. Although I do not doubt the existence of such a venous plexus, I must agree, on the other hand, with *Schwalbe* and *Waldeyer*, who maintain the existence of the so-called *Schlemm's* canal, besides the venous plexus of *Leber*. The latter is generally the largest of the vessels, and lies nearest the inner surface of the sclerotic. It is lined with a layer of endothelial cells, and the corneo-scleral fibres which form its inner wall, are fenestrated in the manner above referred to. The anterior chamber and its endothelium are therefore in more or less direct communication with *Schlemm's* canal and its endothelial lining. While it is easy to fill the venous plexus by injecting the blood-vessels with a colored fluid, I was never able to inject *Schlemm's* canal from this side. It is, however, comparatively easy to fill it by injecting a tinted fluid into the anterior chamber. I must further state, with *Waldeyer*, that I never yet found blood, which is hardly ever wanting in the vessels of the venous plexus, in this vessel :

The blood-vessels of the sclerotic proper come from the anterior and posterior ciliary arteries. *Waldeyer* states that they are all surrounded by a sheath, called by him, " perithelium-sheath."

The nerves of the sclerotic, according to *Helfreich*, are arranged in a similar manner to those of the cornea. His statement has not yet been confirmed by others. My own researches, by staining the sclerotic with chloride of gold and osmic acid, have not been successful.

The vorticous veins (4, 5 or 6) perforate the tissue of the sclerotic at an acute angle, from before backwards. They are surrounded by a lymphatic sheath, as are the ciliary arteries and nerves, passing through the sclerotic, which opens into the suprachoroidal space on one side and *Tennon's* space on the other side. The cilary nerves, while passing through their canals in the sclerotic, are frequently accompanied by posterior ciliary arteries, which is of great importance in the pathological processes observed in these organs.

2. PATHOLOGICAL CONDITIONS

A. Scleritis and its Results.

Scleritis, like keratitis, is histologically characterized by a larger number of round-cells, which may leave the fibres of the sclerotic intact, and only separate them slightly from each other, or may entirely destroy them. True, scleritis is, it seems, never a primary disease, unless caused by an injury; it seems to be always caused by an inflammatory process in the neighboring tissues. There are two kinds of scleritis, viz., infiltration-scleritis, and purulent-scleritis. The large number of blood-vessels piercing the sclerotic are in such cases of inflammation hyperæmic, and sometimes new blood-vessels are seen to spring from them. Infiltration-scleritis is always of a chronic character, and by aggravation may become puru-lent.

a. Infiltration-Scleritis.

Infiltration-scleritis is always found in the parts of the sclerotic which are pierced by blood-vessels. It affects the fibres of the sclerotic comparatively little, if at all. The primary diseases leading to it are corneal affections, iritis, iridocyclitis, not purulent choroiditis, and intra-ocular new-formations. From this it is evident, that we shall find infil-tration-scleritis chiefly, or perhaps only, at the corneo-scleral margin, and where the vasa vorticosa, the posterior and anterior and ciliary arteries perforate the sclerotic. We then find these blood-vessels in a state of hyperæmia, and fre-quently, in higher degrees of inflammation, always new-formed vessels starting from them and entering the tissue of the sclerotic. The interstices between the fibres of this latter membrane are filled with round-cells. I am, however, not able to state whether these cells (like those found in the cornea during keratitis) are immigrated as well as proliferated ones from the fixed scleral cells. It is certainly very probable that they also come from both sources. Infiltration-scleritis generally involves the whole thickness of the sclerotic, and may reach into the episcleral tissue.

When the primary disease heals, the scleritis generally also disappears, without leaving a trace. In other cases, however, if the primary disease is of a very chronic kind, the sclerotic begins to become stretched and atrophic (staphyloma), or a new-formation of connective-tissue takes place between its fibres, which leads to an hypertrophic condition, such as we find, for instance, in the sclerotic of phthisical eyeballs. Wounds of the sclerotic also heal with the symptoms of infiltration-scleritis. (See later on.)

b. Purulent Scleritis.

The characteristic feature of purulent scleritis, is an abundance of round-cells, which causes a rapid destruction of the fibres of the sclerotic. This kind of scleritis also attacks by preference the placet where the sclerotic is pierced by blood-vessels and nerves. Purulent scleritis generally originates from purulent affections of the uveal tract, and is one of the symptoms of purulent panophthalmitis. It may also be caused by foreign bodies. I have never had occasion to see a genuine abscess such as we find in the cornea in the sclerotic. Purulent panophthalmitis is sometimes incorrectly called scleral abscess.

Since purulent scleritis is, as a rule, caused by purulent affections of the uveal tract, it is not astonishing that it chiefly (and often only) involves the inner layer of the sclerotic. In consequence of circumscribed abscess-like cell-aggregations in the choroid, which mostly perforate the lamina vitrea and enter the vitreous body, a very small part of the sclerotic may become ulcerated. In such a place the purulent inflammation may then cause an excessive new-formation of connective-tissue, which may grow through the choroid and retina into the vitreous body.

The inflammation, however, does not always remain confined only to such a circumscribed part, or to the inner layers of the sclerotic, but the new-formation of cells, and with it necrosis of the sclerotic tissue, may progress, until this membrane becomes perforated on its outer surface. Such perforations usually happen in the region of the equator of the globe, where the vasa vorticosa pierce the sclerotic.

Although this kind of inflammation of the sclerotic is generally chronic, it is in rare cases found to run its course in a very acute manner. In these cases the new-formation of cells is so excessive, that the destruction of the fibres of the sclerotic cannot go hand in hand with it. Consequently this membrane must become very much thickened, and may, therefore, be mistaken for total staphyloma of the sclerotic.

I had the opportunity to examine such an eye, which was enucleated in a homœopathic eye-hospital with the diagnosis of total staphyloma of the sclerotic, and was shown to me as a highly interesting and rare case of acute staphyloma with hypertrophy of the sclerotic. It is true, to the naked eye the sclerotic appeared to be about six times as thick as a normal one. The microscope, however, revealed at once an immense number of round-cells which lay between the fibres of the sclerotic in the episcleral tissue, and pressed these fibres, which were not as yet necrotic, far apart.

In case the sclerotic becomes perforated in a circumscribed spot, the pus escapes on its outer surface, and choroid and retina become adherent to the scar-tissue, which afterwards closes the perforation. The result of such a perforation, with subsequent synechia between sclerotic, choroid and retina, may be staphyloma.

As was above stated, purulent scleritis is chiefly found in the parts surrounding the blood-vessels and nerves which pass through it; and this inflammation may, too, become the cause of sympathetic affections in the fellow-eye.

The Results of Scleritis.

a. Formation of Scars.

Scars in the sclerotic are only found in consequence of purulent scleritis. The conditions are then the same as when the sclerotic has been pierced by an injury, and will be treated of under that head.

b. Prolapse and Incarceration of Iris, Ciliary Body, Choroid, Retina, Crystalline Lens and Vitreous Body in the Sclerotic.

These conditions will also be spoken of in the chapter on injuries of the sclerotic.

c. Hypertrophy of the Sclerotic.

A chronic inflammatory process of the whole eye-ball, or of the uveal tract, frequently causes chronic infiltration-scleritis leading to new-formation of connective-tissue, which produces a hypertrophic condition of the sclerotic. From the fact that it is impossible at a later period of these affections to find cellular elements in the hypertrophied connective-tissue, and since, moreover, the lymphatic canals and their lacunæ are then more or less obliterated, we may with some probability conclude that the fixed cells of the sclerotic take an active part in the new-formation of this connective-tissue. It is not impossible, however, that they are destroyed only during the period of retraction of the new-formed tissue. In spite of this retraction, the sclerotic sometimes remains considerably thickened. This hypertrophic condition of the sclerotic always precedes total phthisis of an eye-ball, and the process leading to it begins, without exception, in the posterior parts of the sclerotic, around the entrance of the optic nerve.

The blood and lymphatic vessels become obliterated, and this again results in grave disturbances in the nutrition of the interior of the eye-ball. Later on, the hypertrophy progresses more and more towards the corneo-scleral margin, and in the highest degrees of phthisis of the globe nearly the whole of the sclerotic is equally thickened. It frequently happens that while this is going on, inflammatory processes in the interior of the globe, which produce shrinking, force the sclerotic to fold itself. The episcleral tissue in such cases is also nearly always inflamed, and takes an active part in the new-formation of connective-tissue, and sometimes *Tennon's* space thus becomes perfectly obliterated.

In examining two eyes which were enucleated in consequence of gun-shot wounds, and were in the earlier stages of
phthisis, I had an opportunity to find alterations in the posterior ciliary blood-vessels within the sclerotic, which show
that these blood-vessels not only become obliterated by
pressure exerted upon them by the shrinking new-formed
connective-tissue, but that they may, moreover, take an active
part in this new-formation. I found the endothelium of these
vessels in a high degree of proliferation. Its cells were enlarged and had several nuclei, and they filled the whole of the
lumen of each vessel so altered. In some of them I also
found giant-cells with from six to fifteen nuclei. While most

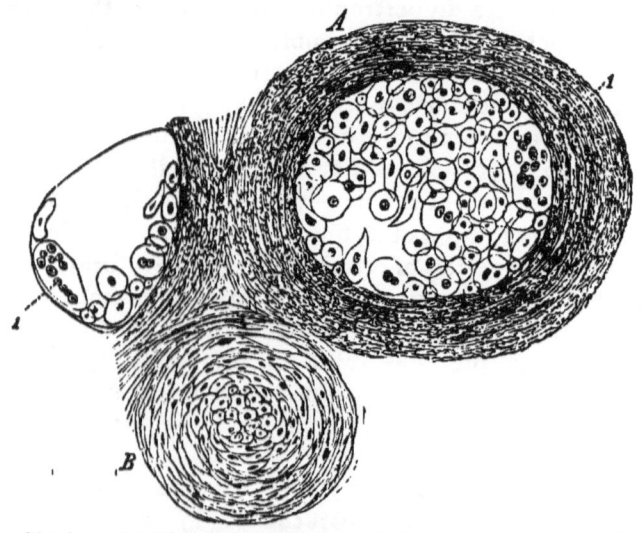

FIG. 18.—Blood-vessels of the sclerotic from a wounded eye in the process of phthisis bulbi.
A. Proliferation of the endothelial cells. 1. Giant-cells. B. Transformation into connective-tissue.

of the changed endothelial cells appeared round and vesicle-
like, some of them had one or two offsets, and passed gradually over into the spindle shape. (See Fig. 18.)

d. *Atrophy of the Sclerotic and Ectasy* (*Staphyloma of the Sclerotic*).

Both kinds of scleritis (but especially infiltration scleritis) very frequently produce staphyloma of the sclerotic.

The characteristic features of this affection are atrophy and stretching of the scleral tissue. Although synechiæ between the sclerotic and some part of the uveal tract are very frequent in cases of such staphyloma, they are not always found, and are therefore not essential. This atrophy and ectasy may concern only a part of the sclerotic or the whole of it. We have therefore a total and a partial staphyloma scleræ.

Total staphyloma of the sclerotic is but seldom observed, and then it forms only a part of the total ectasy of the eyeball. We find, in these eyes, an abnormal extenuation and stretching of the sclerotic, which may occasionally be combined with adhesions between this membrane and the uveal tract. Even where such adhesions are wanting, the uveal tract shows varying pathological alterations. All the blood-vessels which either nourish the sclerotic or only pass through it become, as a rule, obliterated. Also the nerves gradually disappear, but generally much later than the blood-vessels.

Partial scleral staphyloma is of frequent occurrence, and a characteristic feature of it is, that we nearly always find an adhesion between the uveal tract and the bulging part of the sclerotic. It may, of course, be found in any part of the sclerotic. The following are the three kinds most frequently observed.

1. *Anterior Staphyloma of the Sclerotic.*

Concerns those parts of the sclerotic which lie in front of the equator of the eye-ball. There are two varieties, *viz.*, corneo-scleral and ciliary staphyloma.

a. Corneo-Scleral Staphyloma (formerly called Intercalar-Staphyloma).

This form of staphyloma lies in the beginning just at the corneo-scleral margin. In all such cases which I have examined, I found iritis or iridocyclitis either to be present, or unmistakable signs that they had existed. The periphecal parts of the iris are united to the corneo-scleral tissue by a fine layer of newly-formed connective-tissue, which is formed by the proliferating endothelial cells of *Descemet's* membrane and the anterior surface of the iris. In consequence of this adhesion of the anterior surface of the peripherical part of the iris with the corneo-scleral tissue, *Fontana's* spaces become obliterated. During the progress of the new-formation the ligamentum pectinatum and the periphery of *Descemet's* membrane are obliterated, and since the soft tissue of the iris cannot replace the resistance which is lost with the disappearance of *Descemet's* membrane, these parts become gradually stretched and atrophied. Their blood-vessels and lymphatic canals are found obliterated.

The stretching of these parts (where the iris is adherent to the corneo-scleral tissue gradually, removes the free part of the iris from the ciliary body. If the affection progresses still farther, more and more of the anterior surface of the iris becomes adherent to *Descemet's* membrane and more and more of the latter membrane is destroyed. This leads, of course, to a gradual diminution of the area of the free iris, and the size of the anterior chamber, and furthermore to dilation of the pupil, which is alway sobserved in such eyes. (See Fig. 19.)

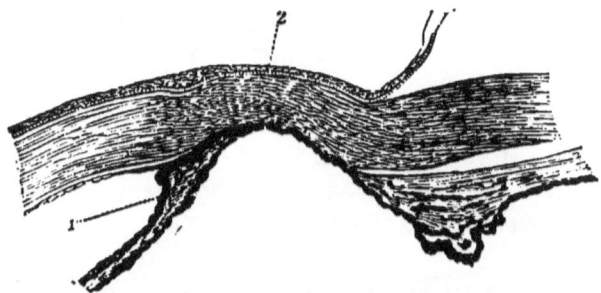

Fig. 19.—Corneo-scleral staphyloma. 1. New insertion of the iris which adheres to Descemet's membrane by means of a tissue formed from the endothelial cells. 2. The ectatic part ; the membrana Descemetli has disappeared.

b. Ciliary Staphyloma.

Ciliary staphyloma concerns the ciliary region only, and involves the ciliary body and the part of the sclerotic covering it. The affection takes its origin from a chronic cycloscleritis. This leads to an adhesion between the ciliary body and the sclerotic, and to atrophy and stretching of these parts. The muscular tissue of the ciliary body disappears totally in the later stages of this process, and we frequently find only a layer of pigmented cells lining the bulging parts, as the remains of this body. The staphyloma is often bounded anteriorly by some atrophic ciliary processes, while posteriorly it slopes gradually down into the more or less normal equatorial region. The blood-vessels and lymphatic canals of the involved parts are, of course, again found to be obliterated and the nerves atrophied. (See Fig. 20)

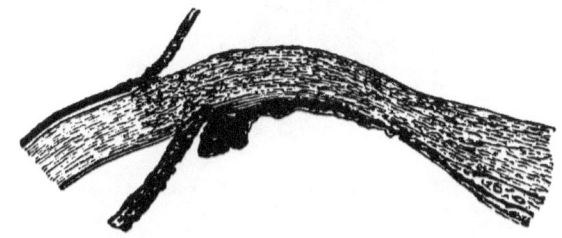

Fig. 20.—Ciliary staphyloma. Ciliary body adherent to the sclerotic and atrophic. Beginning ectasia.

Both of these two kinds of anterior staphyloma of the sclerotic are frequently seen to travel around the whole of the circumference of the eye-ball, and have therefore been called "annular" staphylomata.

2. *Equatorial Staphyloma of the Sclerotic.*

This form of scleral staphyloma lies either just in the equator of the globe or a little behind it. It is caused by chronic chorio-scleritis leading to adhesion between choroid and sclerotic and atrophy, and is mostly found just where, in the normal eye, a vorticous vein passes through the sclerotic. The histological conditions are the same as in the other forms of scleral staphyloma.

3. *Posterior Staphyloma of the Sclerotic.*

Is the result of a chronic sclerochorioiditis, which, however, does not always leads to an adhesion, and which is nearly without exception confined to region of the optic

nerve and macula lutea.   Sometimes it is caused by a congenital defect.   Since the point of direct vision (the
macula lutea) is gradually more and more removed from the
anterior surface of the globe in consequence of the staphyloma, it influences vision in a very important way, viz., it
makes the eye myopic.   The histological conditions are also
here in no way different from what has been described above.
(See Fig. 21.)

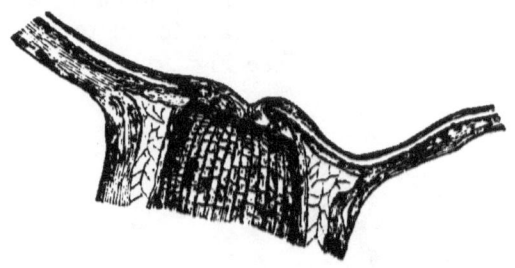

F<small>IG</small>. 21. —Posterior staphyloma from a myopic eye.   Choroid and sclerotic adhere to each
other and are atrophic.

All these different varieties of staphyloma of the sclerotic
may at any time become stationary.   In rare cases they progress, until the eye becomes ruptured.   In this way, and
in consequence of changes in the interior of the eye-ball,
such staphylomata lead to total destruction of the organ.
Staphylomata also usually cause an increase of the intra-
ocular pressure (glaucoma), with all its consequences.   This
is probably due to the alterations in the uveal tract, and
especially to the obliteration of so many lymphatic canals
and blood-vessels, by which the veinous blood and lymphatic
fluids ought to be carried out of the eye.   Glaucoma is chiefly caused by anterior and equatorial scleral staphylomata.
Since in posterior staphyloma the choroid is less frequently
found to adhere to the sclerotic, and it is generally confined
to a smaller part of the eye; and, moreover, seems rather
to influence the entrance than the exit of the blood from
the eye-ball, glaucoma is but seldom found these eyes.
This latter argument seems especially to be proven by
the experiments of *Kniess,* which led this author to the
conclusion, that the lymphatic fluids in the eye-ball run

from behind forward. I cannot, however, agree with the views of the same author when he finds the universal cause of glaucoma in the obliteration of *Fontana's* spaces As I have stated, glaucoma is frequently found as a consequence of all these different kinds of staphyloma, especially anterior scleral staphylomata, I have, however, examined quite a number of glaucomatous eyes which showed no obliteration of *Fontana's* spaces, that is, no corneo-scleral staphyloma.

The great influence exerted by all forms of scleral staphyloma upon the nerves of the affected eye makes it evident that they are frequently the cause of sympathetic affections of the fellow-eye.

Several authors have observed deposits of lime in the sclerotic, and even osseous formations, in consequence of chronic scleritis have been described. *Coccius* and others found a fatty degeneration of the sclerotic analogous to the arcus senilis of the cornea. I never have seen any one of these affections.

B. Injuries to the Sclerotic and their Results.

a. Wounds without Subsequent Retention of a Foreign Body.

We have to speak under this head of ruptures of sclerotic and wounds caused by cutting instruments.

The healing process after the infliction of such injuries to the sclerotic greatly resembles those observed in the cornea under similar circumstances. Very soon after the injury has been received the blood-vessels become hyperæmic, and the edges of the lips are infiltrated with round-cells. We then find the same histological conditions as in genuine infiltration-scleritis. Somewhat later a fibrinous exudation into the canal of the wound takes place, and this, too, becomes filled with round-cells, and is gradually transformed into connective-tissue. The new-formed tissue then becomes denser and begins to shrink. This scar-tissue nearly always runs in a direction which is different from the general one of the fibres of the sclerotic, and therefore always admits of an easy diagnosis with the microscope. (See Fig. 22.) The result is the same whether the instrument pierces the whole thickness of the sclerotic or only a part of it, or when purulent processes have produced perforation or partial ulceration of this membrane.

As purulent processes, which lead to perforation of the sclerotic, are, as a rule, finished as such as soon as the perforation has taken place, we then, usually find, only the symptoms of infiltration-

Fig. 22—Scar in the sclerotic.

scleritis. The healing process is in such cases as described above.

Since, however, an injury or rupture of the sclerotic but seldom occurs, which does not also at the same time affect at least one of the neighboring membranes, the healing-process may be a more complicated one, and, in fact, is so in most cases. If the injury has been inflicted from the outside, at least the conjunctiva bulbi must also be wounded ; but the injury may just as well pierce all the internal membranes of the globe and the vitreous body. If the wound of the sclerotic is received from its inner surface, the inflicting instrument must have passed through nearly all the remaining parts of the eye before reaching it. In this way a great many variations and complications may be observed during the healing process. The most frequent complication is the prolapse, and afterwards incarceration in the sclerotic of the iris, the ciliary body or choroid. The histological conditions in these cases are the same as those we found in incarceration of the iris in the cornea. In rare cases one of these parts of the uveal tract may simply become adherent to the wound in the sclerotic. Furthermore, we may find the crystalline lens, the retina and the vitreous body prolapsing into the scleral wound. If the injury did not at the same time rupture the capsule of the crystalline lens, the latter may escape *in toto* through the wound, and remain lodged under the conjunctiva. If the capsule has been ruptured, the same may take place, or the crystalline lens, after prolapsing into the scleral wound, may there become adherent. During the healing process the lens-substance is then, as a rule, absorbed, and later on we find only the capsule embedded in the scar. If prolapse of the retina has occurred, this membrane always takes part in the formation of the scar-tissue, and its nervous elements disappear. The vitreous body, also, where it is caught in the wound, is transformed into connective-tissue, and becomes adherent to the scar.

When the injuring instrument reaches the sclerotic from its inner surface, it must, as stated, have pierced the vitreous body, retina and choroid before reaching the sclerotic. We therefore find in such cases all these parts adherent to the sclerotic, whether the injury concerns the whole or only a part of the thickness of this membrane.

Whenever the uveal tract has also been injured, or has only prolapsed into the wound of the sclerotic, we find molecules of pigment in the lymphatic canals of the sclerotic adjoining the wound. Hæmorrhages of varying size of the wound-lips are of frequent occurrence, and are absorbed during the healing process.

b. *Wounds with Subsequent Retention of a Foreign Body.*

Since the scleral tissue is a great deal more tolerant of injuries than the tissue of the cornea, we very frequently find foreign bodies embedded in the sclerotic without causing any serious reaction. Where such reaction takes place, a circumscribed purulent scleritis ensues, during which the foreign body is thrown off with the pus.

The more common result is, that in consequence of chronic infiltration-scleritis new-formation of connective-tissue takes place, in which the foreign body becomes *F* embedded. All the injured membranes take part in the formation of this tissue. (See Fig. 23.)

Scars in the sclerotic may become ectatic and lead to scleral staphyloma.

Fig. 23—Foreign body (F) embedded in the sclerotic.

Since most of the scleral injuries at the same time involve a part of the uveal tract, they may produce sympathetic affections of the fellow-eye.

C. Tumors of the Sclerotic.

Fibroma, sarcoma and osteoma of the sclerotic have been described.   They were all found at the corneo-scleral margin, and certainly were tumors of the episcleral tissue.

III.

CONJUNCTIVA BULBI AND EPISCLERAL TISSUE.

1. NORMAL CONDITIONS.

THE epithelium which covers the conjunctiva bulbi is always thicker near the cornea-scleral margin than it is farther backward. The peculiar superficial epithelial layer of the conjunctiva palpebrarum, consisting of cylinder and cone-shaped cells, is more and more changed into a layer of flat cells, like the superficial layer of the corneal epithelium, the nearer it comes to the corneo-scleral margin, and we find nearest the cornea several layers of flat cells with an oval nucleus, which frequently have one or two nucleoli. The more cuboid epithelial cells of the inner layer of the conjunctiva palpebrarum remain very much the same, until they join the basal layer of the corneal epithelium. Near the corneo-scleral margin we find at first a small, then rapidly increasing intermediate layer, consisting of the same forms of cells which we found in the middle layer of the corneal epithelium. Just where the conjunctiva joins the cornea—that is, where *Bowman's* layer of the cornea begins—the epithelium forms two or three papillæ, which dip into the underlying tissue.

The so-called mucous-cells peculiar to the epithelium of the conjunctiva are especially numerous upon the conjunctiva bulbi. They are to be considered as metamorphosed epithelial cells (*Waldcyer*), and are large, round, vesicle-like bodies. When viewed from above they appear as round circles, and seem to contain a transparent fluid. In transverse-sections they show the same shape as the "goblet-cells" of the intestinal tract, and are found to have their base in the basal layer of the epithelium.

Among the cells of the basal layer, nearer the cornea and the middle layers, I found frequently cells with two nuclei or cells which show evident signs of being of a recent date. It appears therefore that the regeneration of the epethelial cells of the conjunctiva takes place in the same way as it does in the cornea.

Under this epithelium lies a tissue which by clinicists is usually considered to form two layers, viz., the subconjunctival and the episcleral tissue. Histologically such a separation does not exist. There is only one conjunctival or episcleral tissue, and we may yield to the clinicists only so far as to call the part of this tissue which lies close to the sclerotic, episcleral, and the part just under the epithelium, subconjunctival. Near to, and just at the corneo-scleral margin, the possibility of even such an ideal separation is wanting.

The conjunctival tissue is formed by a network of fine connective-tissue fibres and elastic fibrillæ.

The meshes of this network of fibres are comparatively wide, except just under the epithelium and upon the sclerotic, where they become smaller and the tissue denser. This condensation is caused by additional fibres coming from *Bowman's* layer and the sclerotic, which enter the conjunctiva. I observed above, that the fibres of the conjunctival tissue enter the sclerotic. Within the meshes of the conjunctiva lie a number of cells of two distinct kinds. The first are flat cells and nuclei, which are adherent to the fibres, probably belong to the class of endothelial cells, and are comparatively rare. The second are lymphatic cells, suspended in the fluid which fills the interstices, and generally lie together in small clusters. These cells are more numerous in the conjunctiva than in other tissues, and give it the typical structure of what by older anatomists was called *adenoid* tissue. I have never seen lymphatic follicles in the normal human conjunctiva (*Waldeyer*).

Small clusters of fat-cells have also been found by *Waldeyer* in the conjunctival tissue.

The small yellowish tumor which is so frequently seen on the inner or outer side of the cornea-scleral margin, in that part of the conjunctiva bulbi which lies just behind the palpebral fissure, has wrongly been called *pinguecula*, as it was thought to consist of fat-tissue. *Sæmisch* changed this name into " palpebral fissure-spot " (Lidspaltenfleck). The little tumor consists chiefly of very dense connective-tissue, which contains scarcely any blood-vessels or cells, and is covered by a strangely thick layer of epithelial cells. I always found among these epithelial cells such a large number of serrated ones that the condition was very similar to that of an epithelial tumor. The erroneous opinion, that this tumor consisted of fat-tissue, was first corrected by *Weller* and *Robin*.

The blood-vessels of the conjunctiva all come from the anterior ciliary blood-vessels. Their structure has nothing peculiar. They are very numerous, especially in the sub-conjunctival tissue, and the veins have a comparatively wide lumen. The capillary blood-vessels which lie under the epi-thelium form an irregular network with small interstices. Contrary to *Waldeyer*, I cannot find any papillæ (*Gefasspa-pillen*) in the conjunctiva bulbi.

The nerves of the conjunctiva bulbi first form a net-work of non-medullated fibres under the epithelium (*J. Arnold*) and then enter the latter. *Longworth* has lately been able to prove beyond doubt, that these nerves really end in peculiar little bulbous structures (Endkolben), as first described by *Krause* and denied by a large number of exam-iners, especially *J. Arnold* and *Waldeyer*.

The lymphatic vessels of the conjunctiva are (*Waldeyer* and others) in direct communication with the corneal and scleral canals, which is a very important fact in pathological processes.

2. *Pathological Conditions.*

Before speaking of the different kinds of inflammation of the conjunctiva, I would like here to mention that kind of œdema of the conjunctiva which is clinically known as in-filtration-œdema, and is found so frequently after operations and wounds near the cornea-scleral margin, especially when the conjunctival wound is healed and the corneo-scleral or scleral one as yet only partly, or not at all closed. In conse-quence of the peculiar structure of the conjunctival tissue with its network of open canals, the fluids coming from the cornea and anterior chamber can, of course, easily escape into it. Histologically we find only the meshes filled with lymphatic fluid, and more or less distended.

Similar conditions are found in cases of so-called subconjunctival hæmorrhage. Whether such a hæmorrhage was caused by an injury or came on spontaneously, we simply find the meshes and canals of the conjunctival tissue filled with blood and distended. The blood gradually becomes absorbed, and leaves, only in rare cases, some pigment behind. It is very probable, but as yet not proven by histological examination, that pathological alterations in the walls of the conjunctival blood-vessels give rise to these hæmorrhages.

A. Conjunctivitis (of the Conjunctiva Bulbi) and its Results.

When examining into the different forms of inflammation of the conjunctiva bulbi, we find the same forms we meet with in other mucous membranes, viz., catarrhal, blennorrhoic, croupous and diphtheritic conjunctivitis. Such an inflammation of the conjunctiva bulbi is nearly always only a symptom of inflammation of the whole conjunctiva. This is, however, not the case with two types of inflammation which are not among those just enumerated, viz., phlyctenular conjunctivitis and clinically so-called episcleritis, which are, as a rule, local diseases. A farther form of inflammation, but rarely observed in the conjunctiva bulbi, is trachoma.

a. Conjunctivitis Catarrhalis, Episcleritis, Phlyctænula.

Catarrhal inflammation of the conjunctiva bulbi is observed only when the whole of the conjunctiva is subject to a catarrhal inflammation. The blood-vessels in such cases are very hyperæmic. Thus an increased transudation, at first of the serous fluid of the blood, and later of white blood-corpuscles into the meshes of the conjunctival tissue is caused, which is accompanied by an increased secretion from the mucous-cells. This condition can heal perfectly by removal of the hyper-secretion from the conjunctival surface and by absorption, or it may become chronic. In rare cases new-formation of connective-tissue in the conjunctiva may take place during the process of such a chronic catarrhal conjunctivitis.

The disturbances in the circulation caused by the considerable degree of hyperæmia always found in cases of conjunctivitis, may also lead to affections of the cornea, or, as is frequently the case, to hyperæmia of the iris. While the latter is often found complicating with an acute catarrhal conjunctivitis, the former affections result more frequently from a chronic one.

Clinicists make a distinction between catarrhal conjunctivitis and episcleritis. They maintain that in the latter the conjunctival tissue nearest to the sclerotic is the seat of the inflammation. As far as I know, cases of such clinically diagnosticated episcleritis have not yet been examined with the microscope. Where episcleritis is a primary disease (and not secondary to inflammation of the sclerotic, etc.), it is, as a rule, a local and very chronic affection. In rare cases it may travel all around the cornea and cause internal complications, such iritis is, choroiditis, and even neuro-retinitis. Episcleritis is always accompanied by a local catarrhal conjunctivitis, and there is probably no catarrhal conjunctivitis of a more serious degree which is not combined with, or causes some degree of episcleritis.

Another *local* form of inflammation of the conjunctiva, which is, however, as a rule, combined with a local, often even with a general catarrhal conjunctivitis, is phlyctenula.

As far as I know, phlyctenula of the conjunctiva have not yet been histologically examined. The process is clinically, however, so similar to that in the cornea, that we shall probably not be very far from the truth in assuming that we here also find a sub-epithelial infiltration with round cells. This infiltration may later on, be again absorbed, or lead to the destruction of the epithelium above it, and thus cause the formation of a superficial ulcer. The phlyctenula may appear singly or we may find a number at the same time. A variety of this affection is the so-called miliary phlyctenula.

b. Conjunctivitis Blennorrhoica (purulenta, gonorrhoica), Ulcer of the Conjunctiva.

In blennorrhoic conjunctivitis, the characteristic secretion

is at first muco-purulent, later on, entirely purulent.   Blennorrhoic conjunctivitis of the conjunctiva bulbi is nearly always
caused by an inflammation of the same nature of the whole
conjunctiva, and probably always combined with an inflammation of the episcleral tissue.

The conjunctival blood-vessels are, in these cases, always
highly hyperæmic, and this hyperæmia is followed by the
emigration and new-formation of numerous round-cells.
These symptoms are combined with œdema and swelling of
the conjunctiva, which again cause stasis in the veinous blood-
vessels and passive œdema, and thus a *circulus vitiosus* is
formed.   The infiltration and new-formation of round-cells
are followed by a lively proliferation of the epithelial cells,
and it seems later they not only allow the pus-cells to pass
through them, but themselves take an active part in the
formation of the pus.   During this process small superficial
ulcers are frequently formed.   Such small ulcers heal by
proliferation of the surrounding epithelium, and it seems that
all the layers take an active part in this restorative process.
The same healing-process, combined with a local blennorrhoic
conjunctivitis, is observed after the breaking of the pustule
formed by a phlyctenula.

After having lasted some time, blennorrhoic conjunctivitis
generally goes over into the catarrhal form, which may soon
lead to the normal condition or become chronic.   Such a
chronic catarrhal conjunctivitis after blennorrhœa often produces trachoma.

Serious cases of blennorrhœa of the conjunctiva are nearly
without exception combined with inflammatory processes in
the cornea, which may lead to partial or total destruction of
this membrane, or even of the whole eye-ball.   It is as yet
an unsettled question whether these complications originate
in an inoculation of pus-cells into the corneal-tissue, or only
in impaired nutrition, or in both combined.   It seems to me,
however, that the latter is the most probable.

As a result of blennorrhoic conjunctivitis (especially when
combined with ulcus corneæ), we find the formation of pterygium, as I have already above stated.

The swelling of the papillæ, which is so conspicuous in the

conjunctiva of the lids, in cases of blennorrhœa, is not observed in the conjunctiva of the bulbus, since, as stated, it has
no papillæ.

c. *Conjunctivitis Crouposa and Diphtheritica.*

Although these two forms of conjunctivitis do not seem
to have been as yet histologically examined, their analogy
with the same forms of inflammation in other mucous membranes will help to explain the conditions. We therefore
probably find in croupous conjunctivitis that a fibrino-puru-
lent exudation is deposited upon the surface of the conjunctiva, without implicating the epithelial layer. Croupous
membranes, taken from the conjunctiva, consist invariably
of a dense network of fibrinous threads, among which round-
cells lie in large quantity. The same exudation is probably
found in diphtheritic conjunctivitis; but here it materially
involves the epithelium and the underlying tissue. The
croupous exudation, therefore, when cast off, leaves only an
inflamed conjunctiva behind, while the diphtheritic membrane
is never cast off without causing a deep ulcer.

The croupous as well as the diphtheritic form of inflammation are only rarely found to involve the bulbar conjunctiva.
When healing they go over into a blennorrhoic, and this later
on into a catarrhal conjunctivitis, which may either soon lead
to the normal condition or become chronic. In the latter case
they may, too, produce trachoma.

Both these kinds of conjunctivitis often result in destruction of the cornea, or even of the whole eye-ball.

d. *Conjunctivitis Trachomatosa.*

Although trachoma is frequently the result of chronic
catarrhal, blennorrhoic, or in some cases croupous and diphtheritic conjunctivitis, it is also observed as a primary disease. It is only found in the bulbar conjunctiva, after it has
affected the whole of the remaining conjunctiva. My own
examinations of trachomatous conjunctiva have taught me
that its characteristic feature is the formation of tubercle-like
aggregations of round-cells. These clusters of round-cells are
more or less globe-shaped, and force the surrounding tissue
(which is also filled with round-cells) aside, at the same time

compressing its fibres in such a way, that a number of authors thought the granules were surrounded by a membrana propria, and were hypertrophic lymph-follicles. But there are no lymph-follicles in the human bulbar conjunctiva, and the apparent membrana propria is, as stated, formed by the compressed fibres of the conjunctival tissue. If the blood-vessels of the conjunctiva are injected with some tinted fluid, it

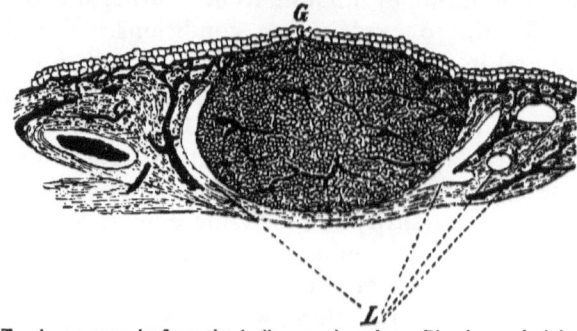

Fig. 24.—Trachoma-granule from the bulbar conjunctiva. Blood-vessels injected with a stained fluid. L. Enlarged lymph-canals.

is easily seen that they pass through these accumulations of round-cells. (See Fig. 24.) Besides the blood-vessels, I always found enlarged lymphatic vessels in and around the granules.

These granules may reach the corneo-scleral margin, and sometimes they are even found to lie in the córneal tissue near this place.

Trachomatous conjunctivitis is usually a chronic affection, and produces a hyper-secretion of mucous, or the secretion of a muco-purulent fluid. The granules may undergo fatty degeneration, and thus be absorbed, or they are transformed into a tough connective-tissue (*Preuss*). This new-formed tissue causes the obliteration of blood-vessels and lymph canals and destruction of the mucous-cells. The latter leads to xerosis of the cornea. Corneal affections are, moreover, very frequent complications in cases of trachomatous conjunctivitis. It produces, however, comparatively seldom internal affections or the perfect destruction of the eye-ball.

The Results of Conjunctivitis, viz., Argyrosis, Xerosis, and Pterygium.

Argyrosis of the conjunctiva is not caused by the conjunctivitis itself, but by a too prolonged use of the chief remedy employed in its treatment—nitrate of silver. This condition, according to *Junge*, is due to the precipitation of the silver in the epithelium and the superficial layers of the conjunctival tissue.

Xerosis conjunctivæ we call an affection which is caused by the dryness of the conjunctiva and the transformation of its epithelial cells into horny scales. This process may be combined with the formation of scar-tissue in the conjunctiva or exist without it (xerosis parenchymatosa and xerosis simplex), and originates in a want of moisture dependant upon chronic forms of conjunctivitis, especially trachoma. The mucous-cells are found either undergoing a colloid metamorphosis or altogether destroyed. Xerosis conjunctivæ is generally accompanied by the same affection of the cornea.

Pterygium, as stated above, may originate in a marginal ulcer of the cornea, combined with blennorrhoic conjunctivitis. I have, however, learned by clinical observation that it may just as well be caused by catarrhal conjunctivitis (especially in the acute form), without the existence of an ulcer.

B. INJURIES TO THE CONJUNCTIVA AND THEIR RESULTS.

1. *Injuries without the Retention of a Foreign Body.*

Injuries to the conjunctiva, without retention of a foreign body, are either cuts, rents or scratched wounds. The cuts we observe on the bulbar conjunctiva are chiefly those caused by an operation. If the tissue has simply been severed healing by primary intention, generally takes place and no trace is left behind. If the cut, however, causes a loss of substance, or for some reason the wound-lips are not allowed to become well applied to each other, the healing process occurs by secondary intention. We then find, similar to those conditions seen after a corneal wound, an exudation of a fibrinous nature covering the loss of substance, or between the wound-lips, which is gradually transformed into connective-tissue, and then covered by new-formed epithelium. In the new-formation of the latter, all the layers seem to participate.

If the wound lies at the corneo-scleral margin, it is, as stated above, covered to the larger extent by the conjunctival, to the smaller by the corneal epithelium.

2. *Wounds with Subsequent Retention of a Foreign Body.*

If a foreign body remains in the conjunctiva after having pierced only the epithelium and the layers under it, it nearly always produces a general catarrhal and a local blennorrhoic conjunctivitis. The latter leads to the formation of an ulcer around the foreign body, which then is thrown off with the pus, and the ulcer heals in the usual way.

If the foreign body has entered the deeper layers of the conjunctiva, and is small enough to remain embedded there, it is usually soon surrounded by dense connective-tissue capsule, which is the result of chronic conjunctivitis. Among such foreign bodies we find little pieces of wood, iron or stone.

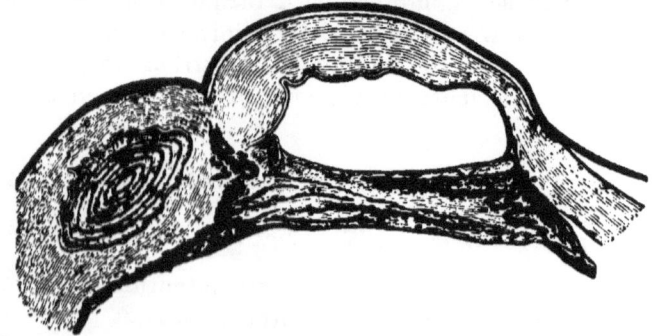

FIG. 25. Crystalline lens dislocated under the conjunctiva and there encapsuled.

Lenses dislocated under the bulbar conjunctiva produce the same results. (See Fig. 25.)

3. *Burns with Lime.*

Burns of the conjunctiva, like those of the cornea, are mostly caused by lime. The epithelial cells and the under-lying tissue are infiltrated with the lime, become necrotic, and then acting as foreign bodies, produce a local blennorrhoic conjunctivitis, besides the general catarrhal conjunctivitis. Thus the burned parts are thrown off, and an ulcer is formed which heals in the manner described.

If the conjunctiva of the lids has been burned at the same time and the two ulcers lie close to each other, their surface may heal together. This condition is called symblepharon posterius. If the burn be extensive enough, it may cause the formation of an anchyloblepharon.

C. TUMORS OF THE CONJUNCTIVA BULBI AND EPISCLERAL TISSUE.

In chapters I and II, I remarked that the so-called tumors of the cornea and sclerotic as a rule, take their origin from the limbus conjunctivæ, which is so well supplied with blood-vessels, and not from either cornea or sclerotic. The literature on this subject and the clinical experience of others as well as my own numerous histological examinations have thoroughly convinced me that no genuine corneal or scleral tumors are observed, at least, that no tumor has so far been described which undoubtedly took its origin in either the cornea or the sclerotic alone. I have therefore thought it proper to place the description of all these tumors here.

Metastatic tumors in these parts, resulting from intra-ocular new-formations, do not of course, belong under this head.

a. Lymphangiectasia and Serous Cysts.

I am not aware that the result of a histological examination of a lymphangiectasia of the conjunctiva has ever been published before the following one which I had occasion to examine and to describe in my paper on the nature and anatomical causes of sympathetic ophthalmia. The conditions were, as follows ;

In the conjunctiva bulbi I found a system of cavities and canals, perfectly independant of the blood-vessels, which were hyperæmic and therefore well defined. These cavities and canals are in direct communication with each other, and press the surrounding conjunctival tissue aside. Some of them are separated from each other only by a very thin septum. They contain a serous fluid, in which a small number of lymphatic cells are suspended. Their walls have an endothelial lining which, however, does not seem to be continuous. The walls themselves are formed by the compressed fibres of the conjunctival tissue (See Fig. 26).

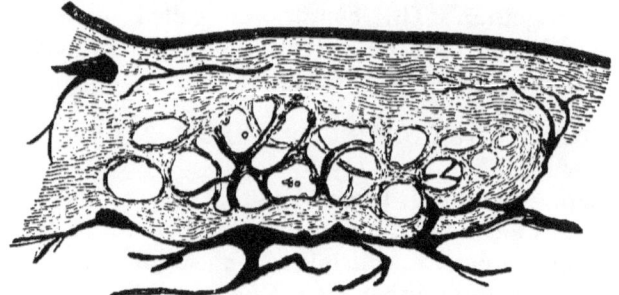

FIG. 26. Lymphangiectasia of the bulbar conjunctiva.

If the ectasia of such lymph-canals increases still further and the septa disappear altogether, all the different small cavities may coalesce into one large one and form a serous cyst. That serous cysts acquired after birth may be developed in such a way, has also been stated by clinical observers (*Schoen, von Wecker*).

I have had no occasion to examine congenital, uncomplicated serous and dermoid cysts of the conjunctiva.

b. Granuloma (*Polypus*).

Granuloma of the conjunctiva is but seldom observed upon the bulbar part of this membrane. It is caused by chronic inflammatory processes, or by traumatic and operative influences. In cases where the eye-ball is phthisical, it appears sometimes, as if the granuloma had originated in the corneal tissue, which is, however, not the case. According to my experience, there exists no granuloma of the cornea, although *Pagenstecher and Geuth* have described such a tumor. If the eye is as yet a useful organ granulomata are seldom allowed to grow to a considerable size but are removed at an early stage. Upon phthisical (blind) eye-balls these tumors sometimes grow very large. All the tumors belonging under this head and examined by me, were built up of simple granulation-tissue, *viz.*, round-cells, new-formed blood-vessels and very little, if any, connective-tissue (See Fig. 27).

Fano's decription of a " fibrous " polypus in this region, may be taken as a proof that this granuloma-tissue may later on

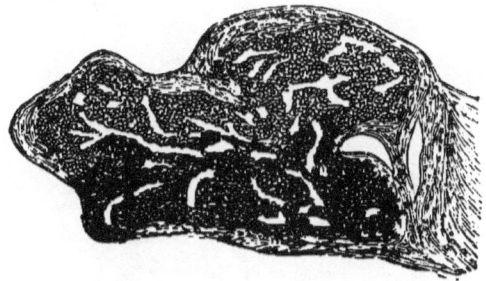

FIG. 27. Granuloma (polypus) of the bulbar conjunctiva.

become transformed into dense connective-tissue. Mucoid polypi (*Saemisch*) have never come under my observation in this part of the eye.

c. Dermoid and Lipomatous Tumors.

Dermoid (*Ryba*) tumors of the conjunctiva are, it seems, always independent new-formations. In all of the cases hitherto described the tumor was situated just upon the corneo-scleral margin in such a way, that one half was adherent to the cornea, while the remaining half lay upon the sclerotic. All authors agree as to the benign character of these tumors, and all describe them as consisting of the constituents of the normal skin. In rare cases in the latter periods of life dermoid tumors through some cause or other may become irritated and begin to grow. They are then, of course, with regard to the usefulness of the eye of a malignant character. In a very large majority of the cases, however, dermoid tumors remain stationary.

The histological appearance of three, such new-formations which I myself had occasion to examine is described in the following. (See Fig. 28).

The dermoid tumor is covered with a continuous epithelial coat, which consists of the same layers and elements as the epidermis. The most superficial layer is formed by flattened epithelial cells, which, however, are not always horny. Cells undergoing colloid metamorphosis seem to be frequent in this layer. The layer under the flattened cells has well marked serrated cells. Mucous-cells as they are found in the

conjunctiva, are also found among the epithelial cells of dermoid tumors.   This epithelial coat has as uneven a surface

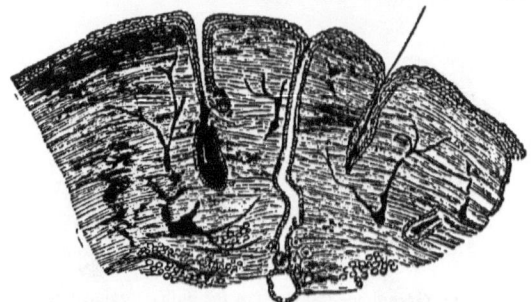

Fig. 28.—Dermoid tumor of the bulbar conjunctiva.

as that of the skin, and sends numerous offsets into the underlying tissue surrounding the papillæ of the tumor.   In
nearly all of these indentations, we find a hair or the orifice
of a gland.   The latter are of the acinous type and probably
all sudoriferous.   The hairs are very thin and have very little
pigment.   Under the epithelium lies the connective-tissue,
which appears very tough and dense, and contains a few elastic
fibrillæ.   At the base of the tumor the connective-tissue, becomes looser and includes a varying amount of fat cells.   It
seems thus far only tumors, which had been removed from the
globe have been subjected to anatomical examination, and that
their basis is always found to consist chiefly of subcutaneous
fat-tissue.   In other tumors the fat-tissue may form the bulk
of the tissue, and such tumors have by several authors been
described as lipomatous dermoid tumors.   Purely lipomatous
tumors of this part have also been spoken of by some authors,
but I am inclined to think that they were actually dermoid
with a large amount of fat-tissue.

It has been stated by others that most of the dermoid tumors contain only very few blood-vessels.   In the three cases
which I examined, the blood-vessels were as numerous as in
the skin and the network of capillaries in the papillæ was
especially well developed.   Nerves have not been found in
these tumors, which, however, does not altogether prove that
they really do not exist.

In one of my own cases, I found the connective-tissue
which lay directly under the epithelium, filled with round-

cells and the blood-vessels were very hyperæmic. I think that this dermoid tumor was in a state of irritation that would have enabled it to grow.

The connection between these tumors and the under-lying tissues has, as far as I know, not yet been described, as all the published cases concerned dermoid tumors which were removed from the living eye-ball. From clinical observation we know, however, that while they are only loosely connected with the conjunctiva (resp. sclerotic), they adhere firmly to the cornea.

d. Fibroma and Osteoma.

Fibroma and osteoma of the bulbar conjunctiva have but seldom been observed.

A fibroma described by *Saemisch* was found upon the posterior part of the bulbar conjunctiva. It consisted of dense connective-tissue with a few cells. The latter showed all the stages of development of a cell into connective-tissue fibre.

Osteoma (*von Graefe, Saemisch*) was found to be lying in a capsule of tough connective-tissue and to be true osseous tissue. *Watson* described an osteoma in the conjunctiva as springing directly from the sclerotic.

e. Papilloma, melanoma and melanocancroid new-formations.

Among the benign tumors of the bulbar conjunctiva papilloma and melanoma have been described.

Skokalsky's case of papilloma corneae is the only one which has been carefully studied, and seems to allow of no doubt as to the diagnosis. (*Horner's* case of a "fibroma papillare" will be mentioned later on). The description clearly shows, however, that this case, too, was not a corneal tumor, but sprang from the corneo-scleral margin, that is, from the conjunctival or episcleral tissue. It formed, cauliflower-like, a number of cylindrical excrescences which consisted of spindle-cells, containing blood-vessels, and was covered with epithelium.

The "pure" melanoma is generally described as a benign tumor. The benign character seems, however, very doubtful, as most of authors, including *Sœmisch*, report that at any time it may become malignant. The anatomical conditions of melanoma of the conjunctiva generally mentioned do not appear to warrant its being called a distinct species of new-formation. Such a melanoma described by *Heddaeus* and taken from the corneo-scleral margin, consisted of "detritus, epithelial cells with and without pigment, free nuclei, free pigment, numerous large round cells with large nuclei and nucleoli." Probably most of these tumors belong to the sarcomata.

Once only I had myself the opportunity to examine such a tumor, which had been removed from the conjunctiva as a benign melanoma, and I found the following conditions.

On the whole the new-formation was very much like that of a dermoid tumor. Under a thick layer of epithelium came first connective-tissue with numerous, then one with scarcely any cells, and the base of the tumors was formed by a loose tissue containing fat-cells. The blood-vessels were very numerous and they formed papillæ like those found in the skin.

The epithelium however, had several remarkable peculiarities. (See Fig. 29.) From the epithelial layer large papillæ spring forward like pointed condylomata, and these epithelial papillæ contain cavities and small canals which can sometimes be traced to the lymphatic vessels in the tissue underneath the epithelium. The epithelial cells bordering these cavities and those at the base and top of the papillæ are pigmented to a varying degree. The granular pigment lies in the protoplasma of the cells as well as in the cementing substance between them. The inner layers of the epithelium consist of well defined and large serrated cells. The nearer the surface the more they go over into flattened epithelial cells and horny scales. Some of the papillæ show pearl-nodules.

Furthermore, the tumor contains glands and hair. The hairs are very thin, only slightly pigmented and two of them generally stand together. The glands are very much like the Meibomian glands in the lids but I do not know their exact nature. A strong nerve-branch enters the base of the tumor.

The question now is, what is the anatomical diagnosis of

this "melanoma"? In the whole of its structure the growth throughout most resembles a dermoid tumor, with the differ-

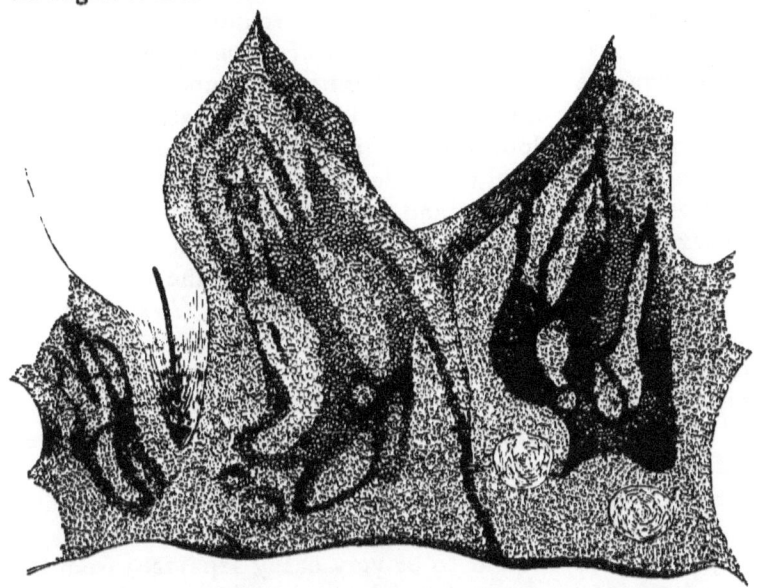

Fɪɢ. 29.—Partially pigmented epithelial papillæ from a dermoid tumor of the bulbar conjunctiva.

ence that it has papillary and epithelial excrescences. There are, however a great number of pigmented cells, among the latter which may have led to the clinical diagnosis of melanoma. Those, however, who consider pearl-nodules as a sure characteristic feature of an epithelioma, will perhaps call it a melano-cancroid.

I consider it to be a peculiar variety of the dermoid tumor and, perhaps, some of the new-formations described as melanomatous and melano-cancroid tumors may belong among the same class. Some of them were undoubtedly cases of *melanosarcomatous* tumors.

f. Leucosarcoma and Melanosarcoma.

Sarcomata of the episcleral region are comparatively rare, and among them the leucosarcomata are but very seldom found, therefore, the number of these new-formations described in literature is but very small.

Only one case of leucosarcoma of the episcleral region has come under my own observation. The tumor had about the size of a pea and consisted of large round, mingled with a few spindle-cells. A great number of these round-cells had more than one nucleus. Furthermore, I found among them a larger number of giant-cells. The new-formation contained a great many blood-vessels, lifted the conjunctival and corneal epithelium off the underlying parts and thus grew in between *Bowman's* layer and the corneal epithelium, without, however, materially altering the tissue of the cornea.

Later on the elements of the tumor enter the sclerotic and cornea proper (*Pagenstecher* and *Genth*). *Hirschberg* described such a case of a leucosarcoma of the conjunctiva with intra-ocular metastases. In what way the tumor reaches the inner membranes does not seem to be known.

Melanosarcomata of the conjunctiva have been observed and histologically examined more frequently than leucosarcomata. All authors agree in the prominently vascular character of these new-formations. In the beginning stages they were always found to be very easily separated from the underlying tissue, especially from the cornea. Very frequently an injury to the eye-ball has to be considered, as the origin of the sarcoma, and it is therefore not improbable, that the hemorrhage caused by the injury has something to do with the formation of the pigment.

I have examined three such melanosarcomatous tumors of the conjunctiva, myself, and the conditions were very much alike in all of them.

The new-formation seems to always start in the vascular limbus conjunctivæ, to gradually spread between the corneal epithelium and *Bowman's* layer, until at a certain stage, it is found to lie upon the cornea, like " pannous-tissue " without as yet having changed this membrane at all. Later on, however, the periphery of *Bowman's* layer is destroyed and the elements of the new-formation, enter the parenchyma of the cornea. *Bowman's* layer is, however, so resistant, that the elements of the tumor when they have once entered the corneal parenchyma progress much quicker towards the centre than *Bowman's* layer is destroyed. It is even possible for the new-formation to encircle the whole of the cornea, before it can pierce this layer, and thus grow into the deeper parts.

The elements of melanosarcomata, are round or spindle-cells, which vary considerably, with regard to the amount of pigment they contain. We find, therefore, in one and the same tumor, parts which are nearly unpigmented, while in other parts the cells, contain so much pigment, that it is utterly impossible to recognize their nuclei. It seems from my specimens that the highest degree of pigmentation is always found in the cells which lie nearest to the blood-vessels. The more superficial parts are generally the least pigmented ones. The cells are generally larger than white blood-cells and have one or more nuclei. I have never found any giant-cells in these tumors. (See Fig. 30).

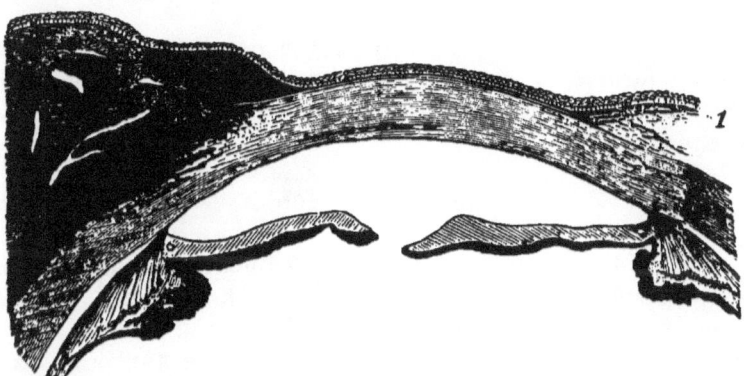

FIG. 30.—Melanosarcoma of the bulbar conjunctiva. 1. Shows how the pigmented cells creep along the blood-vessels of the conjunctiva and upon Bowman's layer under the epithelium of the cornea.

Most of the authors on this subject, mention the scarcity of an intercellular substance. In my cases, too, I could only clearly demonstrate the intercellular substance, in the peripheral parts of the tumor. The large number of capillaries form a dense network. Besides them I find a number of well distinguished veinous and arterial branches. The vascularity of these tumors readily explains the recent and old hæmorrhages usually found therein.

From my specimens it appears that in the progress of the tumor, the blood-vessels play an important part. In one of

the cases I found in the part of the episcleral tissue, which
lay diametrically opposite the original tumor a network of
pigmented stripes. Examining this part with a higher magnifying power I found the network to be formed by blood-
vessels, which were not only surrounded by a sheath of pigment but which also contained pigment molecules within their
lumen. The progress of the tumor into the parenchyma of
the cornea or sclerotic, is always preceded by the new-formation of blood-vessels and the emigration and proliferation
of cells. Along these new-formed blood-vessels the pigmented elements of the tumor, are then seen to creep into
the corneal and sclerotic tissue and to gradually destroy the lamellæ of these membranes. It does not seem to be known
whether such new-formations lead later on to rupture of the
cornea, or whether they may grow into the interior of the
eye-ball.

The periphery of the tumor in the tissues so involved, is
always formed by the well known zone of inflammation, and
their surface is covered with the conjunctival or corneal epithelium.

g. Epithelioma.

Epithelioma is the most frequently observed, of all the
tumors of the episcleral tissue. Consequently it has already
often been examined and described. The authors on this
subject (*Althoff, Classen, Horner, Knapp* and others), however, disagree in their opinions upon important points so
much, that in the following I only give the results of my
own examinations, which up to this time embrace fourteen
cases. I will only mention here that a tumor described by
Horner as a "fibroma papillare" belongs most probably to
the same class of tumors, as the patient died from carcinoma.
Furthermore, old epitheliomata of the conjunctiva, very frequently show the pupillary form known under the name of
"cauliflower"-cancer.

Epitheliomata originate in a true hyperplasia of the epithelial layer of the conjunctiva, whether they start directly
from the corneo-scleral margin or from a place somewhat remote from it. It usually begins just where *Bowman's* layer

joins the conjunctiva, and where, as stated above, the normal conjunctival epithelium dips into the underlying tissue in the shape of one or two papillæ. It seems that epithelioma never originates from the epithelium of the cornea proper.

We find, in the beginning, the epithelial layer considerably thickened, and this thickening is caused by an abnormally increased number of epithelial cells. It is in this stage furthermore, impossible to recognize the normally so distinct layers of the corneal and conjunctival epithelium, since the cells vary considerably in shape and size. In most cases nearly the whole of this original tumor consists of serrated cells, in others the cells are flat and partially horny. Every cell (except the horny ones) have a large round or oval nucleus and several nucleoli, cells with two or more nuclei are very rare. If the tumor progresses, the surrounding conjunctiva becomes hyperæmic and filled with cells, while the cornea proper remains for a long time unaltered. Gradually, however, new blood-vessels enter the cornea or sclerotic and round-cells begin to emigrate in their tissue, which process is followed by the proliferation of their fixed cells. Only then the elements of the tumor seem to be able to perforate the peripheral parts of *Bowman's* layer (as in cases of sar-

FIG. 31.—Epithelioma of the bulbar conjunctiva.

coma) and grow into cornea and sclerotic, arranged in the well known characteristic gland-like and cylindric way. (See Fig. 31). Epithelioma enters the hard membranes of the eye-ball, without having first destroyed the peripheral parts of *Bowman's* layer; the progress of the destruction of this layer however, does not necessarily go *pari passu* with the progress of the tumor in the corneal tissue, *Descemet's* membrane can resist much longer and may be found perfectly intact, even if the whole of the corneal parenchyma is taken up by the new-formation.

The following are the more minute histological details to be observed in these new-formations.

If the surface of the epitheliomatous growth is ulcerated, the conditions are altered accordingly. Where no such ulceration exists, I find the superficial layer of the tumor to consist of flattened, often horny, epithelial elements. Under these layers come the cells of the new-formation, varying in size and shape and mostly serrated, and they dip into the underlying parts forming the well known cylinders. These are the primary epithelial cylinders. They are surrounded by a tissue filled with blood-vessels and round-cells. These round-cells frequently lie so close together, that their form is altered by the pressure. They, too, vary in size. We find among them free nuclei, cells with one or two, and larger ones with even three and four nuclei.

The outlines of these primary epithelial cylinders are mostly sharply defined and their periphery is formed by a single layer of cylindrical or cone-shaped cells, which are also frequently serrated. The centre of the cylinders, consists of epithelial cells of very different size and shape; pearl-nodules are frequently found among them.

If we follow up such primary cylinders under the microscope, we see that some of them have a blunt end, others branch off into secondary and tertiary cylinders of the same kind, while others again pass over into round-cell cylinders, which then are gradually lost in the surrounding cellular tissue. (See Fig.32). Although *Knapp* states distinctly that all cylinders consist of epithelial cells and that he never saw epithelial cell cylinders go over into round-cell cylinders, my own specimens all show this condition undoubtedly. In some specimens I found even large networks of such secondary and tertiary cylinders, which consist solely of round-cells.

Sometimes I saw a number of epitheloid cells (which are similar to epithelial cells in shape, and like them, by *Muel-ler's* hardening fluid tinted darker than the surrounding

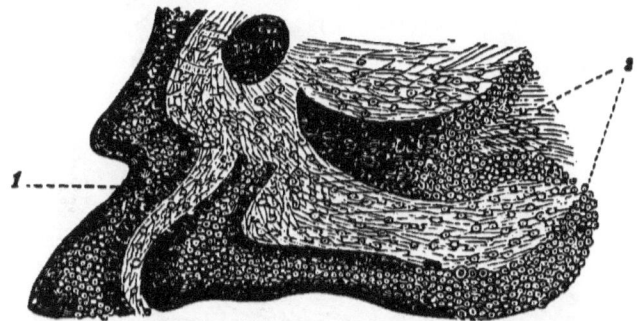

Fig. 32.—Epithelioma of the bulbar conjunctiva. 1. Epithelial cylinder filled with round-cells. 2. Epithelial cylinders ending in round-cell cylinders.

tissue) lying just in the angle where younger cylinders branched off from older ones. Although I was never able to see directly the transformation of round into epithelial cells, I could not explain the conditions, without assuming that such a change occurs. This seems to be still more probable, as I frequently found also round-cell cylinders whose periphery was formed by a single layer of epithelial cells. (See Fig. 32). I want to state here, furthermore, that while the round-cells very distinctly show the phenomena of proliferation, the number of undoubtedly proliferating epithelial cells, is but very small.

The epithelial cylinders seem in the beginning to grow along the corneal canals (*Knapp*). Later on, however, the condition of the lamellæ becomes changed in such a way, that we can no longer speak of corneal canals. The lamellæ are broken up and destroyed. We then find the cylinders surrounded by a tissue, consisting of very fine spindle-cells. (See Fig. 33).

When the tumor has grown over the whole cornea, *Bowman's* layer is always wanting. During the growth of the tumor, however, this layer is not as quickly destroyed, as the elements of the new-formation spread in the corneal tissue. *Descemet's* membrane, which as stated above, resists much longer, may in consequence of ulceration and an increased

intra-ocular pressure, at a later period be also perforated.
When this perforation takes place the capsule of the crystalline lens is often ruptured, or the lens may escape from the

FIG. 33.—Epithelioma of the bulbar conjunctiva. The tissue of the cornea is changed into
one consisting of long fine spindle-cells.

eye-ball *in toto*. When the perforation occurs, the iris probably always prolapses, and thus becomes adherent to the
new-formation. In this manner one channel is opened, by
which the elements of the tumor can enter the interior of
the eye-ball. In one case which I examined, the epithelioma
entered the anterior chamber by this channel and was found
spreading upon the surface of the iris, as well as into its parenchyma. (See Fig. 34). Doubtlessly the tumor can also

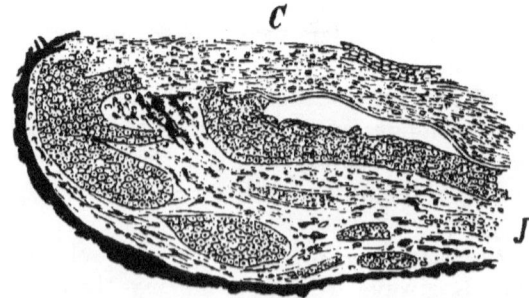

FIG. 34.—Epithelioma of the bulbar conjunctiva. The tumor has perforated the cornea,
and is spreading upon the surface and into the parenchyma of the iris. C. Cornea.
I. Iris.

enter the remaining membranes of the interior of the eye in
such a manner.

Another way (perhaps, a more frequent one) by which the elements of the epithelioma enter the interior of the eye-ball, are the lymphatic sheaths of the anterior ciliary arteries. This I saw in two cases. (See Fig. 35). While in the one

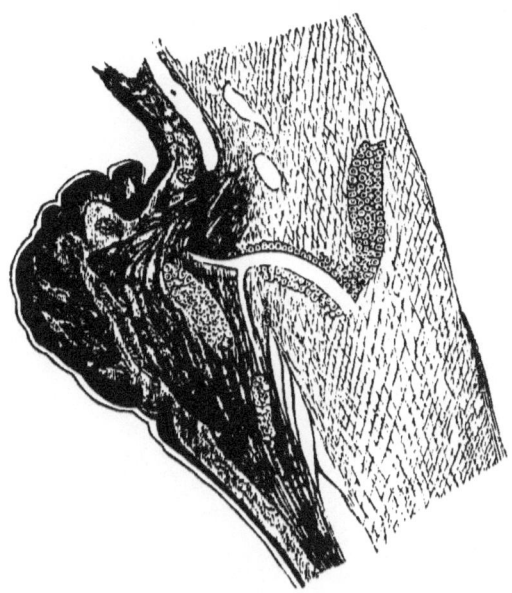

FIG. 35.—Epithelioma of the bulbar conjunctiva. An anterior ciliary artery surrounded by epithelial cells. Nests of epithelial cells in the tissue of the ciliary body.

case the epithelioma had only entered the ciliary body, it had also invaded the choroid in the other. The alterations produced in these tissues by epithelioma, resemble those above described with regard to conjunctiva, cornea and sclerotic.

My examinations have thus proven, that epithelial tumors of this region originate in a true hyperplasia of the preëxisting epithelial cells, and, furthermore, that the connective-tissue, especially the round-cells, undoubtedly play (not to say more) an important and active part in their progress.

Gummata, lupus and tubercles, in these parts which have but rarely been described, do not show any peculiar structure.

Angiomata of the conjunctiva, do not seem to have been histologically examined and they are also most probably, in no way different from similar tumors in other parts. I may' here mention that cysticercus and filaria medinensis have been observed under the bulbar conjunctiva.

IV.

IRIS.

1. NORMAL CONDITIONS.

THE iris consists of the anterior unpigmented endothelium, the parenchyma and the posterior pigmented and uveal layer.

The question whether the anterior surface of the iris is covered by a cellular coat, has up to a recent date been unsolved. *Faber*, however, has lately proven that a continuous endothelial layer covers the anterior surface of the iris. I have never been able to see this endothelial coat in hardened specimens, but only in fresh ones. I found the conditions several times materially as stated by *Faber*.

The endothelial layer covers the whole of the anterior surface of the iris from the ligamentum pectinatum to the pupillary margin. Its cells are flat, varying in size, but mostly oblong and quadrangular and have a large round nucleus. These cells, however, do not lie in one plain next to each other, but are arranged like tiles, partially, covering each other as *J. Arnold* has stated before *Faber*. The endothelium forms, as it seems, only a single layer. *Faber* states that the nuclei of these cells are also flattened, and appear rod-shaped in transverse sections, like those of connective-tissue and organic muscular fibres. These cells are always unpigmented. According to *Faber* the endothelial layer ends by papillary excresences at the pupillary margin.

It appears that these endothelial cells are only loosely connected with the underlying tissue or are very perishable, which would explain why it is so very difficult to see them.

The parenchyma of the iris appears to be composed of three layers, viz., a dense anterior, a loose middle, and a dense fibrous posterior layer. They, however, do not exist in reality, as distinctly separate layers, but they gradually merge into each other, and the anterior and posterior layers form.

—so to speak—only a condensation of the middle one. The chief elements of which the parenchyma of the iris consists, are connective-tissue and blood-vessels. The former is in different individuals, developed in a different degree ; its cellular elements are, however, always far more numerous than the fibres. The cells are partially unpigmented, partially pigmented to a varying degree. Those of the anterior and especially the posterior layer are mostly spindle-shaped ; those of the middle layer have two or more offsets, and frequently anastomose with each other. Moreover, we find, also in the parenchyma of the iris, as in other tissues, a number of wandering cells.

The arteries of the iris come from the circulus iridis major and run in a radiating direction towards the pupillary margin, meanwhile giving off numerous smaller branches. Near the pupillary margin they form the circulus iridis minor and then a capillary network between the fibres of the sphincter pupillæ muscle, or go directly over into veins (*Faber*). The veins run again in a radiating direction back to the ciliary bodies and empty the blood into the vorticous veins. According to *J. Arnold* the blood-vessels of the iris have an abnormally thick muscular layer. The adventitia also is more developed than is commonly the case in blood-vessels of the same size.

The nerves of the iris which are hardly less numerous than the blood-vessels, are on the whole arranged like these. They come from the ciliary nerves and form very soon after entering the iris a network with narrow meshes from which branches run to the anterior and posterior surface, and into the sphincter pupillæ. Nothing certain is known with regard to where and how they end. *Faber* also describes numerous ganglion-cells in the iris.

The parenchyma of the iris contains, moreover, near the pupillary margin the sphincter pupillæ muscle. This is a muscular ring which lies nearer the posterior than the anterior surface of the iris. It consists of organic muscular fibres, with a rod-like nucleus. While the existence of this muscle is proven beyond a doubt, the same cannot be said of the dilatator pupillæ described as its antagonist. The fibres of the latter are said to run in a radiating direction, from the cil-

iary margin towards the sphincter and to unite with this muscle, after being bent in an arch-like way. In the eyes of animals, especially of rabbits, these conditions are plainly to be
seen. I have, however, never yet been able to distinguish a
dilatator pupillæ in the iris of the human eye. *Iwanoff* recently tried to convince us that the spindle-cells of the posterior layer of the iris are muscular fibres. This question can,
however, hardly be decided by the microscope alone, since
we all know, how difficult it is to distinguish by the mere
form and shape between organic muscular—and connective-
tissue cells. The effects of the different agents and staining
materials, upon the tissue give us more certainty, with regard
to this matter and even in the finest sections, I have never been
able to see anything which convinced me of the existence of a
dilatator pupillæ in the human iris.

The posterior surface of the iris is covered by the very
darkly pigmented uveal layer. *Bruch* discovered between it
and the posterior layer of the iris a lamina vitrea, like the
one upon the choroid and identical with it, (" *Bruch's* membrane,"). *Faber*, too again recently maintained the existence
of this membrane. My own observations force me, however,
to agree with those authors who deny its existence in the
human iris.

It is very difficult to distinguish the elements which constitute the uveal layer. With great care, it is, however, possible to recognize a number of round or oblong and irregu-
lary formed cells, which are densely crowded with pigment-
molecules, so that we can scarcely ever see the round nucleus.
These cells do not seem to possess a cell-membrane. *Faber*
describes still another kind of round cell with a cell-membrane. It appears to me, however, that the whole of the
posterior part of the uveal layer is formed by a continuous
layer of protoplasma in which pigment-molecules are suspended and which in transverse sections is often seen as a
fine light streak, forming the posterior margin of the iris.

This streak has been described as lamina pigmenti or
limiting membrane, and was lately by *Faber* again considered
to be a separate membrane. It is, however, impossible to detach it, and pathological conditions, of which we shall speak

later, do not allow us to recognize this streak as a separate limiting membrane of the iris.

The uveal layer covers the whole of the posterior surface of the iris and reaches somewhat farther than its pupillary margin.

2. PATHOLOGICAL CONDITIONS.

A. *Iritis and its Results.*

The different forms of iritis which are clinically distinguished can not be so separated histologically. The large number of blood-vessels embedded in the parenchyma of the iris must needs be the most important factors in causing the symptoms of the different forms of iritis. Every inflammation of the iris is preceded by hyperaemia of the blood-vessels. Such a hyperaemia of the iris must be considered as a distinct clinical affection from iritis. Histologically it does, not however, appear to produce pathological alterations in the tissue of the iris. The different forms of iritis are chiefly characterized by the products of inflammation, the exudates found upon the surfaces or in the parenchyma of the iris. We consider in the following 1. *serous* (sero-fibrinous ; hemorrhagic), 2. *fibrinous* (plastic) and 3. *purulent* (parenchymatous) forms of iritis.

a. *Iritis serosa (sero-fibrinosa, hemorrhagica).*

As in every other tissue, we find in the iris, as soon as it is inflamed, a considerable degree of hyperæmia of the blood-vessels and an increase of cells. In the beginning these cells are exclusively emigrated, white blood-corpuscles, and no signs of proliferation are to be found in the preëxisting parenchymatous cells. The latter begin to proliferate at a later period only. Besides these new cells, we find that the meshes of the iris tissue, contain serous fluid, which makes them appear distended, and renders the whole of the iris thicker than normal. At the same time some serous fluid is exuded upon the anterior and posterior surfaces of the iris, *i. e.* into the posterior and anterior chambers.

Serous iritis does not seem to materially alter the anterior endothelial coat. The uveal layer, however, is mostly altered in such a way, that its elements become remarkably glutinous and the posterior surface of the iris thus becomes adherent to the anterior capsule of the crystalline lens. I have tried in vain in a large number of specimens to find cellular elements which might unite the iris with the lens-capsule. (I speak here only of cases of serous iritis). This may explain why the posterior synechiæ caused by serous iritis are comparatively easier severed. If the pupillary edge of the iris has thus become glued to the anterior lens-capsule, it often happens that the exudate in the posterior chamber, presses the periphery of the iris forward into the anterior chamber, and thus causes the iris to become, what has been styled " crater-shaped." (See Fig. 36). It seems that this

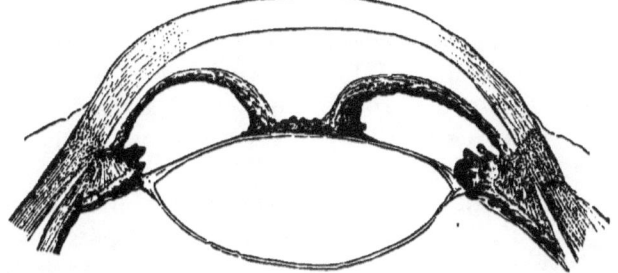

FIG. 36. –Serous-iritis. The pupillary edge of the iris is adherent to the anterior lens-capsule. The peripheral parts of the iris are protruding into the anterior chamber (crater-shaped iris).

pressure from behind may produce atrophy of the blood-vessels and the parenchyma of the iris, which conditions were at least present in one such case which I examined.

As stated above, the endothelial cells upon the anterior surface of the iris do not seem to be altered by serous iritis. The latter, however, always produces pathological changes in the endothelial cells lying upon *Descemet's* membrane. These become irritated (probably by the pressure exerted upon them) and begin to proliferate partially while others become destroyed. In this way small deposits are formed upon *Descemet's* membrane which consist of round-cells, free nuclei and detritus. These sometimes become detached and then fall to the bottom of the anterior chamber. These changes in the endothelial cells of *Descemet's* membrane, make it very probable that the endothelial cells upon the anterior surface of the iris, do not remain unaltered, although I have never been able to see any changes.

Serous iritis may perfectly recover and leave either no trace, or only posterior synechiæ behind. If this is not the case it will become a chronic iritis, and will then lead to a more active cell-proliferation in the parenchyma of the iris which, ends in the new-formation of connective-tissue, and the gradual atrophy and destruction of the preëxisting cellular elements. Later on the blood vessels too, become atrophic, which atrophy again produces atrophy of the whole of the iris-tissue. This *circulus vitiosus* is materially aided in its progress, by the pressure exerted upon the iris-tissue by the exudation.

A variety of serous iritis is the sero-fibrinous and hæmorrhagic iritis. As far as I know, this kind of iritis has only once been examined histologically, and described by myself. Clinically it has been called iritis with a spongy exudation. (*Gunning, Knapp, Gruening*).

The characteristic features of this kind of iritis are numerous larger and smaller hæmorrhages into the parenchyma of the iris. While the fluid parts of the blood, are transuded into the anterior chamber, its cellular elements remain lying in the parenchyma of the iris, and there undergo the well known changes of fatty destruction. The fibrine of the blood coagulates in the anterior chamber, and is later on gradually dissolved again from the cornea backwards. It happens that at some time we find two different kinds of exudation in the anterior chamber, *viz.*, a gelatinous part near the cornea, and a sero-fibrinous part upon the iris. (See Fig. 37). The latter appears under the microscope as a network of very fine fibrinous threads, not unlike those found in the alveoli in croupous pneumonia, and filled with serum and a small number of lymphatic cells. The former is a perfectly uniform transparent substance, which differs from the aqueous humor only by being gelatinous. The dissolution and absorption of this peculiar exudation, always begins in the parts nearest the cornea and progress more or less concentrically. This mode of absorption explains why at some time the exudation is in shape and appearance very much like an opaque lens,

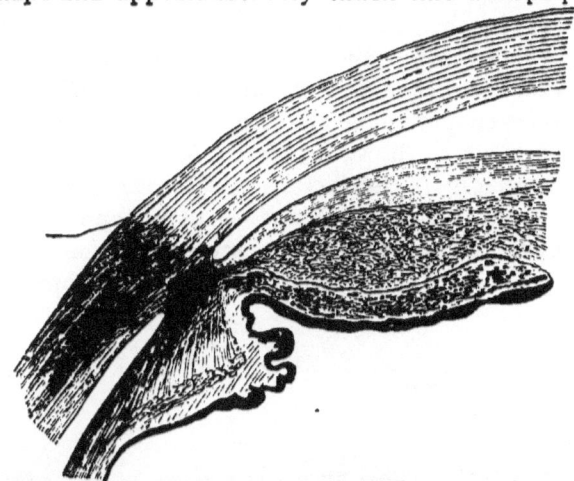

FIG. 37.—Hæmorrhagic iritis (with spongy exudation). Hæmorrhages in the parenchyma of the iris. In the anterior chamber lies a fibrinous and a gelatinous exudation.

which before it was duly recognized, led to frequent errors with regard to the treatment of this affection.

Serous inflammation of the iris may spread upon the ciliary body and choroid and thus produce more serious symptoms. It is also frequently combined with keratitis leading to sclerosis of the involved part of the cornea.

b. Iritis fibrinosa (plastica).

Fibrinous iritis shows besides hyperaemia of the blood-vessels and an increase of cellular elements in the parenchyma of the iris, a fibrinous exudation. This exudation generally appears first at the pupillary edge and we then find besides the adhesion between the posterior surface of the iris, and the anterior lens-capsule (which we also found in cases of serous iritis), an amorphous fibrinous coagulum upon the pupillary region of the anterior lens-capsule. The exudation is but seldom found upon the posterior, and yet more rarely upon the anterior surface of the iris in the earlier periods of the disease. The fibrinous coagulum usually contains some

round-cells. If the process be arrested at this period the
fibrine may be dissolved, and totally absorbed. It is, however
very frequently found that the disease progresses and the
fibrine becomes an organized tissue. More round cells wander into it and assume the spindle-shape, while the fibrine
is destroyed. We then find at some later period instead of
the fibrinous coagulum, a delicate membrane consisting of
spindle-cells, which however, later on is changed into a
fibrous and tough connective-tissue. This membrane, generally called pupillary membrane, usually spreads a short
distance upon the anterior and posterior surface of the iris.
(See Fig. 38). At a later period we frequently find that the

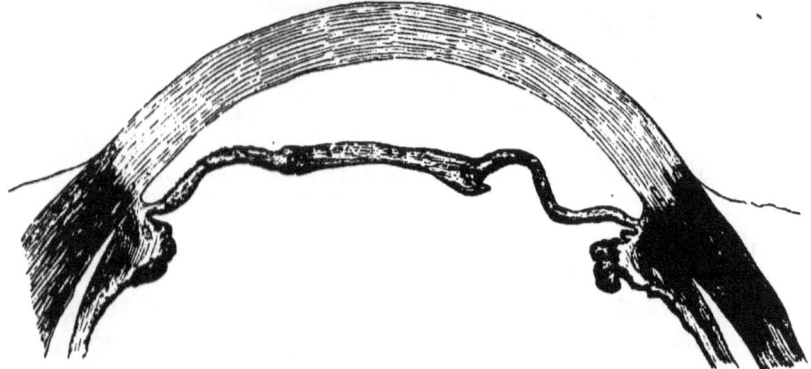

Fig. 38.—Plastic iritis. Pupillary membrane.

blood-vessels of the iris have grown into the pupillary membrane. When this new-formed connective-tissue shrinks,
it, of course drags upon the iris, which thus is drawn towards
one side or towards the centre of the pupil and becomes
atrophic. If at the same time some fibrine has been exuded
upon the posterior surface of the iris, this may also be transformed into connective-tsssue, which later on produces an
adhesion between iris and lens-capsule, materially different
from the common pupillary adhesion.

As above stated, fibrinous exudation, is but seldom deposited upon the anterior surface of the iris. It seems to
me that this happens only when the changes in the pupillary
region have taken place, and the posterior surface of the iris
has become adherent to the lens. In rare cases this fibrinous

exudation is deposited in such a quantity, upon the anterior surface of the iris that the anterior chamber is perfectly filled with it. The exudation may here also become organized and vascularized. Membranes thus formed, generally have a lamellar structure, similar to the corneal tissue. They frequently contain old or recent hæmorrhages. (See Fig. 39).

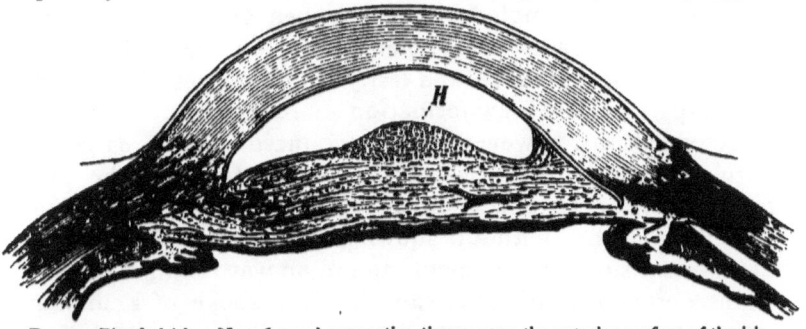

FIG. 39. Plastic iritis.—New-formed connective-tissue upon the anterior surface of the iris. This tissue is lamellar and contains blood-vessels. H. A large hæmorrhage.

The alterations, caused by the above described conditions in the parenchyma of the iris, produce perfect atrophy of this membrane. The uveal layer frequently shows a very peculiar appearance. In the beginning of the affection. it is very much thickened, and when the fibrinous exudation lying upon it becomes organized, it seems that the protoplasma, in which the pigment-molecules are suspended is consumed. The pigment molecules, thus freed, are drawn into the new-formed connective-tissue, and the uveal layer appears several times thicker than it does in the normal condition.

Fibrinous inflammation may, of course, also spread from the iris upon the ciliary body and choroid. Furthermore, the communication between the vitreous body and the anterior chamber being perfectly cut off, the intra-ocular pressure, may become increased and lead to results to be detailed farther on.

c. Iritis purulenta (parenchymatosa).

While in iritis serosa and fibrinosa we found the exudation to contain but few cells, the latter are the prevalent part of the exudation of a purulent iritis.

Hyperæmia of the blood-vessels is at once followed by a considerable emigration of round-cells, and proliferation of the parenchymatous cells of the iris. This causes the iris to become rapidly swollen, and pus-cells wander into the anterior chamber, at first probably through the meshes, of the ligamentum pectinatum. If the changes progress, we find that all the elements forming the tissue of the iris are gradually destroyed. The proliferating parenchymatous cells lose their pigment-molecules, which then are lying free between the cells, and free nuclei. Later on, the endothelial cells, the muscular fibres, and lastly the blood-vessels take an active part in the new-formation of round-cells. We find these conditions, however, well pronounced only in cases of purulent panophthalmitis, and we may then see the iris replaced by a mass of round-cells and free nuclei, filling the anterior chamber without showing any traces of muscles, blood-vessels or even pigment, and in no way reminding one of the normal conditions of the iris. We spoke of a similar affection observed in the cornea, and called keratomalacia; it might be very appropriate to call this condition of the iris iridomalacia. (See Fig. 40).

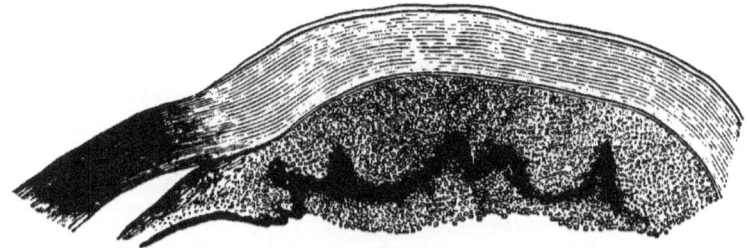

FIG. 40.—Purulent Iritis.

Parenchymatous iritis may also appear as a merely local affection, in the shape of a gumma or tubercle. In both cases we find local swelling and accumulation of round-cells. *Colberg* described a case of gumma of the iris. He found free nuclei, gummy intercellular substance and new-formed connective-tissue. These cell accumulations gradually undergo a fatty metamorphosis, and the detritus is usually emptied into the anterior chamber, after the anterior surface of the iris has been ruptured. A small scar is generally the only remaining trace of such a local parenchymatous iritis. Gumma as well as tubercle may, however, grow so large as to touch the posterior surface of the cornea. Anterior synechia may be thus formed with or without perforation of the cornea. This is probably the only way in which anterior synechiæ of the iris, is formed without preceding perforation of the cornea.

Diffuse purulent iritis, as stated above is chiefly found in cases of purulent panophthalmitis. It may, however, also be the primary affection, and lead to purulent panophthalmitis.

The Results of Iritis.

If iritis does not heal at an early stage, or if the inflammation, does not lead to the perfect destruction of the eye-ball, by spreading over the remaining parts of this organ, it leaves changes behind which always enable us to make a a sure diagnosis, with the aid of the microscope.

a. Synechiæ of the Iris.

The most frequent results of iritis are synechiæ of the iris, especially posterior ones, anterior ones being only in exceptional cases caused by iritis. The name synechiæ is here applied to the adhesion between the iris, (especially of its pupillary edge), and the anterior capsule of the lens. Synechiæ are caused by all the three forms of iritis. In cases of simple synechiæ, I never could. find an organized tissue, between iris and lens-capsule. In transverse sections the uveal layer simply lies close upon the lens-capsule. If we try to sever the synechiæ, the uveal layer, is torn and remains partly upon the lens-capsule, partly in connection with the iris. I suppose chemical processes cause these adhesions which the microscope cannot possibly detect. The conditions are very different when the whole of the posterior surface of the iris is glued to the lens, in the pupillary membranes and the new-formed tissue upon the anterior surface of the iris. Here we always find a new-formed connective-tissue, which at first contains a large number of cells, and later on becomes tougher, denser, and loses the cellular elements. It is then generally vascularized by new-formed blood-vessels starting from the blood-vessels of the iris. (See Fig. 41.) During the period of retraction, this new-formed tissue drags upon the tissue of the iris and causes it to atrophy.

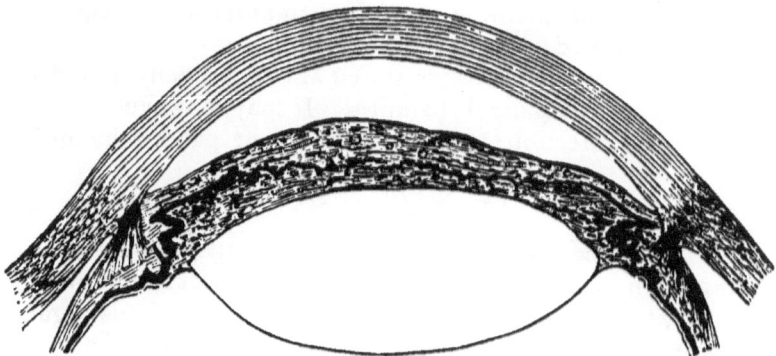

FIG. 41.—New-formed connective-tissue uniting the posterior surface of the iris with the anterior lens-capsule after plastic iritis.

b. Atrophy of the Iris.

Besides the just mentioned atrophy of the iris, caused by pressure and tearing from parts outside the parenchyma of the iris, atrophy of the latter may be, and is frequently the result of chronic iritis. The atrophy is then the direct consequence of the new-formation of connective-tissue, in the parenchyma of the iris, or the pressure exerted upon it by the exudation of serum into its meshes and interstices. It seems that the first to suffer from atrophy, are the pigmented parenchyma cells. They undergo fatty degeneration, become granular, and are broken up. Their pigment is then found scattered about in the tissue; later on it may nearly altogether disappear. The last to become atrophic are the uveal layer and the muscular tissue of the sphincter pupillæ, and even in the highest degrees, of atrophy of the iris, they are not totally destroyed.

In one case of very far advanced atrophy of the iris, I found the anterior endothelium, in a state of colloid metamorphosis. (See Fig. 42.) With a low magnifying power it appeared like a new-formed transparent lamella, covering the anterior surface of the iris. (Similar vitreous lamellæ, upon the iris have been described by a number of authors, and declared to be inflammatory new-formations; perhaps, they ought to have been explained in the same way as the one under consideration). With a high power it was easily seen to consist of endothelial cells, filled with colloid substance.

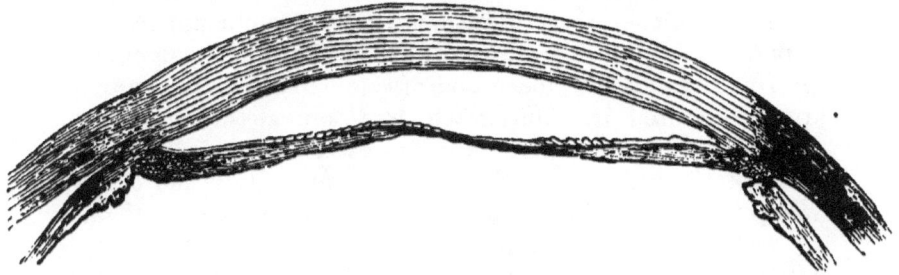

Fig. 42.—Iritis chronica. Atrophy of the iritis and colloid metamorphosis of its anterior endothelial coat.

Atrophy of the whole iris, of course, involves also its blood-vessels and nerves.

B. *Injuries to the Iris and their Results.*

Injuries to the iris are mostly combined with an injury to the cornea or sclerotic or even more parts of the eye-ball. It is easily understood that the histological conditions are accordingly complicated. We will however, here mention only those injuries which involve cornea, or sclerotic and iris, and those which concern the iris alone.

Foreign bodies which enter the eye, only very seldom remain lodged in the tissue of the iris. They either perforate it and pass farther on, or rebound and fall into the anterior chamber. If however, they remain lodged in the iris, they produce at first a local, later on a diffuse iritis, which generally assumes a purulent character. More does not seem to be known, with regard to the anatomical conditions. Foreign bodies intentionally brought into the iris of animals, lead also to the growth of sarcomatous new-formations.

The injury may sever the tissue of the iris to a varying extent. The wound may lie at the pupillary edge, or in the part between it and the ciliary margin, or at the latter, or the whole of the breadth of the iris, may be rent apart in a radiary direction, or it may reach from the sphincter or ciliary edge, into the part between the two. If the iris tissue is thus once severed, the gap generally remains a permanent one.

The edges of such a wound heal through a small amount of
fibrine which becomes exuded and organized upon them.
The healing process after wounds caused by operations too,
show nothing peculiar.

Rents of the sphincter edge of the iris (coloboma) and the
separation of the ciliary edge of the iris from the ligamentum
pectinatum and the ciliary body (iridodialysis) are not unfrequently caused by injuries which do not at the same time
rupture either of the hard membranes of the eye-ball. Ruptures of the part of the iris, between its pupillary and ciliary
margins, are probably always combined with wounds of one
or both of the hard membranes.

If the cornea or the corneo-scleral margin has been ruptured by the injury, the aqueous humor will flow out, and
the either wounded or normal iris, becomes entangled in the
wound-lips, or is thrown further into the wound-canal. This
causes the formation of an anterior synechia (leucoma ad-
hærens) or a prolapse of the iris, which may either become
reduced or remain stationary. If the prolapse of the iris
remain stationary, the prolapsed part may either decay, and
fall off (and thus again an anterior synechiæ be the result) or
it may become the starting point of a granuloma of the iris,
of which more later on.

The histological conditions in cases of anterior synechiæ,
of the iris have been spoken of above (See chapter I). I
must mention here, however, a condition resulting from
anterior synechiæ, and involving the iris only. I mean the
formation of serious cysts of the iris. *Von Wecker & Knapp*
have stated (and I once had occasion to confirm their
statement) that serous cysts of the iris may be formed, if
a fold of this membrane, becomes adherent to the posterior
surface of the cornea (or to a wound-canal in the latter), that
is, that the parenchyma of the iris takes no active part in the
formation of these cysts. The walls of such a serous cyst of
the iris which I had occasion to examine were two-thirds
formed by the atrophic iris, and one-third by the posterior
surface of the cornea, and were thus perfectly lined with the
endothelium of the anterior chamber. (See Fig. 43.)

The cavity formed in such a way inside the anterior chamber, becomes larger through the pressure of the aqueous humor secreted by it. *Von Wecker* states that such a cyst

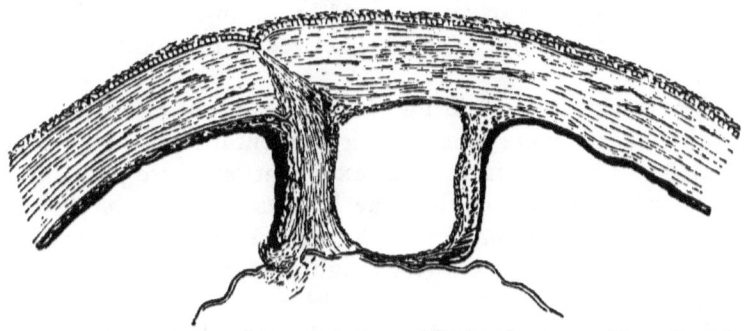

Fig. 43—So-called cyst of the iris, formed after an injury to the cornea. The walls of the cyst are formed by Descemet's membrane, the atrophic iris and some new-formed connective-tissue, and lined with the endothelium of the anterior chamber.

may separate itself at a later period from the cornea. This appears rather improbable from the anatomical conditions, and, moreover, clinical experience shows that these cysts are firmly adherent to the cornea, and therefore are nearly always ruptured in the attempt to remove them by an operation.

What we described above as crater-shaped iris, that is, the bulging and atrophy of the periphery of this membrane, subsequent to circular posterior synechia of the pupillary margin, is by *von Wecker* enumerated among the cysts of the iris.

Some authors described another variety of cyst, in the parenchyma of the iris filled with atheromatous substance, and always resulting from an injury which has been called " epidermoidoma." *Krause's* observations leave no doubt that these cysts are caused by epithelial cells, from the hair-follicles of the eye-lashes, which are thrown into the parenchyma of the iris during the infliction of an injury, are there retained, and then begin to proliferate. This is the more probable, as generally in these cases one or more ciliæ were found in the anterior chamber or in the tissue of the iris.

It follows therefore from the facts above stated, that serous cysts of the iris are improperly so-called, and originate in an injury followed by the adhesion of a fold of the iris to the cornea. Atheromatous cysts lie really in the parenchyma of the iris, and are usually caused by an injury without the formation of anterior synechiæ between this membrane and the cornea.

The conditions resulting from prolapse of the iris, were studied by me some time ago, experimentally on the eyes of animals. The results of these examinations were published, without however, applying the lessons they taught unconditionally to the human eye. Numerous specimens from the human eye have since then, taught me, that I would have been justified in doing so.

Very soon after the iris has prolapsed into a wound-canal of the cornea or sclerotic, it becomes infiltrated with blood in consequence of the stasis of its blood-vessels. If the prolapse protrudes through the cornea, it may become necrotic and be thrown off. The outer orifice of the wound-canal is then covered by new-formed connective-tissue and epithelium, and we thus find again the conditions of an anterior synechia. If the prolapse is small, it may be covered *in toto* with scartissue (See Fig. 44), into which a fibrinous exudation coming

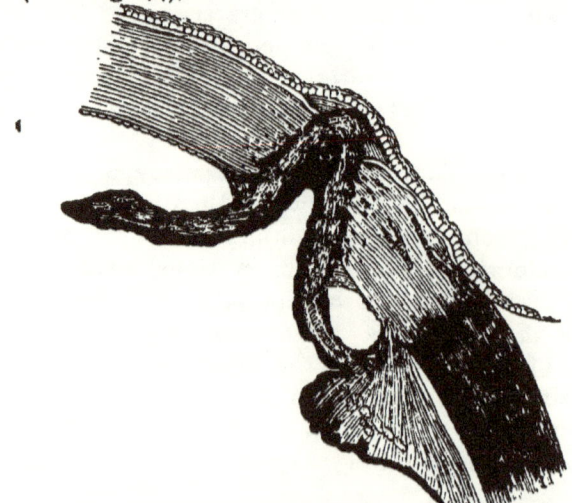

Fig. 44.—Incarcerated iris. Small prolapse of the iris into a corneal wound, covered with new-formed connective-tissue and epithelium.

from the iris is gradually transformed. This is especially the case when the iris has prolapsed at the corneo-scleral margin (for instance after operations in that region). The epithelium which finally covers such a prolapse in the corneo-scleral region, takes the greater part of its origin from the conjunctiva. The final stationary condition has received the name of " incarceration " of the iris.

Injuries to the eye without inflicting wounds may sometimes cause a part, or the whole of the pupillary edge of the iris to be tilted backwards. Such cases have, however, it seems, never been microscopically examined.

C. Tumors of the Iris.

a. *Granuloma Traumaticum.*

Although clinicists have described a genuine (non-tranmatic) granuloma of the iris, only the traumatic one has so far been microscopically studied. The results of my own examinations of three such cases, perfectly agree with those of *Hirschberg* and *Steinheim.*

Prolapse of iris, or those parts which are exposed to the air through the destruction of the cornea, often become the origin of such tumors. The latter consist of round and small spindle-cells, between which are found a small amount of connective-tissue and new-formed blood-vessels. (See Fig. 45). The tumor may or may not be covered by epithelium. It is probable that, like other granulomata this, also may be transformed into connective-tissue and thus heal by itself.

Hirschberg and *Von Wecker* also count among the granulomata of the iris a vascular tumor, described by *Mooren*, but not examined anatomically. *Schirmer* mentioned a " cavernous " tumor of the iris which probably belonged to the same class.

b. *Melanoma.*

Knapp was, as far as I know, the first to describe simple melanoma of the iris after having seen a specimen of *J. Arnold's.* It " consisted of circumscribed accumulations of stroma-cells of the iris, the larger part of which were pigmented, had many offsets and anastomosed with each other.

They passed without a sharp boundary into the neighboring tissue, and the remainder of the iris was normal." This kind

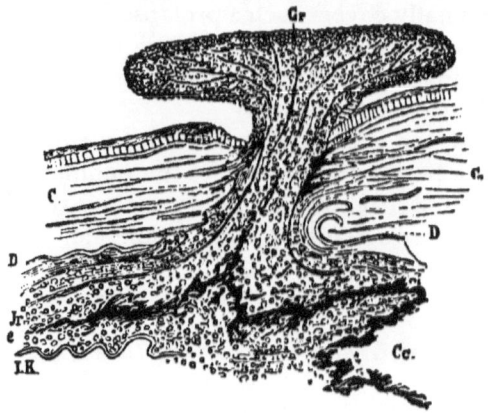

FIG. 45.—Traumatic granuloma of the iris after this membrane has prolapsed. Gr. Granuloma. C. Cornea. D. Descemet's membrane. Ir. Iris. Cc. Ciliary body. L.C Lens-capsule.

of tumor is certainly very rare. Like all the so-called benign melanomata, it is said to be able at any time to assume a malignant character.

c. Leucosarcoma and Melanosarcoma.

Primary sarcomata of the iris are very rarely met with. Only four such cases have so far been anatomically examined and described (*Dreschfeld, Knapp, Hirschberg, Kipp.*)

It seems that the new-formation takes its origin from the parenchyma of the iris. In *Dreschfeld's* case only, it was said to have started from the connective-tissue between the muscular fibres.

From these different descriptions, we know of unpigmented (*Kipp*) pigmented (*Hirschberg*) spindle-cell sarcoma, and pigmented round-cell sarcoma. All of the tumors were very vascular. Judging from the structure of the iris, we may expect (and the descriptions prove it), that the pigmented tumors have also some unpigmented parts and *vice versa*. *Dreschfeld* found some small nests of organic muscular fibres in his case, and considered this proof, that the tumor originated in the intra-muscular connective-tissue.

Sarcoma of the iris seems to grow comparatively slowly.

It causes, like other intra-ocular tumors, glaucoma, and leads to destruction of the eye.

Metastic tumors caused by primary sarcoma of the iris, have been clinically observed.

V. Corpus Ciliare.

1. *Normal Conditions.*

The tissue of the ciliary body consists of the same elements as that of the iris. We find here as the outermost layer (near the sclerotic) an endothelial coat, then the parenchyma and inwards from this, the pigmented uveal layer which, moreover, is here covered by another layer, *viz.*, the ciliary part of the retina. While the surfaces of the iris are comparatively smooth, the inner surface of the ciliary body, has a large number of processes and corresponding indentations. The former are called the ciliary processes.

The parenchyma of the ciliary body, like that of the iris, consists in the main part of cellular elements. We here again find round unpigmented cells, and cells with offsets which are either pigmented or unpigmented. The pigmented cells with offsets are very numerous, only in the eyes of negroes. In the eyes of the white races, the tissue of the ciliary body has chiefly unpigmented cells. Besides the cells, we find a larger quantity of connective-tissue fibres, and elastic fibres in the ciliary body, than in the iris. The connective-tissue prevails in the outer parts (near the sclerotic), while the cellular elements form mainly the inner layers of the ciliary body.

Embedded in this tissue is the ciliary muscle. It consists, as well known, of circular (equatorial) and longitudinal (meridional) fibres. The longitudinal fibres lie in the outer, the circular ones more in the inner part, of the ciliary body. The two kinds of fibres are, however, not perfectly distinct from each other, as a fibre may at first run in a longitudinal and then in a circular direction and *vice versa*. The elements of this muscle are organic muscular fibres.

Iwanoff was the first to point out that the proportion, between the two kinds of fibres (circular and longitudinal),

varies in different eyes.   He found that in myopic eyes, that
is, eyes which are very long, the longitudinal fibres prevail
(See Fig. 46), while in hypermetropic, that is, short eyes, the

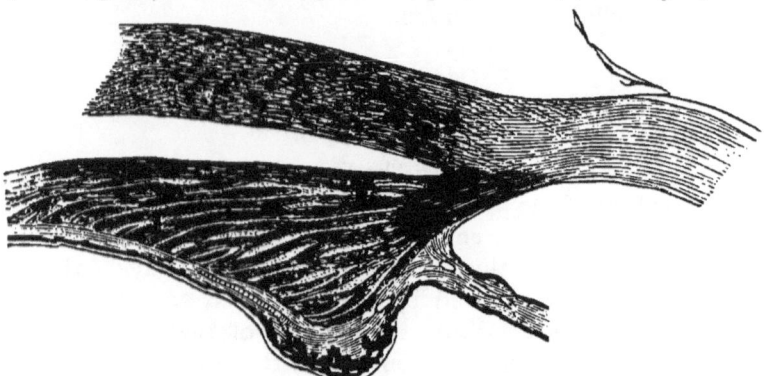

Fig. 46.—Ciliary body from a myopic eye.

circular fibres, which are but few in an emmetropic eye, are
very numerous. (See Fig. 47). *Iwanoff*, however, has at

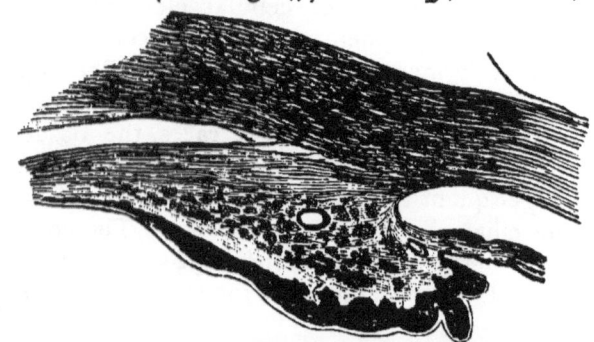

Fig. 47.—Ciliary body from an hypermetropic eye.

the same time to confess there are many exceptions to these
conditions.

To explain the mode in which accommodation takes
place, a number of hypotheses have been put forward and,
strange to say, most of them would presume just the reverse
condition, of the ciliary muscle from that which we frequently
find.   This has already been pointed out by *Loring*.   It is
not the place here to speak of the physiological action of this
muscle, but I have to state, that in eyes suffering from ciliary

or total staphyloma we find the same conditions, with regard to the ciliary muscle as in myopic eyes, *i. e.* only longitudinal fibres. This would show that any stretching of the ciliary muscle, is enough to produce such conditions.

The question, how the ciliary muscle acts, when the eye accommodates, can only be satisfactorily solved, by closely studying the development of this muscle, and it would, be very important to know, for instance, whether in a case of non-progressive myopia this muscle presents the same arrangement soon after birth, that it does in the later periods of progressive myopia. The authors on the development of the eye have, it seems, all neglected to study this point, which is of such great importance. In the eyes of two newly born children I only found longitudinal fibres, although the shape of the eyes impressed me as being that of emmetropic ones.

The fibres of the ciliary muscle are joined anteriorly in a tendon which passes over into *Descemet's* membrane, and the posterior lamellæ of the cornea in the way, described above (See Chapter I). Posteriorly the muscular fibres end in the outer layers of the choroid in peculiar star-like formations (*Ierophceff, Iwanoff*), some of them pass into the sclerotic.

On equatorial sections through the ciliary body, it is seen that the separation into longitudinal and circular fibres, which is so well pronounced in meridional sections, is only apparent, and that the fibres interlace at all sorts of angles.

The blood-vessels of the ciliary body come from the arteriæ ciliares posteriores longæ and the arteriæ ciliares anteriores. Their structure shows nothing peculiar. The larger part of their branches lie in the layers to the inner side of the ciliary muscle. The veins of the ciliary body conduct the blood either to the small veins coming from the cornea (resp. conjunctiva), or to the vorticous veins (*Leber*).

The nerves constituting a net-work of the ciliary body, come from the ciliary nerves. They lie chiefly upon the outer surface of the ciliary muscle, from where smaller branches enter the latter. It is not known how and where they end.

If we sever the ciliary body (or choroid) from the sclero-

tic, a number of fibres will remain in connection with the
latter, which have been called the lamina fusca. This
lamina is, however, not an independent membrane. As
stated above, some of the fibres of the ciliary muscles insert
themselves into the sclerotic, moreover, connective-tissue
fibres from the sclerotic enter the ciliary body, (and choroid)
and *vice versa.* It is therefore easily comprehended that in
separating the two layers, we tear these fibres apart. The part
remaining adherent to the sclerotic is the lamina fusca, the
part remaining connected with the ciliary body (or choroid) is
the so-called lamina suprachorioidea. Both of these parts are
formed by the fibres joining the hard membranes of the eye
and the uveal tract which (*J. Arnold*) have one and the same
origin in the embryo. A structureless, homogeneous interfibrillar substance, as described by *Iwanoff*, I cannot find.
The meshes between the fibres contain, however, a serous
(lymphatic) fluid which coagulates when the eye is hardened.

Between these fibres lie a large number of pigmented
cells. These are very irregular in shape, and have mostly
short, broad offsets, and are flat. Their large oval or round
nucleus is unpigmented. Besides these pigmented cells of
various shapes, (*Iwanoff* also described round ones), there
are unpigmented endothelial and lymph-cells. The latter
have nothing peculiar. The existence of the former is proven
by staining with nitrate of silver. They form a continuous
coat upon the inner surface of the sclerotic, and the outer
surface of the ciliary body (and choroid), perforated only by
the fibres running from one of these parts to the other
Endothelial cells also lie upon the latter in the same way in
which we found them, adherent to the fibres of the ligamentum pectinatum.

The parenchyma of the ciliary body is, on its inner surface, covered by a thin, elastic vitreous membrane which is,
however, only continuous upon the so-called *pars non-plicata*
Anteriorly to this it is perforated, and thus forms a net-work,
the meshes of which are oblong in a longitudinal direction
(*Iwanoff*). I can not, however, perfectly agree with *Iwanoff*,
who could trace this vitreous membrane even upon the ciliary
processes, for I never found it there.

The uveal layer of the ciliary body, lies on the inner surface of this vitreous membrane. It consists of cells which vary considerably in shape and size. They are densely filled with pigment-molecules, which leave only the round nucleus free. The cells are united to each other by a structureless cementing substance and form one, or sometimes several layers. It is very difficult to distinguish the single cells upon the ciliary processes and the uveal layer here greatly resembles that of the iris. Where the lamina vitrea forms the above described network, the pigmented cells lie in the meshes.

Upon the inner surface of the uveal layer of the ciliary body, lies the pars ciliaris retinæ. The elements of this membrane are according to the latest authors, to be considered as the continuation of *Mueller's* supporting fibres of the retina.

The ciliary part of the retina, consists of one layer of more or less cylindrical cells, which gradually decrease in size towards the insertion of the iris. They are unpigmented and have a round or oval nucleus which lies near their basis. Where the vitreous body lies upon them, they are flat or cone-shaped, and some of them have small offsets. We find sometimes a very thin vitreous membrane lying upon them, which is probably the remainder of the *membrana limitans interna* of the retina.

2. PATHOLOGICAL CONDITIONS.

A. Cyclitis and its Results.

From the similarity which exists between the structure of the iris and the ciliary body, and their direct connection, we may *a priori* expect to find the pathological processes of the ciliary body analogous to those of the iris.

The three forms of cyclitis which will be spoken of presently, and which mostly are found at the same time with similar affections in the iris or choroid, are: 1. serous (serofibrinous), 2. fibrinous (plastic) and 3. purulent cyclitis.

a. Cyclitis Serosa.

Serous cyclitis is hardly ever found without coëxisting

serous iritis.   The ciliary body in this disease appears very
hyperæmic, and the tissue around the blood-vessels contain a
few emigrated white blood-corpuscles.   The exudation characteristic of this kind of cyclitis is found in the posterior
chamber and the vitreous body, sometimes also in the tissue
of the ciliary body itself.   If the pupillary margin of the iris
is at the same time adherent to the anterior capsule of the
crystalline lens, the exudation in the posterior chamber
will press the periphery of the iris forward, and give it the
crater-shape, above referred to.   The pressure may be such
as to bring the peripheric parts of the iris in direct contact
with the posterior surface of the cornea, and if the condition does not soon heal, it induces atrophy of the tissue of
the iris.   With the secretion of the serous fluid in the anterior part of the vitreous body an increased emigration of
cells nearly always occurs.   In this way larger agregations
of cells are formed in the anterior part of the vitreous body,
and not infrequently deposited upon the posterior capsule
of the crystalline lens.   In the latter case, the exudation is
mostly not of a purely serous, but of a sero-fibrinous character, and the cells upon the lens-capsule are then embedded
in threads of fibrine. (See Fig. 48).

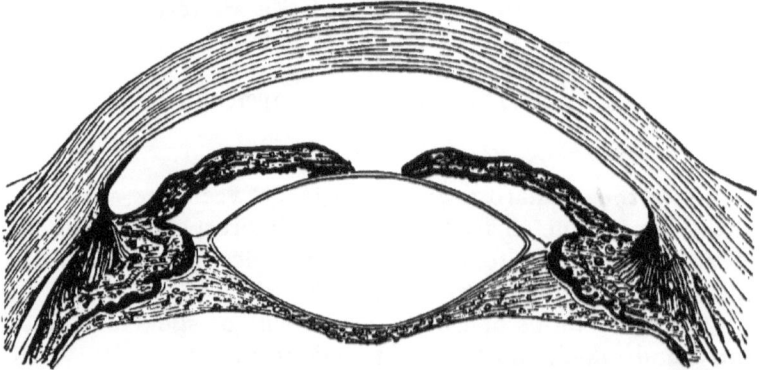

FIG. 48.—Sero-fibrinous cyclitis.   Amorphus fibrine, containing numerous round-cells, lies
upon the posterior lens-capsule.

If the exudation is secreted by the tissue of the ciliary
body itself, it forces the fibres of the ciliary muscle apart,
and if this condition persists, they become atrophic. (See
Fig. 49).   In rare cases only, we also find the inner cellular

layers of the ciliary body, *viz,,* the uveal layer and the ciliary part of the retina to take an active part in the serous inflammation. They then show a small degree of proliferation. If the intra-ocular pressure, as is not seldom the case, becomes increased during the process, these layers suffer accordingly.

Serous cyclitis like serous iritis, may recover without leaving a trace. More frequently, however, it does not pass off so simply. The results of complications to which it leads, will be discussed further on.

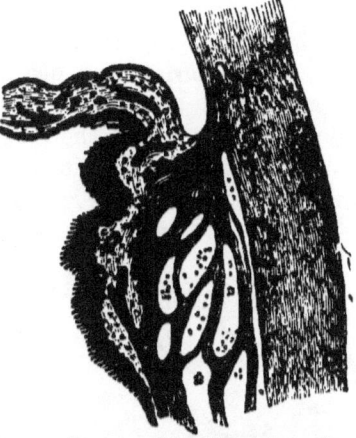

Fig. 49.—Serous cyclitis. The exudation lies in the tissue of the ciliary body itself, and presses the muscular fibres apart.

b. *Cyclitis Fibrinosa (Plastica).*

The form of cyclitis most frequently met with, is the fibrinous or plastic. Although this form may be found uncomplicated, it is in the majority of the cases combined, with inflammatory processes, in other parts of the eye-ball (especially of the iris.)

We here again find the blood-vessels hyperæmic, and the surrounding tissue more or less infiltrated with emigrated white blood-corpuscles. Characteristic of this form of cyclitis, is the fibrinous exudation. This is at first deposited upon the inner surface of the ciliary body and zonula *Zinnii.* In more serious cases we find it filling the whole of the posterior chamber and traversing the eye-ball between the iris and the crystalline lens, and behind the latter.

Doubtlessly this exudation may at an earlier period be again absorbed, and so the serious results of plastic cyclitis may be prevented. The affection is, however, more frequently observed to progress, and the fibrine becomes organized. After it has been filled with round-cells, blood-vessels are seen to grow into it, coming from the ciliary body, and sometimes from the peripheral parts of the retina, and thus the amorphus fibrinous substance is gradually changed into a delicate connective-tissue. In this way the periphery of the iris frequently becomes adherent to the ciliary processes, and the posterior chamber obliterated. Moreover this new-formed connective-tissue may cover the remainder of the ciliary body, enclose the zonula *Zinnii*, and lying upon the posterior capsule of the crystalline lens, traverse the whole of the eye-ball. (See Fig. 50.)

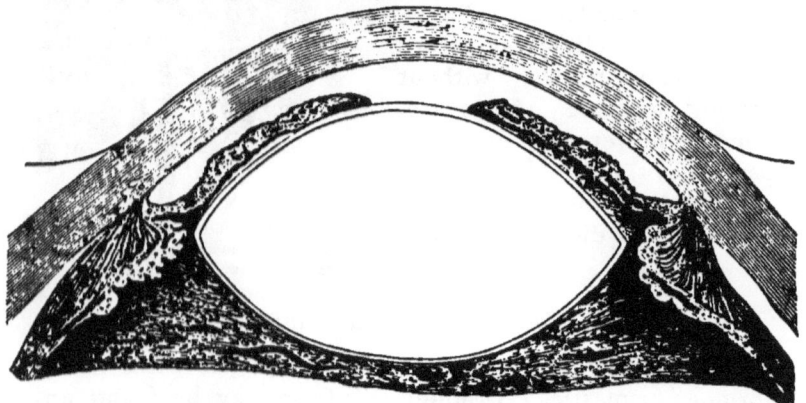

F<small>IG</small>. 50.—Plastic cyclitis. Cyclitic membrane upon the posterior lens-capsule. The posterior chamber is obliterated. Lens and iris are pressed forward.

This whole process may go on without materially altering the uveal and retinal layers of the ciliary body. More frequently, however, we see that these layers take an active part in the formation of the cyclitic membrane, especially the retinal part of the ciliary body. The cylindrical cells of this layer proliferate and begin to grow out into long spindle-shaped cells, and finally into long connective-tissue fibres. This alteration of the retinal layer, always begins at the junction between *pars plicata* and *pars nonplicata* of the ciliary body. The parts lying more anteriorly are only involved later on and never to so great an extent. (See Fig. 51.)

Meanwhile the cells of the uveal layer have also undergone proliferation. The whole layer appears very much thickened and grows into the cyclitic membrane in an irregular way. We also observe, however, frequently a more typical kind of proliferation of the cells of the uveal layer in the shape of cylindrical tubes, which grow into the cyclitic membrane and give off branches. In longitudinal and transverse sections, these tubes appear like the glandulæ tubulosæ or

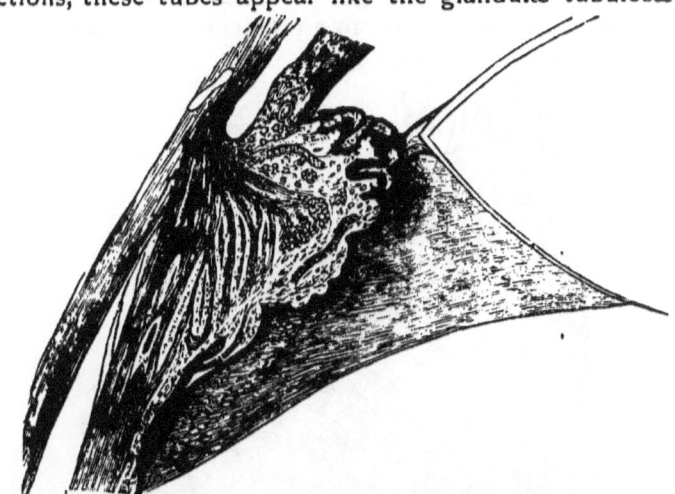

FIG. 51.—Plastic cyclitis. Shows how the cells of the retinal layer of the ciliary body are changed into spindle-cells and aid in the formation of a cyclitic membrane.

the epithelial cylinders of an epithelioma. The cells of these tubes are either free of pigment or pigmented. Their shape and arrangement with their branches have given some authors, (*Schiess-Gemuseus*) the idea that they were blood-vessels, whose walls were filled with pigment. Specimens in which the blood-vessels have been injected with a colored fluid, however, plainly show that they are widely different from blood-vessels. They appear, as stated, just like glands or epithilioma-cylinders. (See Fig. 52).

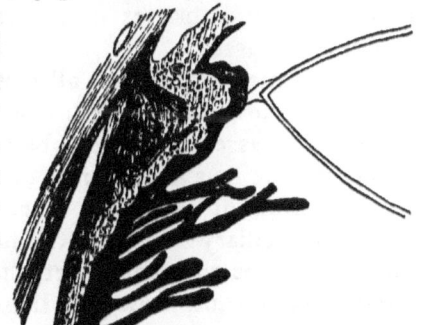

FIG. 52.—Plastic cyclitis. Tubular excrescences of the pigmented (uveal) layer of the ciliary body.

Not all the cells originating by proliferation from the uveal layer are pigmented, and I am even convinced that the young cells of this layer are at first always unpigmented and form their pigment only later on. For this reason we find in cyclitic membranes also the same tubular formations without any pigment at all, which can nearly always be traced backward to a pigmented cell-tube or the uveal layer itself. (See Fig. 53).

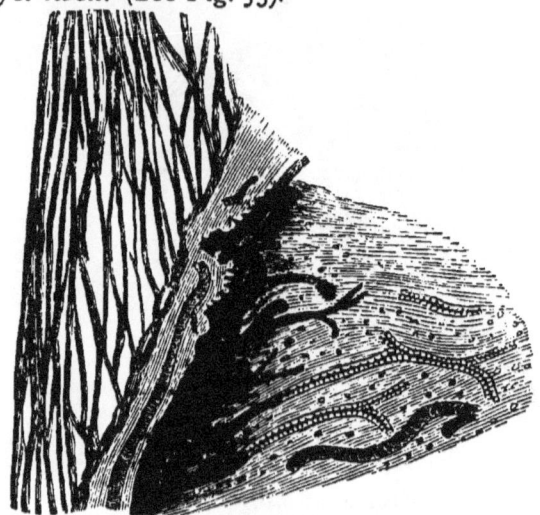

FIG. 53.—Plastic cyclitis. The same tubular excrescences. The younger ones as yet unpigmented.

Small and large hæmorrhages are frequently found in cyclitic membranes, and later on, deposits of lime are very common. Such membranes may furthermore become changed into osseous tissue.

Cyclitic membranes, like all new-formed connective-tissue, begin at some period to shrink, and thus cause further pathological processes in the eye-ball. At first the nutrition of the crystalline lens is impaired to such a degree, as to cause the formation of cataract. Then the retraction, influences directly the ciliary body, and the neighboring part of the choroid. These parts become detached from the sclerotic, and drawn inward—and forward. It is evident, that this detachment could not take place if the consistency of the vitreous body had not before been materially altered, and that it must at the same time lead at least to the peripheral detachment of the retina. (See Fig. 54). Plastic cyclitis may, also, produce detachment of much larger parts, or even the whole of the retina, and give rise to chronic inflammatory processes in all parts of the eye-ball, which finally produce phthisis bulbi.

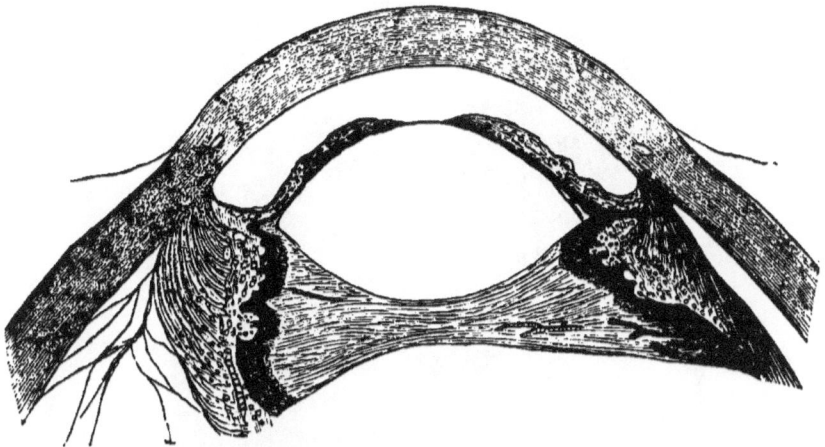

FIG. 54.—Plastic cyclitis. Cylitic membrane. Detachment of the ciliary body.

c. *Cyclitis Purulenta (Parenchymatosa)*.

This form of cyclitis is observed especially after injuries to the ciliary body itself, and as a part of purulent panophthalmitis. Hyperæmia of the blood-vessels is always here followed by the rapid formation of pus-cells. In the earlier periods, the affection lies chiefly in the inner layers of the ciliary body, and we find its inner surface covered with a fibro-purulent substance. Gradually, however, the disease spreads, and then later on we find that nearly all the layers of the ciliary body, take an active part in the formation of the pus-cells. The last to become involved, are the fibres of the ciliary muscle which, like the nerves, seem to be very resistant. When the disease has advanced so far, we find the whole of the tissue of the ciliary body transformed into a mass of round cells, between which lie the free pigment-molecules and some muscular fibres. (See Fig. 55).

Raab at a recent date thought that in a case of purulent panophthalmitis described by him, the origin of the affection was to be found in embolism of a ciliary blood-vessel. This, I think, is for obvious reasons highly improbable, and has not been observed by others.

Purulent cyclitis may as it seems, heal again at an early period.   If it does not, it leads to the perfect destruction of the involved tissue.

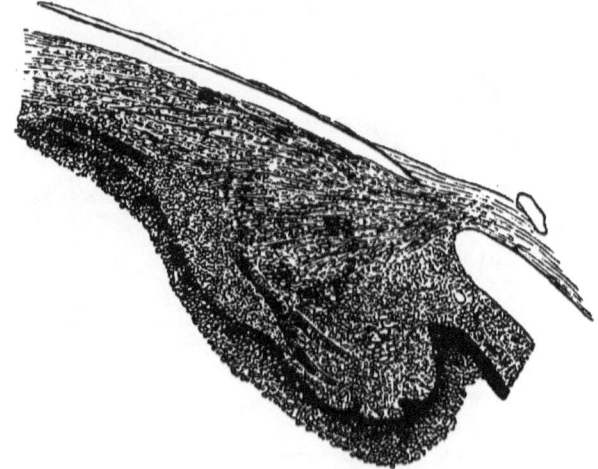

FIG. 55.—Purulent cyclitis.

In most cases of purulent cyclitis, we find the anterior portion of the vitreous body, also filled with threads of fibrine and pus-cells.

Except after direct injuries to the ciliary body, purulent cyclitis is but rarely a primary disease.   If it is the primary affection, the inflammation spreads very easily over the remainder of the uveal tract.   If the iris becomes involved, we see the formation of hypopyon, if the disease spreads upon the choroid, this is generally the beginning of a purulent panophthalmitis.

This form of cyclitis, like parenchymatous iritis, may also be found perfectly localized in the shape of an accumulation of round cells, as gumma or tubercle.   A gumma of the ciliary body which I once had the occasion to examine, consisted of such an accumulation of round-cells, which were so crowded that they began to decay in the centre of the little tumor. The muscular fibres were simply pushed aside and compressed.   No blood-vessels were found in the tumor.   (See Fig. 56.)

Purulent cyclitis may result from plastic cyclitis.   This we must assume to be the case, whenever we find purulent cyclitis and a cyclitic membrane, since the former never leads to the formation of such membranes.

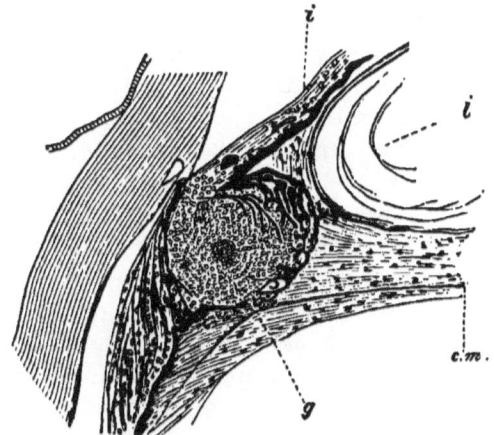

FIG. 56.—Gumma of the ciliary body. I. Iris. L. Lens. G. Gumma. Cm. Cyclitic membrane.

Results of Cyclitis.

Serous cyclitis usually heals without leaving a trace ; but the other varieties generally cause some changes in the tissues of the eye-ball, which allow of a certain diagnosis.

a. Cyclitic Membranes.

I already have mentioned the way in which cyclitic membranes are formed. It is certain that the retinal layer of the ciliary body, when proliferating, is of great importance in these new-formations, and often even their starting point. The latter statement is proven, by the fact that we not infrequently find in eyes suffering from cyclitis, the beginning cyclitic membrane to consist of nothing, but the proliferated cells of the retinal layer. They grow towards the posterior pole of the crystalline lens, and I am in the possession of specimens, where this latter is as yet perfectly free. In these cases the cyclitic product consequently does not form a membrane, but only a ring. In other cases, the centre of this ring is filled with an amorphous fibrinous substance, which is deposited upon the posterior capsule of the crystalline lens.

The cells of the uveal layer of the ciliary body, are mostly destroyed during the formation of a cyclitic membrane, especially those of the *pars non-plicata*, and their pigment, being freed, is with the growing membrane drawn towards the centre. In other cases we find besides, partial destruction of the uveal cells, a very active proliferation and new-formed cells, which grow into the cyclitic membrane arranged in gland-like, cylindrical and tubular formations. These start chiefly from the *pars non-plicata* of the ciliary body.

At the same time with these changes, we find new-formed blood-vessels growing into the cyclitic membrane, which in consequence, is often very vascular. The new blood-vessels not infrequently give rise to hæmorrhages in these membranes. I also mentioned above, that these membranes often contain deposits of lime, and undergo ossification.

At a certain stage, cyclitic membranes, like all new-formed connective-tissues, begin to shrink. If the cyclitis has at the same time produced alterations in the posterior parts of the eye, and especially in the vitreous body, this shrinking will cause the ciliary body and the neighboring parts of the choroid to become detached from the sclerotic. Thus we may find, in a meridional section through such an eye-ball, that two diametrically opposite ciliary bodies have been drawn so much towards the centre, that they nearly touch each other. (See Fig. 57). The same process may further

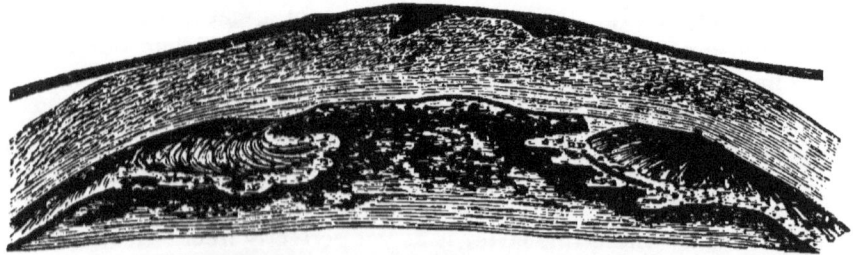

FIG. 57.—Plastic cyclitis from an eye with anterior phthisis. The cyclitic membrane is very considerably shrunken, and brings the ciliary bodies nearly in contact with each other.

on produce total detachment of the retina, which, however, is generally preceded by an increase of intra-ocular pressure, and excavation of the optic nerve entrance.

b. Atrophy.

Although most of the cases of cyclitis, unless they heal, lead to the formation of a cyclitic membrane, there are a number of cases in which such a membrane is totally wanting, and yet we can judge from the conditions of the ciliary body, that cyclitis must have existed during life. I had in one case only, the occasion to find an undoubted hypertrophy, of the muscular tissue in the ciliary body of an eye which had been injured (See Fig. 58). It seems therefore that cyclitis may cause hypertrophy of the muscular tissue. Whether this hypertrophy is only a spurious one, and leads later on to atrophy, or whether it may remain persistent, I cannot decide. In most cases (without a cyclitic membrane) we find atrophy of the ciliary body, as the result of cyclitis. The pigmented and the

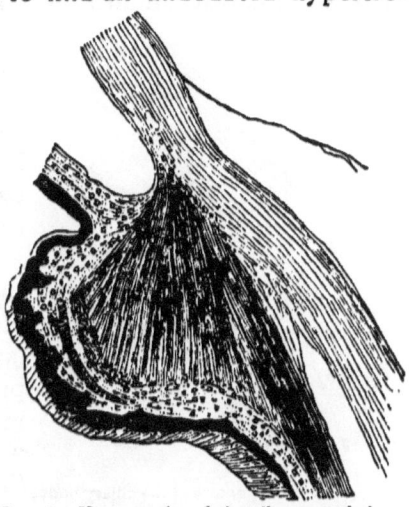

FIG. 58.—Hypertrophy of the ciliary muscle in a case of cyclitis.

retinal layer, as a rule, remain unaltered, while all the elements of the parenchyma of the ciliary body become atrophic. In the most advanced cases, we find but a very thin layer of connective-tissue, separating the uveal and the retinal layers from the sclerotic, as the remainder of the ciliary body. In the blood-vessels and nerves such cases no longer exist.

c. Staphyloma.

The mode in which chronic cyclitis may help in the formation of corneal and ciliary staphylomata, has been explained in Chapter I.

B. Injuries to the Ciliary Body and their Results.

Wounds of the ciliary body but rarely happen except the

part of the sclerotic covering it, has been pierced. The ciliary body, may however, also receive an injury from its inner surface, after the foreign body has perforated other parts of the eye (mostly the cornea, iris and crystalline lens). I found furthermore, in several eyes which had been enucleated for hæmophthalmus subsequent to a contusion, a rupture of the ciliary body. In one case the rupture beginning at its outer surface, reached into the muscular tissue. (See Fig. 59).

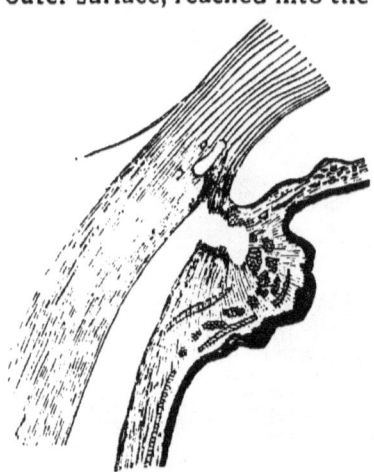

Ruptures of one or more of the blood-vessels of the ciliary body and subsequent hæmorrhagic infiltration, of its tissue, are not rare in eyes having received a contusion.

If the instrument by which the injury is inflicted, has pierced the sclerotic and ciliary body, the latter generally prolapses, and this prolapse may, of course, be combined with an injury to the lens, (iris, cornea, choroid,) and prolapse of the vitreous body. Such wounds heal by the formation of a scar-tissue,

FIG. 59.—Isolated rupture of the ciliary body. The eye was enucleated on account of hœmophthalmus. The tissue of the ciliary body was perfectlyfilled with blood. (The latter has not been drawn, to show the rupture better.)

preceded by the exudation of fibrine into the wound-canal. The scar-formation is as a rule assisted in by all of the wounded tissues (of course with the exception of the crystalline lens). Later on we then find a tough and frequently pigmented band of scar-tissue, uniting the ciliary body firmly with the sclerotic. In a number of cases the inflammation will spread, and then besides the local changes we find in the wound a general plastic, or purulent inflammatory process.

If the foreign body enters the ciliary body from the interior of the eye-ball, the same conditions may be found, as have just been detailed. If the foreign body is very small, it may remain embedded in the ciliary body, and then a capsule of tough connective-tsssue is gradually formed around it. In the large majority of cases, however, such a foreign body will cause purulent cyclitis.

If this local inflammation gives rise to a general purulent inflammation, the eye-ball may be perfectly destroyed. Injuries to the ciliary body are, furthermore, among the most frequent causes of sympathetic affections of the fellow-eye.

C. TUMORS OF THE CILIARY BODY.

a. Myoma.

Iwanoff has so far described the only case of myoma of the ciliary body, known in literature. The tumor of the size of a filbert, consisted of organic muscular fibres in the parts nearest to the sclerotic; the inner parts consisted of connective-tissue.

It appears from this description rather doubtful whether this tumor can be really called a myoma.

b. Sarcoma.

Sarcoma, especially the melanosarcoma, is the new-formation most frequently found to originate in the ciliary body, (perhaps the only one). These tumors come, however, as a rule, under the hands of the anatomist, when their origin can only be guessed at. It therefore happened that

Fig. 60.—Primary melanosarcoma of the ciliary body.

leucosarcomata and melanosarcomata and such sarcomata which were partly pigmented, partly unpigmented, have been described and said to have originated in the ciliary body without a direct proof, that this was really the case. I only once had the occasion to examine a true case of pigmented round-cell sarcoma of the ciliary body. (See Fig. 60). The whole of the ciliary body in this case consisted of darkly pigmented round-cells between which no longer any trace of the muscular fibres could be found.

The mode in which sarcomatous tumors of the choroid spread over the ciliary body, will be detailed when these tumors are spoken of. Primary sarcoma of the ciliary body is certainly of very rare occurrence.

VI. CHOROIDEA.

1. *Normal Condition.*

The choroid consists of the vascular parenchyma, an exterior coat of endothelium (upon its scleral surface,) and the lamina vitrea. Upon the latter, lies the pigmented (uveal) epithelium which was formerly considered to be part of the choroid, but has recently been assigned to the retina. Since it suffers always, however, when the choroid is in a pathological condition, it will be spoken of after the choroid.

The parenchyma of the choroid, like that of the iris and ciliary body, consists of a small amount of connective-tissue, some elastic fibrillæ and pigmented or unpigmented cells. The cells of the parenchyma of the choroid appear to be scattered equally over the whole of its thickness. The pigmented cells are, however, less numerous in the part which lies directly outward from the lamina vitrea (the capillary layer). The pigmented cells of the choroid, have mostly several long offsets, and accordingly vary considerably in shape. Their nucleus is round or oval, and free from pigment. The pigment, filling the main body of the cell and the offsets, is granular and very varying in its tint. While it can hardly be called brown in albinotic eyes, it appears perfectly black in the eyes of a negro, and prevents us frequently from discerning the nucleus of these cells. The unpigmented cells are less numerous, and vary in shape, in the same way as do the pigmented ones. Some of them are undoubtedly lymphatic cells, others appear as free nuclei, without being surrounded by protoplasma.

The blood-vessels are a most important part of the paren-

chyma of the choroid. They form two groups, *viz.*, the
capillary blood-vessels, which lie nearer the inner, and the
venous vessels which lie nearer the outer surface of the
choroid. The arteries which chiefly conduct the blood to
this membrane, are the short posterior ciliary arteries. After
having pierced the sclerotic near the optic nerve entrance
and entered the choroid, they branch off and these new
branches form the capillary network of the choroid, which
ends with an indented margin at the *ora serrata* (*Leber*).
The long posterior and the anterior ciliary arteries, send
small branches backwards to these vessels in the choroid.
The veins into which the blood passes from the capillaries,
collect it into from four to six larger branches, the vorticous
veins, which leave the eye through the sclerotic. The veins
as well as the arteries have perivascular sheaths. *Sattler*
has also proved the existence of such sheaths around the
capillaries, which, as it appears from his researches, lie free in
cavities which are in direct communication with the perivascular sheaths of the larger vessels. The same author found
two endothelial membranes separating the capillaries from
the veins. I have not been able to convince myself by my
own observation, of the existence of these endothelial membranes. Pathological conditions, however, especially the
way in which parenchymatous hæmorrhages may split the
choroid into two layers, make it very probable, that *Sattler's*
statement is correct.

The parenchyma of the choroid furthermore, contains a
great many nerves. They come from the nervi ciliares breves
and longi, and form a net-work of pale nerve-fibres in the
choroid, which follows largely the arrangement of the blood-
vessels, and has great many ganglionic cells. The fibres of
this network end in the capillary layer; the manner of their
termination is, however, not yet known. The ganglionic
cells are very large, and lie together in clusters. Several
authors have found organic muscular fibres in the choroid.
The mode in which the muscular fibres of the ciliary muscle
end in the choroid, has already been explained.

All that has been said in the previous chapters about the
laminæ fuscæ and suprachoroideæ, holds good for the same

parts of the choroid. I may only add, that the larger
branches of the ciliary nerves, pass through this layer of
fibres, and there form a network with wide meshes, before
entering the parenchyma of the choroid.

The choroid and sclerotic adhere more firmly to each other
around the optic nerve-entrance, where a larger number of
blood-vessels and fibres coming from the sclerotic, enter the
choroid. The choroid has no more a large round hole by
which the optic nerve enters the eye-ball *in toto*, than the
sclerotic, as we see fibres from the so-called lamina cribosa,
enter the choroid and vice versa. The question whether
blood-vessels from the posterior parts of the choroid, pass
over into the optic nerve-entrance or retina, is not yet considered perfectly settled. *Knapp* has drawn such a picture
from a diseased eye, and Fig. 61, taken from a normal eye,

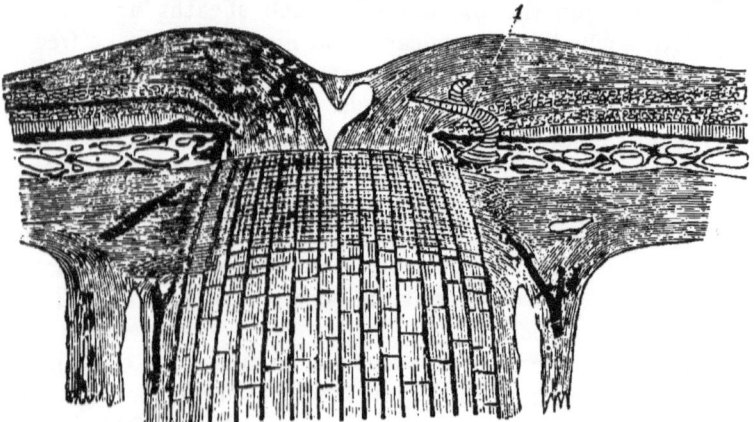

FIG. 61.—Normal entrance of the optic nerve into the eye-ball. 1. A blood-vessel coming
from the choroid and entering the retina.

cannot leave any doubt as to the existence of such blood-
vessels, although they may not be found in every eye.

The inner surface of the choroid is covered by the thin
lamina vitrea. This is an elastic and perfectly transparent
membrane, upon which the (uveal) pigmented epithelium
lies. Recently it has been said to have a fibrous structure.
It is not yet known, how this membrane is united with the
underlying tissue. *Sattler* found upon its outer surface a
network, which he expressly says is not formed by fibres.

The pigmented epithelium, lying between the choroid and retina, has lately, (first by *Babuchin*) been declared to be a part of the retina. *J. Arnold* has, however, more recently stated, that it is not yet, perfectly proven, that the lamina pigmenti, (the pigmented epithelium), is formed from the atrophic posterior lamella of the secondary ocular vesicle in the fœtus, and this conscientious author feels himself able to state only, that the lamina pigmenti, " replaces " the posterior lamella of the secondary ocular vesicle. This is the more important, as the normal or pathological conditions of the pigmented epithelium, are certainly found to depend much more upon the conditions of the choroid, than upon those of the retina. Nearly every pathological condition of the choroid, exerts its influence upon the pigmented epithelium, while the most important changes may happen in the tissue of the retina, without any alteration whatsoever, in the condition of the pigmented epithelial cells. Furthermore, if we take the retina out of a normal eye, these cells do not adhere to it, but remain lying upon the choroid.

Most recently it has been found that this layer of epithelial cells secretes the retinal purple, (*Kuehne, Boll*). It represents therefore a kind of gland, lying between retina and choroid, as an independent organ.

The cells forming this epithelial layer are mostly hexagonal. They are united with each other by a structureless cementing substance, and form one single layer of flattened epithelium. Their nuclei are round and unpigmented : their protoplasm is filled with granular pigment. The pigmentation varies considerably in the cells of one and the same eye. In the eyes of negroes, the pigment is as a rule very dark, but it rarely altogether hides the nucleus.

In some eyes, especially those of old people, the cementing substance between these cells is found to be much broader and thicker, and if the cells are carefully removed, a tough network remains lying upon the lamina vitrea of the choroid, the meshes of which are filled by the cells. (See Fig. 62).

Nearly all of the recent authors on this subject, have described and drawn very fine and long offsets which the cells of the pigmented epithelium are said to send in between the

rods and cones of the retina.   They are said to be either pigmented or unpigmented.   *Schwalbe*, one of these authors,
states, however, that in the human eye they produce only a
very loose union between the retina and the pigmented
epithelium.   I must confess, that I have searched in the human eye in vain for these offsets.   In eyes taken from corpses
which have begun to decay, a condition similar to the granu-
ular offsets, drawn by *Schwalbe*, is frequently seen ; in fresh
eyes, however, or eyes put into *Mueller's* hardening fluid
when perfectly fresh, I cannot find them.

Cells with two or more nuclei are rare among the normal
pigmented epithelial cells, but there are always a number of
small cells, which are probably of a more recent date.

2. Pathological Conditions.

A. *Pathological Changes of the Pigmented Epithelium.*

It seems to me that before we go on to a description of
the different kinds of inflammation the choroid is subject to,
this is the proper place to speak of the pathological changes
observed in the pigmented epithelium.   Nearly every pathological process in the choroid involves this layer, and we
would thus be forced to frequently repeat the same ; on the
other hand, there are a number of pathological changes observed in the pigmented epithelium which are peculiar to it,
and more or less independent of any affection of the choroid.

The most common pathological alteration the cells of the
pigmented epithelium undergo, is that they lose their regular
shape and uniformity in size.   The new forms are very manifold, and the pigment lies mostly in the periphery of the protoplasma, in these cells.   It seems also, as if the pigment
could—so to speak, be secreted by one and taken up by
another cell in its neighborhood.   The latter then appears
perfectly black.   Later on round or oblong, light (empty or
filled ?) structures are seen inside the cells, which by some
authors are considered to be colloid-globules, by others to be
vacuolæ.   If the cells are altered in such a way, the cementing substance is found to be either hardened, and to remain
adherent to the lamina vitrea (See Fig. 62), or to have apparently altogether disappeared.

Combined with these alterations, we very frequently find between the pigmented epithelial cells, round or oval, transparent, hard bodies which adhere to the lamina vitrea. These have by English authors, received the name of colloid excrescences of the lamina vitrea, and have been often described as such. There is, however, no proof that these bodies consist really of colloid substance; their per-

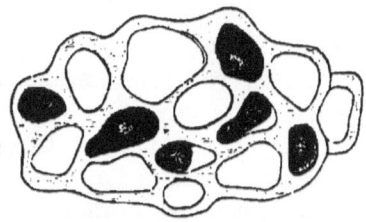

FIG. 62.—Thickened and hardened intercellular substance from the pigmented epithelial layer, lying upon the lamina vitrea of the choroid; 1, containing lime.

fect resistance to all chemical agents, and their hardness would on the contrary tend to prove that they are not of a colloid nature. In transverse sections, they resemble very much the corpora arenacea of the coats of the brain. (See Fig. 63). The fact, that they lie upon the lamina vitrea,

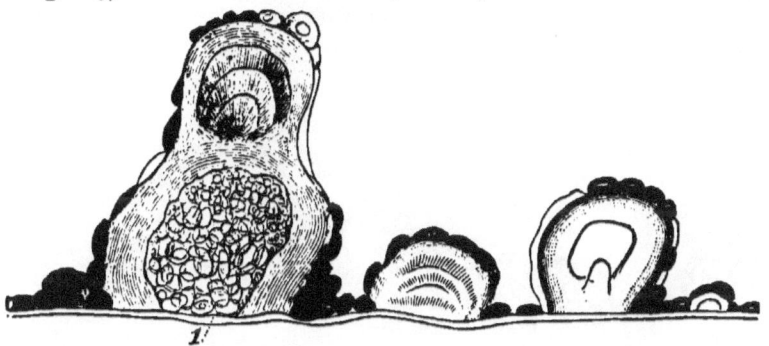

FIG. 63.—Vitreous bodies upon the lamina vitrea of the choroid; 1, containing lime.

and are only found, where the pigmented epithelium is altered in the manner above referred to, seems to prove that their formation is caused by these, and *Mayer* has recently tried to show that these bodies are really secreted by the cells of the pigmented epithelium. I must agree with him in considering this the most probable way in which they are formed, although I have seen a great number of specimens, in which it appeared as if they were the result of a degenerative process of the cells themselves. While the smaller sized vitreous bodies are generally covered by a continous layer of pigmented epithelial cells, part of which are new-formed, these cells are gradually destroyed as the vitreous bodies grow larger and coalesce. This may be simply the consequence of the pressure, but it is possible also, that the protoplasma of the cells is the material, by which these vitreous bodies grow. Through these changes, the pigment molecules become free, and seem to be taken up by the more or less normal cells which surround the basis of the vitreous bodies, and which now appear perfectly dark, and sometimes in a state of proliferation.

It has often been stated that these bodies are peculiar to old age. This may in the majority of cases really be so ; they are, however, found in the eyes of young individuals also, for I found an immense quantity of them once in the eye of a boy twelve years of age.

Later on amorphous lime is frequently deposited inside these vitreous bodies and, in spite of their hardness, it cannot be impossible for cells to penetrate into them, as they may become organized in the form of osseous tissue. (See Fig. 64).

F IG. 64.—Formation of osseous tissue in the vitreous bodies of the lamina vitrea choroideæ.

An undue and pathological new-formation of cells, is not infrequent in the pigmented epithelial layer. It is seen in nearly all of the cases of choroiditis and we have already spoken of it, when describing the changes caused by cyclitis. The new-formed cells are, (as stated already by *Virchow*) at first nearly always free from pigment. They are, however, as it seems, able to form their pigment at any time themselves. The new-formation of cells may produce a simple thickening of the pigmented epithelium, by superposing layer after layer of new cells. The formation of tubular offsets, similar to the epithelial cylinders of an epitheliomata, appears, however, to be more frequent. (See Fig. 65).

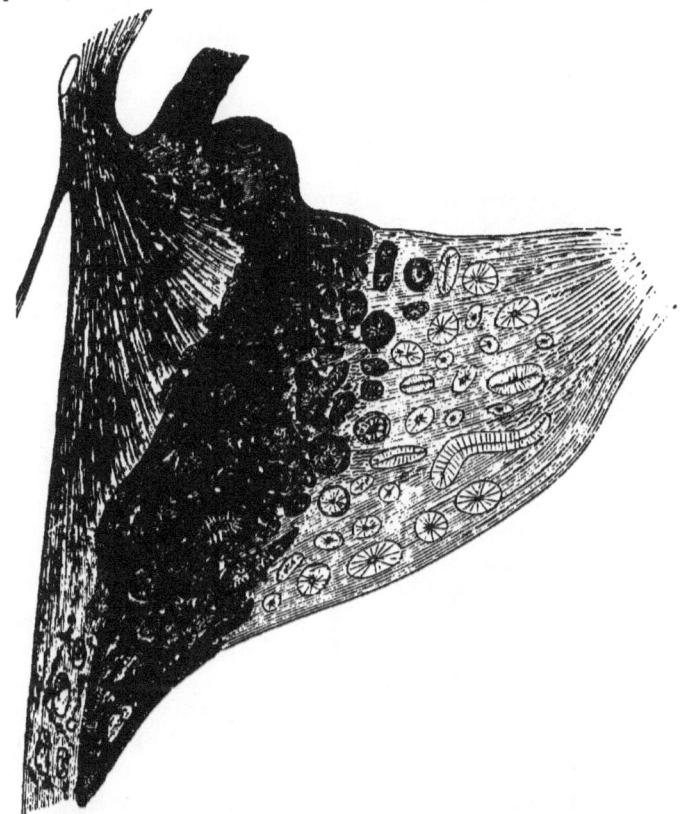

FIG. 65.—Tumor-like new-formation of pigmented and unpigmented cell-cylinders, starting from the uveal layer of the ciliary body and neighboring choroid.

An affection of the retina of great clinical importance, is caused by such an hyperplasia of the pigmented epithelium, without any pathological change in the choroid, *viz.*, pigmentary retinitis. In such cases the tubular offsets of the pigmented epithelium are partly pigmented, partly unpigmented, and grow into the retina, after having first destroyed its outer layers. In the retina, these foreign substances cause a chronic interstitial inflammation, which leads to hypertrophy of the connective-tissue, and to destruction of the nervous elements. (See Fig. 66). Furthermore, new

connective-tissue is formed in the perivascular sheaths of
the retinal blood-vessels (perivasculitis) and these become

Fig. 66.—**Pigmentary retinitis.** Pigmented cell cylinders going over in such cylinders without pigment. Blood-vessel changed into connective-tissue.

gradually obliterated.   It seems that this process often
begins in the peripheral parts of the retina ; in a case which
I described recently, it involved only a zone of retinal tissue,
ten millimetres in width, and equally distant from the *ora serrata* and the optic-nerve entrance.   That the peripheric vision
is at first impaired in cases of this affection, does not depend
alone on the disease usually beginning in the peripheral parts
of the retina, but also upon the diminished quantity of
nutritive fluids, furnished to these parts.

   We shall see later on that some forms of choroiditis, may
be followed by a very similar kind of pigmentation of the
retina.   The genuine pigmentary retinitis is, however, a secondary affection, caused without any affection of the choroid
proper, by the primary pathological new-formation of cells of
the pigmented epithelial layer.

During the process of this disease, the pigmented cells may enter the perivascular sheath of a retinal blood-vessel. (See Fig. 67). The primary disease is, however, not one of the blood-vessels, as has been stated by former authors.

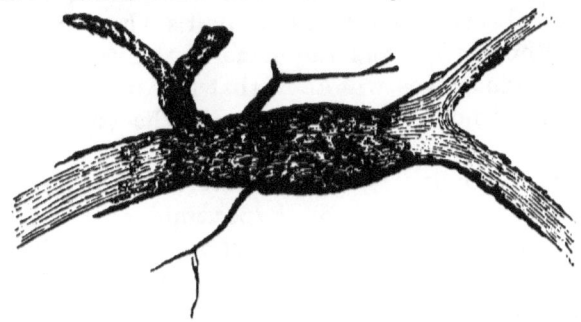

FIG. 67.—Pigmentary retinitis. Pigment in the perivascular sheath of a retinal blood-vessel.

The cells of the pigmented epithelium may undergo fatty degeneration. This seems to be most frequent in eyes with total detachment of the retina. Such cells, are then often transformed into aggregations of round fat-granules (Koernchenkugeln), which may or may not contain some pigment molecules.

B. Choroiditis and its Results.

The large number of different forms of choroiditis which the clinicists treat of, are anatomically summed up under the following three heads, *viz.*, 1. serous (serous-fibrinous), 2. fibrinous (plastic) and 3. purulent (parenchymatous choroiditis). This distinction is made according to the products of the inflammatory process. These are exuded either into the tissue of the choroid itself, or into the parts lying to the inner side of this membrane, (the pigmented epithelium, retina and vitreous body), and we find therefore most cases of choroiditis complicated with inflammatory processes in other parts of the eye-ball, (especially the pigmented epithelium, the retina and vitreous body).

a. Choroiditis Serosa (sero-fibrinosa).

Serous choroiditis, which is not infrequently met with, has recently been perfectly identified with glaucoma. This standpoint has been chiefly accepted by *Schmit-Rimpler* and *von Wecker* in *Græfe* and *Sæmisch's* Cyclopædia. Although, as will be shown further on, it is possible that glaucomatous symptoms result from serous choroiditis, we do not always find serous choroiditis when there is glaucoma. Whoever has had the occasion to examine a number of glaucomatous eyes, will know that it is impossible in most of the cases, to detect any change in the condition of the choroid.

Serous choroiditis, which I therefore do not identify with glaucoma, is ushered in by hyperæmia of the blood-vessels, especially the veins of the choroid. This hyperæmia may concern the whole of the choroid, or be more or less localized. I found it several times to be confined to one vorticous vein, or even only to a large branch of one. This hyperæmia is followed by the exudation of a serous, sometimes a sero-fibrinous fluid. In hardened specimens, it appears that this fluid is but very rarely exuded into the tissue of the choroid itself, which is, however, no proof that the conditions are not different in life. The serous exudation is mostly found inwards from the choroid, between the lamina vitrea and the pigmented epithelium, or between the pigmented epithelium and the retina, or between retina and vitreous body, (especially in their posterior half), or in the vitreous body itself. Furthermore, I frequently found in cases of serous or sero-fibrinous choroiditis, small round and oval cavities in the outer granulur layer of the retina, filled with a sero-fibrinous fluid, the formation of which may be caused directly by the disease of the choroid, before a secondary affection of the retina can be developed.

Some more recent authors have proven that chemical, not histological alterations in the tissues of the eye, are the chief cause of the serous exudation. If this exudation is not soon absorbed, it will produce different pathological alterations, in the condition of the tissues according to the place where it lies. It may lead to partial or total detachment of the retina (with or without the pigmented epithelium), from the choroid, or to detachment of the vitreous body from the retina, or it may simply produce liquefaction of the vitreous body. The consistency of the latter must, of course, have been considerably altered, before either it or the retina can become detached, and especially in cases of total detachment of the retina, the vitreous body must either have been totally liquefied or condensed. The liquefaction of the vitreous body is, however, found too, without being accompanied by detachment. I must state here that every detachment of the retina is not caused by serous choroiditis. There are quite a number of factors, which may come into play in detaching the retina from the choroid, which have already been partially and will be more fully described further on.

The increased production of serous fluid within the eyeball, especially when the means of exit are pathologically altered, or totally obliterated, may so increase the intra-ocular pressure, that we find later on, all the symptoms of glaucoma, including excavation of the optic nerve. This is especially found in eyes suffering from some kind of staphyloma (except posterior sclero-choroidal staphyloma).

Sometimes we find the number of wandering cells in the choroid considerably increased in cases of serous choroiditis. There is, however, in the choroid at least no sign of cell-proliferation to be detected. The vitreous body also is usually filled with a larger number of cells, and the serous exudation contains them. The cells of the pigmented epithelium are partially proliferating, partially undergoing a regressive metamorphosis. If the exudation remains for a long time lying in the same place, we frequently find crystals of cholesterine formed, and lime deposited in it. The former appear always in the well known tablets ; the lime is amorphous. The formation of vitreous bodies upon the lamina vitrea of the choroid, is frequently met with in such cases.

b. Choroiditis Fibrinosa (plastica).

Plastic choroiditis never attacks the whole choroid, but appears in numerous small patches, which may by confluence grow larger. Hyperæmia of the choroid in this form of inflammation, is followed by a fibro-cellular exudation at first into the tissue of the choroid itself. (See Fig. 68). We then find in such a place, a round or oval accumulation of fibrinous substance involving mostly the whole thickness of the choroid, and filled with and surrounded by round-

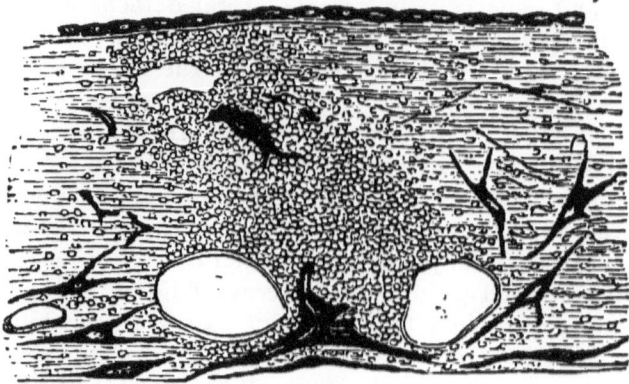

Fig. 68.—Plastic choroiditis. Fibro-cellular exudation in the tissue of the choroid.

cells.   If the process of exudation goes on, the lamina vitrea is perforated, and the fibrinous substance may remain under the thus detached pigmented epithelium.   In the majority of cases, however, this layer, too, is perforated, and the exudation enters the tissue of the retina.   This fibrinous substance, is later on transformed into connective-tissue, which at some period will begin to shrink.   If the fibrine has been exuded only into the tissue of the choroid, we find, later on unpigmented, round and oval patches, which are very thin and consist of connective-tissue, without either blood-vessels or cellular elements.   In these cases, also where the exudation has not directly involved the pigmented epithelium, we find it later on changed, and the cells covering the patch of exudation lose their pigment and may be totally destroyed, which latter condition is caused by the pressure exerted upon them, as well as by impairment in their nutrition.   Their pigment having thus been freed, is taken up by the cells in the periphery of the patch of exudation, which consequently appear abnormally dark.   If the exudation has once perforated the lamina vitrea, the retina is always sure to suffer, although to a greatly varying degree.   The rods and cones alone may be destroyed, and the pigmented epithelium adhere to the retina.   If the pigmented epithelium has been perforated by the fibrinous exudation, the latter will enter the retina and there produce a local interstitial inflammation. When the fibrinous substance has been transformed into connective-tissue and begins to shrink, retina and choroid will thus become firmly adherent to each other. (See Fig. 69). Moreover, the pigmented epithelium cells

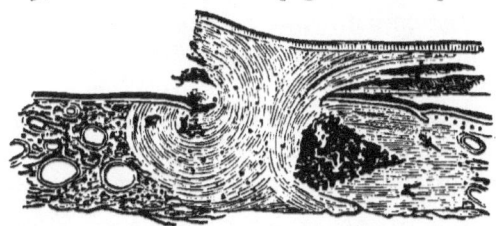

FIG. 69.—Plastic choroiditis. Adhesion between retina and choroid.

may begin to proliferate and so to produce either a thickening of this layer, or form the above described tubular excrescences. If the latter be the case, the retina becomes pigmented in the manner we have seen, in the so called pigmentary retinitis. (See Fig 70). All these processes are clinically called chorio-retinitis.

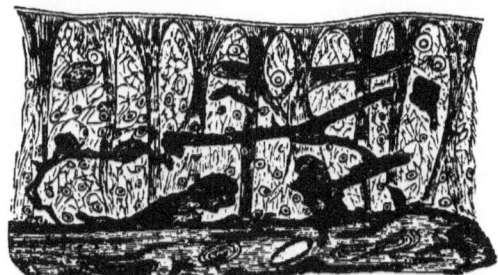

FIG. 70.—Plastic choroiditis. Pigmentation of the retina.

In rare cases the fibrine may be exuded directly upon the inner surface of the lamina vitrea, *i. e.* between lamina vitrea and pigmented epithelium.

Retraction of the new-formed connective-tissue, uniting retina and choroid in the manner above referred to, may cause the neighboring parts of the retina, to become detached from the pigmented epithelium.

The disease may in the first stages, heal by absorption ; in most of the cases, however, it progresses and leads to the local new-formation of connective-tissue and atrophy just

detailed. Vitreous bodies upon the lamina vitrea, are frequently observed in eyes so affected.

There are a number of clinically distinct forms of choroiditis, which anatomically all belong under this head, *viz.*,
choroiditis disseminata, atrophica, exudativa, areolaris, chorio-retinitis disseminata and chorio-retinitis centralis. The
latter name means that the affection is confined to the region
of the macula lutea.

The small patches of exudation may lie very close to each
other, and finally by coalescing, form very large ones. The
original patches are, however, always comparatively small.

c. Choroiditis Purulenta (Parenchymatosa).

The characteristic feature of purulent choroiditis, is the
enormous emigration and new-formation of cells, in the parenchyma of the choroid, which may lead to perfect destruction
of this membrane. The affection is in most of the cases a diffuse one, and concerns the whole of the choroid. We also find,
however, local round-cell accumulations, like, abscesses at the
same time with the diffuse affection. In the very advanced
cases, the whole of the structure of the choroid, is simply
represented by an innumerable mass of round-cells. (See
Fig. 71). *Knapp* says that the formation of pus always be-

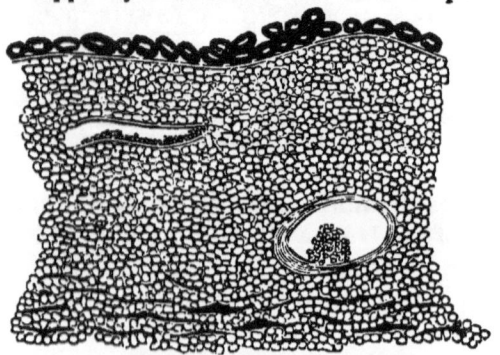

FIG. 71.—Purulent choroiditis.

gins in the capillary layer. This is not, however, without
exception, the case. All of the different elements constituting the tissue of the choroid, even the muscles, take an
active part in the formation of round-cells. The lamina

vitrea is frequently perforated, and thus the pus enters into the parts lying inwards from the choroid. The pigmented epithelium begins to proliferate, and the retina becomes detached. The vitreous body appears very soon pervaded by a large number of pus-cells. The formation of pus may also involve the inner layers of the sclerotic, and, when progressing, lead to perforation of this membrane. The purulent inflammation seldom remains confined to the choroid, but generally spreads over the other parts of the uveal tract, or over all the other membranes of the eye-ball, that is, it produces a purulent panophthalmitis.

This form of acute purulent (diffuse) choroiditis, is either of spontaneous origin, or is caused by an injury. The spontaneous form is frequently called "metastatic" choroiditis, especially when found in individuals suffering from pyæmia. It is, however, not yet undoubtedly proven, that in such cases, the choroiditis must really be considered as a metastic affection. *Raab,* who, as I already stated, found an embolus in a ciliary artery, considered this to be proof of the metastatic character of this variety of choroiditis.

Tubercles of the choroid, are local parenchymatous affections. Although such tubercles have frequently been examined with the microscope, the similar gummatous affection, which from clinical observation may doubtless happen, does not seem to have so far been examined histologically. The tubercles have nothing peculiar in the choroid. They are an

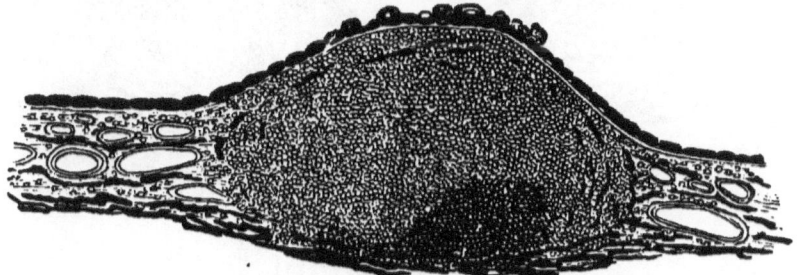

Fig. 72.—Tubercle of the choroid.

accumulation of round-cells in the parenchyma of this membrane, and frequently contain giant-cells. (See Fig. 72). They may be found in all parts of the choroid, single or coalescing.

Acute purulent choroiditis, almost always take on a chronic form. Secretion of pus ceases, the blood-vessels are all destroyed, and formation of connective-tissue ensues. We may thus have the opportunity of examining such eyes at a period, when the tissue replacing the choroid, is six or more times as thick as this membrane appears in the normal condition. This thickening is, however, not persistent, but followed by shrinking of the new-formed tissue, and perfect atrophy of the eye-ball.

The nerves may be found unaltered, even in the most violent forms of purulent choroiditis. When the process has, however, led to perfect atrophy of the choroid, we usually look for them in vain.

Besides acute parenchymatous choroiditis, which goes over into the chronic form, we sometimes observe a purulent choroiditis, which is from the beginning of a chronic character. This frequently leads to the deposition of lime, in the parenchyma of the choroid, and to the formation of osseous tissue. We have seen above, that the formation of osseous tissue may take place in the vitreous bodies lying upon the lamina vitrea of the choroid, and I am inclined to look upon

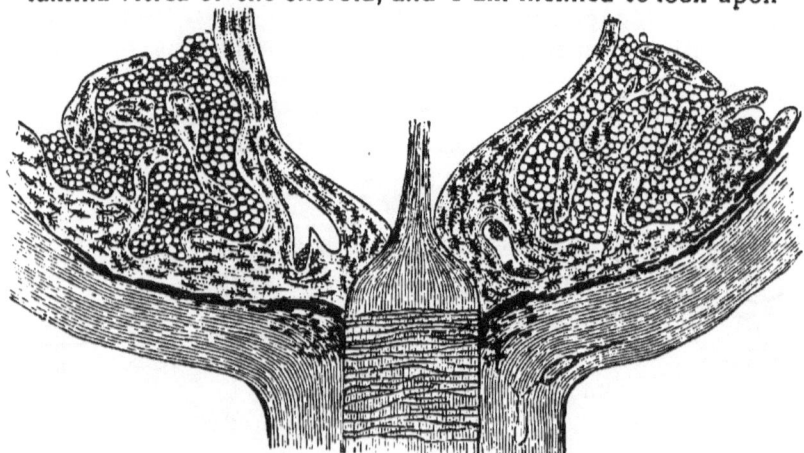

FIG. 73.—Osseous tissue, with marrow in the choroid.

these bodies as being more frequently the origin of the osseous tissue, than we suspect, especially when it is found lying *upon the inner surface* of the lamina vitrea.

The formation of bone *in* the choroid in the beginning, usually takes place in its inner layers (*Knapp*). Later on, the whole choroid may be found thus altered. The osseous shell, formed in such a manner, never reaches farther anteriorly, than to the ciliary body. In its posterier part, it is usually perforated by the optic nerve or retina. The osseous tissue differs in no way from the normal osseous tissue, and in rare cases may even contain cavities filled with marrow. (See Fig. 73).

Since chronic parenchymatous choroiditis usually leads to chronic inflammatory processes of the eye-ball, which cause the new-formation of connective-tissue, we have to look upon it as the chief cause of the shrinking of the whole eye-ball, known under the name of phthisis bulbi, and of consequent sympathetic affections in the fellow-eye.

The Results of Choroiditis.

a. Detachment of the Retina and Vitreous Body.

In consequence of serous choroiditis, we may find, as above stated, the retina detached from the choroid, and the vitreous body from the retina. Detachment of the retina may be total or only partial. We always find in these cases (when the detachment has been caused by serous choroiditis) more or less exudation between the retina and choroid, which, in spite of the means used to harden the eye-ball, remains sometimes perfectly fluid,or may become gelatinous.

It is most probable that during life, the retina too, is saturated by this serous fluid, and is œdematous. Some small round or oval cavities in the external granular layer, filled with a sero-fibrinous fluid, were all I could find in hardened eyes to prove this. The retina, too, clearly suffers from some other pathological processes, which will be detailed presently. With the retina, a number of cells of the pigmented epithelial layer, or even large parts of this layer may be detached. Vitreous bodies from the lamina vitrea may also adhere to the detached retina, and in one case, where I found osseous tissue in the detached retina, this had most probably originated in such detached vitreous bodies.

The vitreous body may be found detached from the retina by serous fluid, whether this membrane is removed from the choroid in the manner just stated, or whether it is in its normal position. The vitreous body then appears condensed and pressed forward towards the ciliary body and the crystalline lens.

b. Liquefaction of the Vitreous Body.

This condition will be detailed further on in Chapter X.

c. Glaucomatous Excavation of the Optic Papilla.

The alterations caused in the " head " of the optic nerve, and later on in the retina, in consequence of increased intra-ocular pressure, will be referred to in Chapters VII and VIII.

d. Atrophy; Synechia between Retina and Choroid, and Pigmentation of the former.

If atrophy of the choroid is diffuse, it has been caused by a purulent (parenchymatous), if it is found in patches, by a fibrinous (plastic) choroiditis. The atrophic patches caused by plastic choroiditis, are round or oval, or when several have coalesced, very manifold in shape. In a plain view, the pigmented epithelium is wanting upon them, and they themselves appear free from pigment and blood-vessels. The pigmented epithelium cells surrounding the patches are considerably darker than the rest. In transverse sections, these atrophic patches appear very considerably thinner than the surrounding parts of the choroid.

As above stated, the retina is very frequently found to adhere firmly to the atrophic patches in the choroid. In such places it is very thin, and drawn towards the choroid. During this process, the rods and cones become destroyed, and thus the pigmented epithelium may grow into the retina, and cause it to become pigmented in a manner closely resembling the conditions seen in cases of pigmentary retinitis. The pigment may even enter the lymphatic sheaths of the blood-vessels, as I must state contrary to *von Wecker's* opinion.

If atrophy of the choroid has been caused by chronic parenchymatous choroiditis, it nearly always concerns the whole of this membrane. We find this condition chiefly in shrunken (phthisical) eye-balls. During this process, the choroid may become firmly adherent to the sclerotic, and, if the retina was involved, choroid and retina may also be found to adhere so firmly to each other, that they can no longer be separated. In some cases, if there is not pigment enough left to mark the line of demarcation, it may, even with the microscope, be impossible to distinguish between the remains of the two membranes. In advanced cases, nearly all the blood-vessels are perfectly destroyed, and the same is the case with the nerves.

e. Ossification.

The formation of osseous tissue in the choroid, is a comparatively frequent result of chronic parenchymatous choroiditis. Most authors consider that this ossification originates in a fibrino-plastic exudation (*Knapp*). It is true, that we often find in cases of ossification of the choroid, a fibrino-plastic exudation lying upon the inner surface of the choroid, and partially ossified. I am, however, of the opinion that the ossification, when lying upon the inner surface of the choroid, very frequently has for its origin, the vitreous bodies of the lamina vitrea, on the other hand I do not deny that it sometimes originates in the new-formed tissue consequent upon plastic choroiditis, to which we have an analogue in the formation of osseous tissue in cyclitic membranes. The osseous tissue within the parenchyma of the choroid, however, seems to me, to be formed chiefly during a chronic parenchymatous choroiditis. The whole of the choroid is sometimes found to be changed into osseous tissue, so that it can only be recognized by the folded lamina vitrea, which is generally preserved.

It is certainly a strange fact that, in spite of the similarity in the structure of the choroid and iris, as yet no ossification has been found in the latter. The osseous formations described upon the posterior surface of the iris, originated in cyclitic productions in that place.

f. Staphyloma.

The manner in which chronic choroiditis may aid in the formation of a scleral staphyloma, has been sufficiently detailed in Chapter II.

C. Injuries to the Choroid and their Results.

The peculiar fact, that a contusion of the eye-ball may cause a more or less isolated rupture of the choroid, has not yet been satisfactorily explained. It is greatly to be regretted, that up till now no such case seems to have been histologically examined and described. It appears from clinical observation, that the rupture chiefly concerns the inner layers of the choroid. The pigmentation of the retina, frequently formed in the surrounding of the rupture, is most probably the result of a simultaneous rupture of the outer layers of this membrane, by which the pigment is enabled to grow into it.

If the injury only leads to the rupture of some blood-vessel of the choroid, a larger or smaller, parenchymatous hæmorrhage will, of course ensue, according to the size of the blood-vessel. The blood may be so distributed in the tissue, that this appears hæmorrhagically infiltrated; or it may split the choroid into two layers and force them considerably apart. (See Fig. 74). These hæmorrhages later

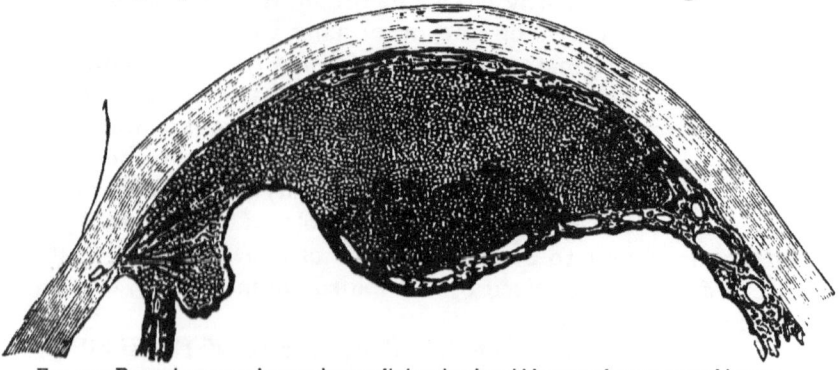

Fig. 74.—Parenchymatous hæmorrhage splitting the choroid into two layers, caused by contusion of the eye-ball.

on undergo fatty degeneration, and become gradually absorbed, leaving behind them a more or less atrophic tissue, filled with crystals of hæmatoidine.

Foreign bodies striking the choroid must, of course, have pierced the sclerotic or the retina before reaching it, and such injuries therefore always produce complicated conditions. If the sclerotic and choroid only have been injured, the latter generally prolapses into the wound of the sclerotic, and the two membranes heal together by means of a local plastic inflammation. The sclerotic then, as a rule, appears pigmented around the wound. If the retina, choroid and sclerotic, have been wounded from the interior, all the wounded parts show this local plastic inflammation. Since, however, the choroid has the most reproductive power of the three, we frequently find a pigmented granulation-tissue growing from it through the retina into the vitreous body. (See Fig. 75). Later on, this granulation-tissue shrinks, and

Fig. 75.—Granulation-tissue starting from the wounded choroid.

we find pigmented scar-tissue, by which the membranes are firmly united with each other. The retina surrounding the scar is nearly always pigmented, and all the parts next to the scar, contain crystals of hæmatoidine.

I have never found a foreign body to be encapsuled in the choroid alone.

The inflammation caused by such injuries remains, however, but seldom a localized one. It generally leads to purulent choroiditis, or even to panophthalmitis. Moreover, the simple scar, as described above, may become stretched, and cause the formation of a traumatic staphyloma of the sclerotic.

It appears, that injuries have in rare cases become the starting point for the formation of malignant tumors in the choroid.

Injuries to this membrane may also finally produce sympathetic affections of the other eye.

D. Tumors of the Choroid.

a. *Cystoid Formations.*

Only once I found cystoid formations in the choroid. They were situated in the peripheric part of this membrane, and formed a number of large round and oval cavities, which (in the hardened eye), appeared to be empty. They had a membrana propria, and an endothelial coating. They probably originated from the lymphatic sheaths of a blood-vessel, and would then be analogous to lymphangiectasia. (See Fig. 76).

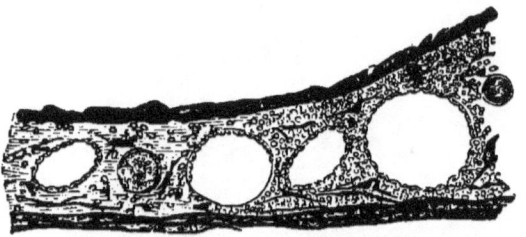

Fig. 76.—Cystoid formation in the choroid.

b. *Granuloma.*

After injuries to the choroid, when abscess-like round cells accumulations in this membrane have perforated the lamina vitrea, we sometimes find granulation tissue starting from the parenchyma of the choroid. Such a granuloma is never very large, and it may either detach the retina from the choroid, or if this membrane too has been perforated, it may grow through it into the vitreous body. These tumors seem at a later period to be always changed into tough connective-tissue, and thus to form a simple scar.

Leber showed to the meeting of oculists at Heidelberg, in 1878, specimens of granuloma of the choroid, from an individual who had suffered from granulated eye-lids (trachoma).

c. *Sarcoma.*

The most frequent new-formations of the choroid, are the

sarcomata. *Knapp* has written a very extensive book on this subject, and to him belongs the merit of having placed our knowledge with regard to choroidal tumors, on a more exact basis. Since its appearance, only very little has been added to this chapter. There are pigmented and unpigmented sarcomata of the choroid. The unpigmented ones are, however rarely altogether free from pigment. The cells of these tumors are either round or spindle-shaped. The pigmented sarcomata consist mostly of large cells, and the latter show a varying degree of pigmentation. Sometimes the cells are so crowded with pigment molecules, that it is impossible to see a nucleus. While the unpigmented round-cell sarcomata consist chiefly of small cells, and are frequently very vascular, the unpigmented spindle-cell sarcomata are tougher, less vascular, and of a more fibromatous character.

According to *Knapp*, the unpigmented sarcomata take their origin from the outer layers of the choroid, which are more fibrous, while the pigmented ones spring chiefly from the inner, especially the capillary layer. It is as yet not known whether and, if so, in what way, the pigmented epithelium may help in the formation of these tumors.

The sarcomata of the choroid may be very vascular, and contain cavernous spaces of varying size. The latter, the so-called teleangiectatic form of sarcoma, seems to be more frequently found in unpigmented than in pigmented tumors, and is often combined with hæmorrhages in the surrounding tissue. In the small-celled sarcoma more so than in any other variety, fatty degeneration of the cells is often seen. Also chalky deposits have been described in sarcomatous tumors. *Knapp*, however, has never seen them, and mine is the same experience. It is therefore likely that the tumors in which they were seen, were retinal and not choroidal new-formations.

Intra-ocular enchondroma of the eye has been described by *Knapp*. I had occasion to describe two cases of choroidal sarcoma with formation of cartilage tissue, and having examined the tumor described by *Knapp*, I am strongly inclined to believe that it belonged to the same class. Hyaline cartilage appears in the choroidal sarcoma in shape of islets which generally lie in the neighborhood of larger blood-vessels. These islets are surrounded by a capsule of connective-tissue. Although it is certainly not impossible that the cartilage is formed by the transformation of the formative cells of a sarcoma, my opinion, based upon anatomical facts, is, that the remains of the vitreous body inclosed in the sarcoma, are its real starting point. (See Fig. 77.)

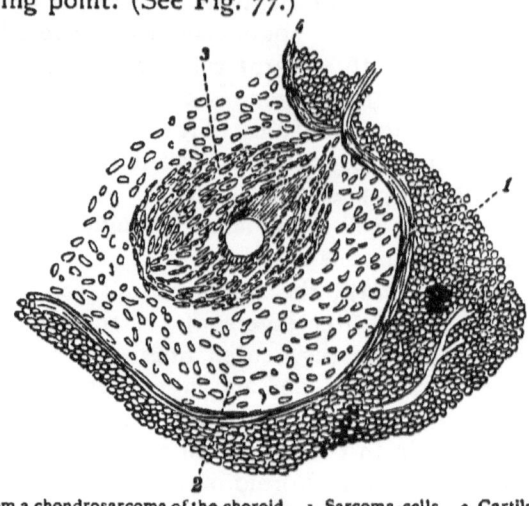

FIG. 77.—From a chondrosarcoma of the choroid. 1. Sarcoma-cells. 2. Cartilage-tissue ; in its centre, (3) remains of the vitreous body changed into delicate, myxomatous tissue. 4. Connective-tissue surrounding the cartilage-tissue.

The formation of osseous tissue in intra-ocular sarcomata, is but rarely observed. I have only once come across such a specimen. (See Fig. 78).

Cowell described a cysto-sarcoma of the choroid. The cysts were filled with a transparent fluid, and were probably formed by the incarcerated exudation, or parts of the vitreous body.

Besides these forms of choroidal tumors, a great many others have been described by other writers, analogues of which the more modern authors have not seen. I consider it therefore better not to mention them at all, as their existence must be proven by more exact anatomical observations.

During its growth the retina may for a long time remain adherent to the choroidal sarcoma. In most cases this mem-

brane is, however, detached by exudation. In the later stages
the retina may altogether disappear.

FIG. 78.—Osseous tissue formed in a sarcomatous tumor of the choroid.

The new-formation later on spreads upon the ciliary body
and iris, either simply by continuous growth or by infection.
The elements of the tumor may furthermore invade the
sclerotic and optic nerve. If the sclerotic becomes perforated
by the tumor, or the optic nerve is destroyed, extra-ocular
tumors are formed.

During the growth of the new-formation the nutrition of
the anterior parts of the eye must needs become greatly impaired, and the intra-ocular pressure increased. This produces the formation of abscesses in the cornea, and sometimes perfect destruction of this membrane. This is another
way, in which the tumor may grow out of the eye-ball.

Finally, the new-formation leads to metastases, which are
of the same structure as the primary tumor in other organs.
Such metastatic tumors are found chiefly in the liver ; they
may appear also in the lungs, pleura, intestines, kidneys,
spleen, brain and other organs.

VII.

NERVUS OPTICUS.

1. *Normal Condition.*

ALTHOUGH this book is meant to deal only with the tissues of the eye-ball itself, it would be impossible to speak of the intra-scleral part of the optic nerve, and to utterly disregard the parts of the nerve which lie farther back. In thus transgressing my programme, I do so in order to aid in a better understanding of the relations of the intra-ocular part of the optic nerve. We will speak in the following pages of the optic nerve near and within the sclerotic and choroid, and of the papilla nervi optici, or the so-called " head " of the optic nerve. The latter I do not consider as *Schwalbe* does, to constitute a part of the retina, although it lies inwards from the choroid.

When speaking of the optic nerve, we have to make a distinction between its outer and its inner sheath, and the nerve itself.

The outer sheath of the optic nerve consists of two parts, *viz.*, the dura mater and the arachnoid. The inner sheath, which lies close to the optic nerve, is analogous to the pia mater.

The dura mater sheath is by far the thickest of the three. It passes directly over into the sclerotic, and its structure is essentially the same as that of the latter membrane. It consists of tough connective-tissue fibrillæ, which, according to *Schwalbe*, in its outer layers run mostly in a longitudinal, in its inner layers in a circular direction. Near the junction with the sclerotic we find only longitudinal fibres. Elastic fibrillæ are also frequently found in the dura mater sheath. Between these fibres lie a number of flat cells (Schwalbe) which are very thin, have an oval nucleus and an nucleolus. If not isolated, they appear like spindle-cells. The inner surface of this sheath is lined with a single layer of delicate endothelial cells. It contains, moreover, numerous blood-vessels and nerves.

The arachnoid sheath which lies comparatively close to the dura mater sheath, is a very thin membrane. It consists chiefly of a network of fine connective-tissue fibres, in the meshes of which lie endothelial cells. Thin connective-tissue trabeculæ unite these two sheaths, while we find much thicker ones connecting the arachnoid sheath with the pia mater sheath.

The pia mater sheath which closely surrounds the optic nerve itself, has a tough outer and a delicate, loose inner layer. It also contains a number of elastic fibres, and is lined on its outer surface with a single layer of delicate endothelial cells. Such cells are furthermore found to adhere to the trabeculæ uniting the outer and inner sheaths with each other. The numerous blood-vessels found in the pia mater come from those of the dura mater, and returning branches of the short ciliary arteries.

The peculiar network of connective-tissue which en-sheathes the nerve fibre bundles of the optic nerve, takes its origin from the pia mater sheath.

The trabeculæ of this network form comparatively small meshes in which the numerous nerve fibre bundles appear embedded. In transverse sections the connective-tissue is seen to form rings (alveoli) of different size. In longitudinal sections we see the trabeculæ regularly arranged in longitu-dinal and transverse directions and intersecting each other. The fibrillæ of this connective-tissue are closely attached to each other, and it has therefore the sclerotic appearance, which we mentioned in connection with the fibres of the ligamentum pectinatum (*Schwalbe*).

The optic nerve is pierced near or just at its axis by a small amount of delicate, loose connective-tissue, in which the central retinal artery and vein are embedded.

The nerve itself is by the connective-tissue divided into a very large number of small bundles of varying size and shape.

The nerve fibre bundles of the optic nerve consist of double contoured nerve fibres, which vary in thickness, and lack a *Schwann's* sheath (*Schwalbe*). These fibres are united with each other by neuroglia, which consists of a homogeneous matrix and numerous cells. The oval short nuclei of the latter in hardened and stained specimens are readily distinguished from those of the connective-tissue. In longitudinal sections they appear arranged in rows in a longitudinal direction. The cells are of a varying shape, but are mostly flat and must be considered as endothelial cells.

At the optic nerve entrance, the dura mater sheath and the arachnoid sheath, now firmly united into one, pass directly over into the sclerotic and make part of its outer layers. The pia mater sheath enters the eye with the optic nerve until it has reached the choroid. It then is united with the inner layers of the sclerotic, and helps in the formation of the lamina cribrosa.

While the space between the pia mater and arachnoid thus becomes obliterated behind the sclerotic, the wider space between the arachnoid and pia mater (subarachnoidal, subvaginal, intervaginal space) can be traced into the sclerotic. Sometimes it even appears to be enlarged within this membrane, and in certain (chiefly myopic) eyes, it is seen to bend at right angles and thus (in transverse sections) to divide the sclerotic into two, generally unequal parts.

The optic nerve itself becomes much thinner after having entered the sclerotic. The cause of this is found in the fact that the double-contoured nerve fibres are changed into non-medullated ones. I would here like to point out a difference in the manner in which this change of the nerve fibres takes place in very short (hypermetropic) and in very long (myopic) eye-balls, which as far as I know has not yet been mentioned elsewhere. While in short eyes the nerve becomes only very gradually thinner, and this attenuation begins already somewhat behind the sclerotic, it takes place in a very abrupt manner in long eyes, and just where the thin sclerotic and choroid surround the nerve. This is caused by the different manner in which the double-contoured nerve fibres go over into non-medullated ones. In the short eyes the boundary line between the two appears in a longitudinal section through the axis of the nerve in the shape of a funnel, the basis of which lies within the outer lamellæ of the sclerotic, while its apex lies considerably farther backward. (See Fig. 79). In long eyes the transformation of the nerve fibres takes place in such a way, that the boundary line is straight or convex towards the front of the eye-ball, and lies just where sclerotic and choroid surround the nerve, that is, within the lamina cribrosa. (See Fig.

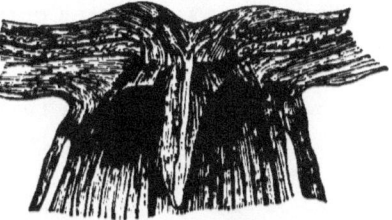

FIG. 79—Shows how the double-contoured nerve-fibres of the optic nerve changed into non-medulatedones in an hypermetropic eye.

80). I am at a loss to explain this fact ; it is, however, also in macroscopical specimens so evident, that it invites further investigations.

After the pia mater has joined the sclerotic, the latter surrounds the nerve directly, and we see numerous thick trabeculæ of connective-tissue spring from it, traverse the optic nerve and thus form, what is called, the lamina cribrosa. In the formation of the latter the choroid also aids. In longitudinal sections of these parts, we see the longitudinal connective-tissue trabeculæ become gradually thinner ; at the same time the number and thickness of the transverse ones is so considerably increased, that while

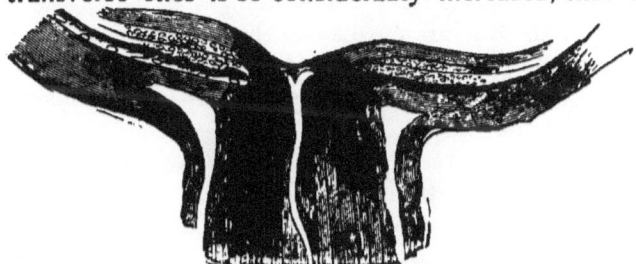

FIG. 80.—Shows how the double-contoured nerve-fibres of the optic nerve are changed into non-medulated ones in a myopic eye.

we find in a part of the optic nerve lying farther backward, but of the same size, perhaps, half a dozen transverse trabeculæ, we find here twenty, thirty and more. In transverse sections of this region we see furthermore, that the meshes between the connective-tissue trabeculæ are much smaller and more numerous, than in those parts of the nerve which lie farther back.

The blood-vessels of the optic nerve come from those of its sheaths and from the central retinal vessels. They form a capillary network between the nerve fibre bundles to which small branches are added within the lamina cribrosa, which come from *Haller's* "vascular ring" formed by the short ciliary arteries.

The subdural and the subarachnoidal spaces are continuations of the intra-cranial spaces of the same name, and must be considered as lymphatic spaces. Through minute fissures in the sclerotic, they are in communication with the suprachoroidal space ; they furthermore communicate with fissures in the nerve itself, and through these with the perivascular spaces in the retina, which we will describe later on.

When the optic nerve has passed through the lamina cribrosa, its fibres are bent nearly at right angles, and before entering the retina, form the so-called papilla nervi optici. Most of these nerve fibres take a radiary direction, and according to *Liebreich*, a larger number run upward and downwards than towards the sides of the eye-ball. The fibres bend gradually, and in the papilla are accompanied by a great many connective-tissue elements, which later on partly disappear and partly enter the retina. The manner in which the nerve fibres enter this membrane, causes the papilla to have a more or less central depression, which is surrounded by walls differing in height according to the distribution of the nerve bundles entering the retina.

The papilla contains a large number of capillary bloodvessels and within it both the central retinal artery and vein are divided into branches. Injections into the lymphatic sheaths show in the papilla a number of fissures radiating from its centre towards the retina.

2. *Pathological Conditions.*

We shall speak only of the pathological conditions of that part of the optic nerve which lies close to the eye-ball and within it. We shall also find here that the affections called by numerous clinical names become but few, when anatomically considered. The nerve-tissue proper is no more prone to independent inflammation here than elsewhere and in many forms of the affections, clinically described as neuritis optica, the nerve-tissue as such, takes but little or no part at all in the inflammatory process.

Anatomical researches have proven beyond doubt, that every affection causing an increase of intra-cranial pressure (especially tumors of the brain) may exert a direct influence upon the optic nerve, especially its intra-ocular part by causing dropsical enlargement of the intervaginal space, and serous exudation into the nerve, consequent upon the former. Furthermore, we may observe an inflammatory process of the sheaths which leads to obliteration of the intervaginal space and consequent inflammatory processes in the connective-tissue of the optic nerve. Nearly as frequent as dropsical enlargement of the sheaths we meet with primary inflammatory processes in the connective-tissue of the nerve, especially the papilla. The rarest affection is certainly an independent inflammation of the nervous fibres themselves.

We shall describe in the following pages, 1. œdema of the optic nerve and papilla ; 2. inflammation of the sheaths of the optic nerve ; 3. interstitial and 4. parenchymatous neuritis.

a. Œdema of the Optic Nerve and Papilla.

As stated above, various causes, producing an increase of intra-cranial pressure, may lead to the filling of the intervaginal space with an abnormal quantity of serous fluid, and thus gradually distent it. The increase of pressure in the intervaginal space, of course, can not exist for any length of time without influencing the condition of the optic nerve. As described, the intervaginal space communicates with the lymphatic canals within the optic nerve, and we must therefore soon also find an increased pressure within these. They appear sometimes very considerably enlarged, and are seen as fissures and small cavities within the connective-tissue trabeculæ. The connective-tissue fibres, by which the sheaths

of the optic nerve are united, and which run through the intervaginal space become atrophied, in rare cases hypertrophied.

These changes in and around the optic nerve cause com-
pression of its blood-vessels, thus leading again to serous
transudation from that source, and to œdema of the papilla
optici. The latter is characterized by hyperæmia, especially
of the veinous blood-vessels, and later on we find serous fluid
between the swollen fibres. Wide canals and cavities sever
the fibres, which, in hardened specimens, appear empty. It
seems that neither the serous fluid in the intervaginal space
nor within the papilla, contains a large quantity of cellular
elements. (See Fig. 81).

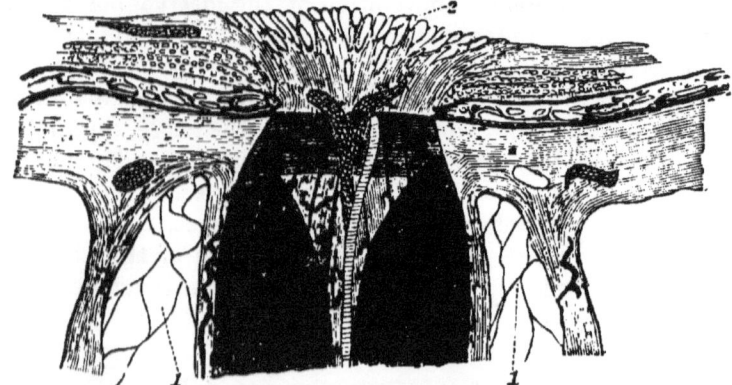

Fig. 81.—Œdema of the intervaginal space and optic papilla. 1. The enlarged intervagina·
space. 2. Spaces in the optic papilla filled with serum.

This œdema of the optic nerve and papilla may again
disappear as soon as the increased pressure becomes reduced,
and the normal conditions may be reestablished. During the
existence of the œdema, hæmorrhages into the optic nerve
and papilla frequently occur. If the disease progresses,
atrophy of the optic nerve fibres, and hypertrophy of the
connective-tissue will be the result. The affection evidently
must also influence the retina. At a later period we find
this membrane also in a state of serous imbibition, and its
nerve fibres swollen ; furthermore, we meet with hypertrophy
of the connective-tissue, hæmorrhages and fatty metamorphosis, especially of the ganglionic cells.

An active inflammation of the parts thus affected, seems to be of rare occurrence.

b. Vaginitis Nervi Optici.

As we may find each of the meninges of the brain separately inflamed (pachymeningitis and leptomeningitis), there are probably also separate inflammatory processes in the outer and inner sheath of the optic nerve. Since, however, the earliest stages of vaginitis optici have as yet not been satisfactorily examined, this is not proven. But there is, no doubt left, that a fibrinous or purulent inflammation of the meninges may cause the same affection in the sheaths of the optic nerve, and influence the conditions of the latter accordingly.

Fibrinous vaginitis is combined with a high degree of hyperæmia in the sheaths. The intervaginal space at first contains a large amount of amorphous fibrine mixed with lymphatic cells. Later on, it is found to be altogether filled with fibrine and cells, and the latter begin to proliferate. Thus the exudation is gradually organized, the proliferation of the endothelial cells of the intervaginal space aids materially in this process. Blood-vessels are seen to spread into this fibro-cellular substance, and soon we find it transformed into connective-tissue. The intervaginal space in this way becomes perfectly obliterated. (See Fig. 82). During the

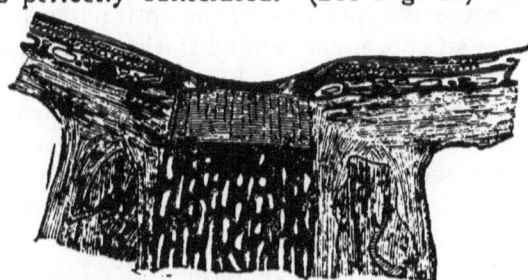

Fig. 82.—Fibrinous vaginitis of the optic nerve. 1. Intervaginal space obliterated by new-formed connective-tissue. Optic nerve atrophic.

progress of this transformation, hæmorrhages frequently occur.

While these changes take place in the intervaginal space,

the optic nerve and papilla cannot remain unaltered. Their connective-tissue is more and more infiltrated with round-cells, and numerous new blood-vessels are formed. Then the connective-tissue becomes hypertrophied, the nervous elements atrophy and simply fade away. During these changes hæmorrhages frequently take place within the optic nerve and papilla.

Besides the fibrinous vaginitis optici, there is a purulent form, which is, however rare, and probably only observed in consequence of purulent meningitis. In such cases we find the sheaths, as well as the intervaginal space filled with round-cells, and later on also the optic nerve and papilla. It seems that in consequence of an early death in these affections, further changes have not been observed.

c. *Interstitial Neuritis.*

Probably the most frequent, certainly the most important affection of the optic nerve, is inflammation of the interstitial connective-tissue. Although such an interstitial neuritis may, as we have seen, arise from œdema of the nerve and inflammation of its sheaths, it is very frequently a primary disease. The inflammatory process involves the neuroglia as well as the connective-tissue trabeculæ, which sever the nerve fibre bundles.

A high degree of hyperæmia of the optic nerve and papilla is followed by an enormous cell-infiltration and proliferation in the connective-tissue. (See Fig. 83). The connective-tissue trabeculæ appear thicker, and in consequence of the large number of new cells in them and the neuroglia, the whole of the nerve appears in fine sections infiltrated with round-cells. (See Fig. 84). The infiltration, however, concerns the nerve fibres themselves but very slightly, if at all. Later on, a large number of new-formed blood-vessels fill the papilla, which in consequence of these changes is sometimes enormously swollen. The blood-vessels of the nerve as well as those of the papilla are frequently found to be surrounded by a mantle of round-cells.

These new-formed cells are gradually changed into connective-tissue. When the trabeculæ become thus hypertrophied, the nerve fibres and blood-vessels are accordingly compressed,

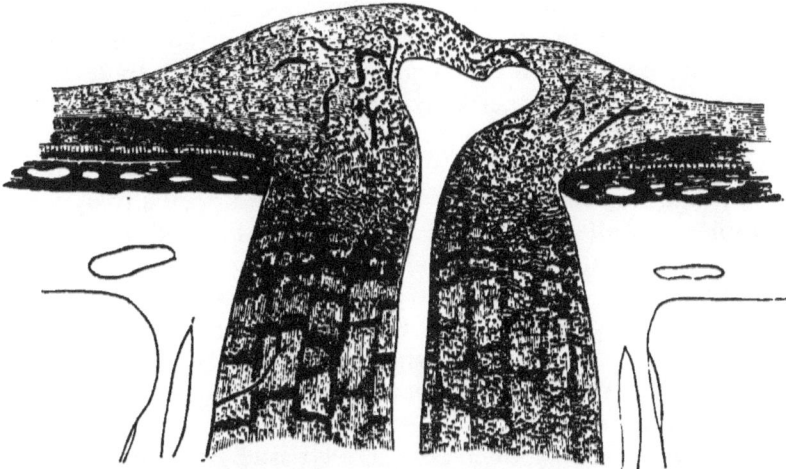

FIG. 83.—Interstitial inflammation of the optic nerve. Longitudinal section.

and the thus impaired nutrition, leads to atrophy of the nerve fibres, of which latter we have two different forms. In one of them the nerve fibres become simply thinner, and we find lying between them a number of fatty cells, probably neuroglia cells undergoing a regresssive metamorphosis; in the

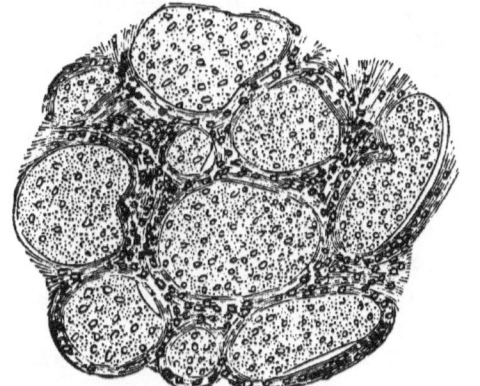

Fig. 84.—Interstitial inflammation of the optic nerve. Transverse section.

other form the whole of the nervous elements is represented by a grumous substance, formed of molecular fat drops, that is, detritus. The connective-tissue grows thicker and thicker and this fatty substance or the simply atrophying nerve fibres disappear more and more. The process as a rule attacks some part of the optic nerve more than the other, and thus the periphery of the nerve or a sector (in a transverse section) may appear perfectly atrophied, while the remainder may as yet be little altered.

At the same time the optic papilla is filled with round-cells, and its connective-tissue also becomes gradually hyper-trophied, while the nervous elements become atrophic. Among the latter we frequently find nerve fibres having a spindle-shaped swelling of varying size, which has been called " sclerotic hypertrophy " of the nerve fibres. I have never been able to see nuclei in these swellings. Cells undergo-ing fatty metamorphosis are also found, and are probably cells of the neuroglia.

When the new-formed connective-tissue gradually shrinks the optic nerve, which had before been greatly thickened, becomes thinner, and its blood-vessels, which are thus com-pressed become atrophied. The formerly much swollen papilla decreases in height and shows a gradually deepening flat excavation, the so-called atrophic excavation of the optic papilla.

Such an atrophy of the optic nerve and papilla must, of course, influence the condition of the retina. We find its nerve fibre layer always thinner than normal. In later stages of the affection, perivasculitis and interstitial retinitis are observed.

Interstitial neuritis may remain stationary at any period, but it is generally progressive. Nerves in which nervous elements can no longer be detected, and which are totally changed into connective-tissue, are, however, but rarely seen.

Hæmorrhages occurring in the optic nerve during the progress of the disease, leave their traces behind in the shape of crystals of hæmatoidine.

The sheaths of the optic nerve also generally become in-flamed and hypertrophied.

d. Medullary Neuritis.

Although the possibility of a primary medullary neuritis

cannot *a priori* be denied, it is certain that the nervous elements are not prone to active inflamation. I have never seen
a case of neuritis in which I thought myself justified in considering the nerve fibres as the seat of the primary inflammation. The description of this form of neuritis given by *Leber*
agrees essentially with mine, of the changes in the nerve and
papilla in cases of interstitial neuritis, but I cannot consider
it as evidence of the existence of such a primary medullary
neuritis optici.

Results.

Besides the dropsical enlargement of the intervaginal
space combined with stretching of the outer sheath of the
optic nerve, and its obliteration by new-formed connective-
tissue, the most important and frequent results of the affections just described, are atrophy of the optic nerve and
papilla, and consequent alterations in the retina.

Even when the nervous elements of the optic nerve
have been totally destroyed, we find the connective-tissue
arranged in a manner resembling the normal condition (at
least in the longitudinal direction). Such nerves, however,
but rarely come under observation. In most cases we find
only the connective-tissue trabeculæ very considerably thickened at the expense of the nerve fibres. Their sclerotic appearance is still more striking than in the normal and the
blood-vessels are greatly reduced in number. The remaining
nerve fibres have either lost their medulla, grown very thin
and lie as indifferent fibres, which can be stained with carmine, between the connective-tissue fibres, or they appear
changed into a yellowish, grumous substance, which cannot
be stained by any staining material, and consists of drops of
fat and myeline of varying size.

Inward from the hypertrophied lamina cribrosa, the connective-tissue of the papillæ is also hypertrophic, and the
nervous elements are destroyed or thin and atrophic. In the
latter case they may still be distinguished from the connective-tissue. Some nerve fibres may be found in a state of
sclerotic hypertrophy, as described above. In later stages

we find that the papilla consists chiefly of a network of areo-lar connective-tissue, the meshes of which appear empty.

In the farther progress of the affection, the new-formed connective-tissue shrinks, and from this shrinkage the so-called atrophic excavation of the papilla nervi optici ensues ; and the gradually flattened papilla may finally be nearly or entirely reduced to the lamina cribrosa, which in this affec-

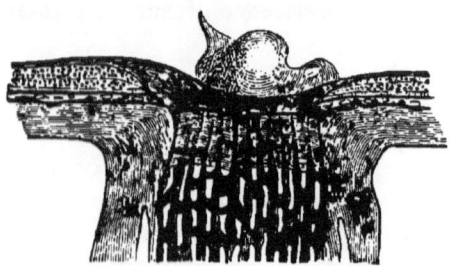

Fig. 85.—Atrophic excavation of the optic papilla filled with a delicate connective-tissue formed in the neighboring vitreous body.

tion always remains in its normal position. (See Fig. 85). The walls of the remaining blood-vessels are thickened and sclerosed. Atrophy of the optic nerve and papilla leaves in its wake atrophy of the nerve fibre layer of the retina, and regressive metamorphosis of the ganglionic cells.

During the inflammatory affections of the papilla nervi optici, the adjacent part of the vitreous body also seem fre-quently to become inflamed. As a result of this inflamma-tion (circumscribed plastic hyalitis) we see a small amount of connective-tissue formed in the posterior parts of the vitreous body, into which blood-vessels starting from the papilla are seen to enter. If in such cases an atrophic excava-tion of the papilla is formed, we may find the latter filled with delicate connective-tissue, which anteriorly is lost in the vitreous body. (See Fig. 85). The granuloma of the optic nerve to be described later on, is not to be confounded with this affection.

APPENDIX.

Glaucomatous Atrophy and Excavation, and Embolic Atrophy of the Optic Nerve.

In the foregoing, we have had occasion several times to state that, in spite of a large number of very careful investigations, we are not yet in the possession of an anatomical explanation of the cause of the array of symptoms to which we apply the clinical name of glaucoma. *Knies,* too, who thought to have found this cause in the obliteration of *Fontana's* spaces, has certainly gone beyond the mark, since, as many have already proven, this obliteration is often found without having caused glaucoma, and on the other hand, is frequently wanting in glaucomatous eyes. My own investigations concerning a large number of glaucomatous eyes, have not taught me any anatomical fact, which can be considered as the common cause of this disease. Its most important symptom is certainly atrophy of the optic nerve, and glaucomatous excavation of the optic papilla. The anatomical conditions of a glaucomatous excavation are so characteristic that they always enable us to make a positive diagnosis.

While simple atrophic excavation is flat, and only reaches to the lamina cribrosa, which, as stated, remains in its normal position, we find in a case of glaucomatous excavation that the fibres of the lamina cribrosa are compressed and forced backward, often behind the outer surface of the sclerotic. The nerve fibres of the papilla which are pressed aside are atrophied, and the optic nerve behind the lamina cribrosa shows the conditions of atrophy after interstitial neuritis. (See Fig. 86).

Led by clinical observation, *Schnabel* sought the cause of glaucoma in an inflammatory process of the tissues surrounding the optic nerve entrance, especially of the choroid. This idea seemed to be rather plausible, and I tried hard to find anatomical facts to prove it. I could not, however, find them. In most of the cases of glaucoma, I had the opportunity to examine, I found the choroid normal; in one case it appeared inflamed on the nasal side of the papilla, and was infiltrated with round-cells; in a number of cases the choroid was atrophied.

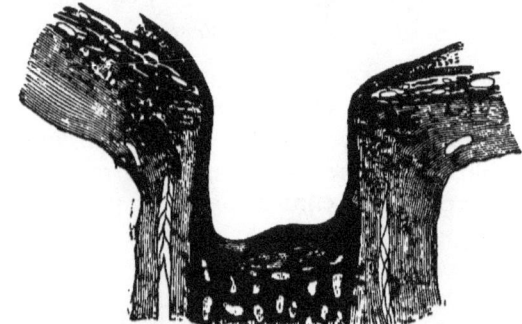

FIG. 86.—Very deep glaucomatous excavation. Atrophy of the optic nerve.

To sum up, the essential difference between an atrophic and a glaucomatous excavation of the papilla nervi optici, is the following, *viz.*, in the former affection the papilla and optic nerve are affected, while the lamina cribrosa retains its normal position, in the latter the lamina cribrosa is pressed outward, while atrophy of the papilla and optic nerve takes place.

According to *Schweigger*, a small secondary excavation may be found in the larger one, if in consequence of the glaucoma the tissue surrounding the central retinal blood-vessels is also distended.

We frequently find also in glaucomatous excavations, a delicate connective-tissue, which is formed in the adjacent part of the vitreous body.

Atrophy of the optic nerve is, moreover, observed after embolism of the central retinal artery. Anatomically, it in no way differs from the atrophy consequent upon glaucoma or inflammatory processes within the optic nerve or its surroundings. Neither has atrophy caused by retinal affections anything peculiar.

Hæmorrhage in the Optic Nerve. Hæmatogeneous Pigment.

Hæmorrhages of a varying size are not rare in the tissue of the optic nerve. They may be caused by injuries or operations, or may occur during inflammatory processes. In recent cases we find the optic nerve or papilla filled with red blood corpuscles, which press the nerve fibre bundles aside. These blood-corpuscles later on are gradually destroyed, and the amorphous or crystallized hæmatoidine remains lying within the connective-tissue of the nerve. (See Fig. 87). It

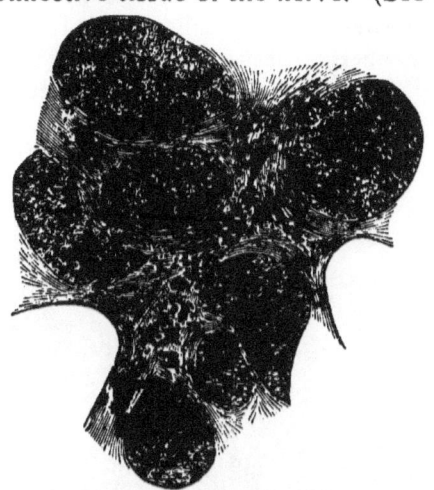

FIG. 87.—From an atrophic optic nerve. Hypertrophy of the connective-tissue. which contains some pigment. The nerve-fibres are broken up into a grumous substance.

is very probable, as *Knapp* conjectured, that the abnormal pigmentation, sometimes seen with the ophthalmoscope in the papilla nervi optici, is caused by such hæmorrhages. Whether hæmorrhages in the intervaginal space (*Leber*) may cause a similar ophthalmoscopic picture, seems to me doubtful.

In transverse sections of such pigmented optic nerves, we frequently find that the nerve fibre bundles surrounded by pigmented connective-tissue are atrophied. This atrophy is probably due to the pressure exerted upon them by the hæmorrhage. The connective-tissue in which the pigment lies embedded, is always hypertrophied. (See Fig. 87).

Tumors of the Intra-Ocular part of the Optic Nerve.

Tumors of the " head " of the optic nerve have, it seems, never been observed. The tumors of the optic nerve reported in literature, all originated in the intra-cranial or intra-orbital part of this nerve, and do not here come under consideration.

It seems that a direct injury to the optic papilla may lead to the formation of a granuloma; I had, at least once, the opportunity of examining such a tumor. It consisted of round-cells and small spindle-cells, which lay between a fine network of connective-tissue and blood-vessels. The connective-tissue and the blood-vessels of the tumor were continuations of those parts in the papilla nervi optici. (See Fig. 88).

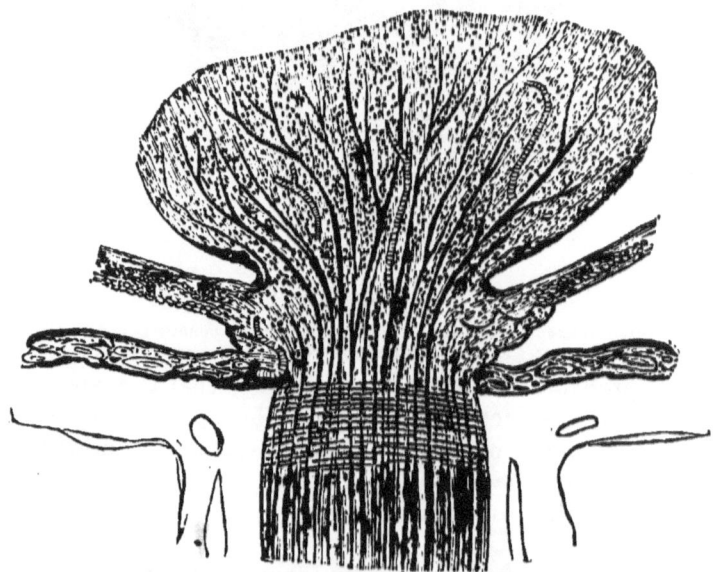

Fig. 88.—Granuloma of the optic papilla.

The similiarity between such an anatomical condition and the one clinically observed by *Manz*, and called retinitis proliferans, and the affections drawn and described by *Jæger* and *Becker* as new-formation of connective-tissue and blood-vessels in the vitreous body, is very striking. In the cases reported by these authors, the eyes however, were, not injured.

VIII.

RETINA.

1. *Normal Condition.*

The retina consists of ten distinct layers, if we count the pigmented epithelium as part of this membrane. We have treated of this layer already, and considered it as a separate one, in which I think we are the more justified, since a direct proof of the genetic connection between the retina and the pigmented epithelium has yet to be found.

The layers of the retina are therefore the following :

1. Internal limiting membrane.
2. Nerve fibre layer.
3. Ganglionic layer.
4. Inner molecular layer.
5. Inner granular layer.
6. Outer molecular layer.
7. Outer granular layer.
8. External limiting membrane (?)
9. Rods and cones.

The first six of these layers have by *Schwalbe* been called the brain layer of the retina, the remaining three the neuro-epithelial layer.

The different elements of the retina are held in position by a common, easily distinguished substance (supporting-tissue) which forms the so-called supporting or radiary fibres of the retina. *Schwalbe* says that this substance is not true connective-tissue. Pathological processes, however, prove it to be in no way different from it.

The radiary fibres traverse the retinal tissue at right angles to its surfaces. They are flat cylindrical structures having on their sides wing-like offsets of varying shape which anastomose with each other. Every radiary fibre has within the inner granular layer an oval nucleus which is either en-closed in a spindle-shaped enlargement, or, as it seems fre-

quently, only adheres to the fibre.   By the site of this nucleus
the radiary fibres are divided into an inner and an outer part.
Their inner part ends with a cone-like swelling within the
nerve fibre layer at the internal limiting membrane.   Their
outer part reaches the limitans externa.   According to
Schwalbe, the cone-like swelling of the inner part of the
radiary fibres also contains a nucleus.   I have never been
able to see it.

Merkel states that the supporting tissue forms a tube-like
sheath for every cone-fibre and every cone-granule, and he
draws a similar sheath around the rods.   In teased specimens
the former may without doubt frequently be seen.

The limitans interna and externa enclose, so to speak, the
retina.   In transverse sections the former always appears as
a double-contoured, vitreous membrane.   Recent authors
have denied the existence of an internal limiting membrane,
and stated that, what appeared to be such, was formed by the
coalescence of the cone-like enlargements of the inner part
of the radiary fibres.   This they declare to be proven, since
in a plain view of the inner surface of the retina, we can see
the basis of these cone-shaped ends, and when they are
stained with nitrate of silver, their outlines are very similar
to those of endothelial cells.   I am not prepared to agree with
these authors, and must insist upon the existence of a separate
internal limiting membrane, which is not formed by the coalescence of the basis of the cone-shaped terminus of the supporting fibres, but which covers these and can become detached by
itself, as we frequently find it in pathological eyes.   Besides
I once had an opportunity to observe vitreous bodies lying
upon it, similar in appearance and nature to those of the
lamina vitrea of the choroid.   I consider this to be a further
proof of the existence of a separate internal limiting membrane, similar to the lamina vitrea of the choroid, and the
membrana *Descemetii*.   This membrane is, however, not to
be confounded with what has been called the hyaloid membrane, and which will be spoken of in Chapter X.

While I thus unite in the opinion of those authors who
acknowledge the existence of an internal limiting membrane,
I do not consider that, what has been called the external

limiting membrane, is really a membrane. In the outer
granular layer, all the parts of the supporting tissue coalesce
in such a way that they fill all the spaces between the fibres
of the rods and cones and their granules. The free ends of
the rods and cones reach beyond this,—*sit venia verbo*—
cementing substance, and the outer surface of the latter represents in transverse sections a single line, which is sharply
defined, but is not a membrane. If the latter were the case,
we would see a double contour.

The sheaths of the outer parts of the rods and cones
reach with them beyond this surface, and are, as *Merkel*
states, probably open towards the choroid.

The nerve fibre layer of the retina consists, as its name
implies, chiefly of the nerve fibres which radiate from the
optic nerve, as soon as it has entered the eye-ball. The majority of fibres continue to run in a radiating direction
towards the periphery of the retina. Only those fibres which
go to the macula lutea deviate from this direction, and
are concentrically bent into arches, by which arrangement
a larger number of nerve fibres are enabled to reach the
yellow spot, than would. be possible, if they approached it in
a radiating direction. The fibres are axis-cylinders of varying thickness, and are united into bundles. Near the optic
nerve entrance there are several layers of such bundles,
which at a short distance from it are spread into one. Towards the periphery of the retina the thickness of the nerve
fibre layer continually decreases, and the fibres end at the so-
called ora serrata in a terminal plexus (*Merkel*). *Schwalbe*
described flat endothelial-like cells with an oval nucleus in
this layer. They are neuroglia-cells, and can be easily recognized as such.

The nerve fibres are said to branch off at acute angles
while on their way to the ora serrata, and to anastomose with
each other. The varicose appearance which they often have,
is probably a post mortem symptom, or is caused by chemical
agents.

Outwards from the nerve fibre layer lies the ganglionic
cell layer. These ganglionic cells form, only in the region of
the macula lutea, several layers. They lie very near each

other in the neighborhood of the optic nerve entrance, and
are found farther apart the nearer the ora serrata. It must
be mentioned here that the ganglionic cell layer is not well
defined, and many of its cells lie in the nerve fibre or in the
inner molecular layer.

The cells themselves vary in size. They are round or
oval, and have a large round or ellipsoid nucleus with several
nucleoli. A nerve fibre coming from the opticus enters into
every such ganglionic cell, and we see springing from the
cells one or more offsets which go into the inner molecular
layer. In the region of the macula lutea, the ganglionic cells
are said by all authors to be oval and to have only one peripheral offset, that is, to be bipolar. The ganglionic cells lie
embedded in notches on the wing-like offsets of the supporting fibres. *Schwalbe* found a homogeneous, lustrous cementing substance between them. The offsets, after entering the
inner molecular layer, give off numerous branches in a radiating or oblique direction. According to *Merkel*, these branches
then enter the inner granular-layer and anastomose with the
central fibres of the inner granules.

The inner molecular layer consists of these fine fibres
just mentioned, and the so-called granular (molecular) substance. *Merkel* and others describe the latter as a homogeneous substance containing numerous small cavities. These
cavities are said to be filled with fluid which refracts the light
in a different manner, or to contain solid granules. (*Merkel*,
Henle, *Retzius*). The inner molecular layer is comparatively
thick, and remains of about the same thickness all over the
retina, except in the region of the macula lutea. The supporting fibres simply pass through it. *Retzius* states that
the offsets from the ganglionic cells have a radiating direction in this layer, others found them to branch off at right or
acute angles before entering the inner granular layer.

The inner granular layer is mainly formed of nuclei.
We stated above that the supporting fibres have a nucleus in
this layer, and besides these we find another kind of delicate
oval nuclei with a nucleolus, and surrounded by a small
amount of protoplasm. These have a central and a peripheral (inner and outer) offset, the former of which is thinner

than the latter. According to *Merkel* and others, the central offsets of these nuclei of the inner granular layer, anastomose with the peripheral offsets of the ganglionic cells in the inner molecular layer. Their peripheral offsets pass through the outer molecular layer in a radiating direction or are bent like a bayonet, and give off several smaller branches. *Merkel* undoubtedly found an anastomosis between these peripheral offsets of the nuclei of the inner granular layer and the central fibres of the cones in the outer molecular layer. Such an anastomosis with the rod-fibres, although it is very probable, has as yet not been found.

The outer molecular layer is very thin. Besides the fibres just mentioned, we find in it a small quantity of the same granular (molecular) substance, with which we already met in the inner molecular layer. I can confirm the statement of *Merkel*, that in transverse sections of this layer, nearly without exception, we see a broken line (Huelfslinie). This is formed by the broader end of the central fibres of the cones and their sheaths, and will be spoken of again later on. *Schwalbe* also found flat cells in the outer molecular layer, the offsets of which took part in the formation of the network of fibres of which this layer partly consists. These cells are said to be of a ganglionic nature.

Rods and cones and the outer granular layer, are according to *Schwalbe* the " neuro-epithelium " of the retina.

Let us first examine the cones. The cone-fibre originates with a cone-shaped swelling in the outer molecular layer, and is there, as proven by *Merkel*, in direct connection with the fibres coming from the inner granular layer. The cone-fibre then becomes a little thinner, until just under the limitans externa, it again swells rapidly, and there forms the cone itself. This part of the cone, inwards from the limitans externa, contains a large oval nucleus with a nucleolus (the so-called cone-granule). Besides these cone-fibres, the rod-fibres originate in the outer molecular layer. A direct connection between the rod-fibre and the fibres coming from the inner granular layer has, as stated above, not yet been found. As soon as the rod-fibre has left the outer molecular layer, it has a small swelling, and somewhat farther on, near the limitans externa, it encloses in a larger swelling the "rod-granule." This swelling has in fresh specimens a peculiar transverse striation, which disappears soon after death. Only then the nucleus is distinctly recognizable. While the cone-granule always lies (except in the region of the macula lutea and the ora serrata) just inwards from the limitans interna, the rod-granules which are much more numerous, form several layers, that is, their distance from the limitans externa is varying. We find therefore the rod-fibres generally thinner again to the outside of the swelling which encloses the granule, until they pass over into the rods themselves.

The rods and cones lie outwards from the limitans externa, as we stated before. The cones are bottle-shaped structures which spring from the part of the cone-fibre containing the nucleus; they consist of the inner conical and the outer thinner cylindrical part. The inner part appears granulated, and encloses in its outer half, the so-called ellipsoid body, a structure the nature of which is as yet not understood. The outer part of the cones consist of a homogeneous substance which refracts the light strongly, and cannot be stained with carmine. After death, or under the influence of several chemical agents, it splits into fine lamellæ.

The rods, too, may be divided into an inner and an outer part. The inner part is generally thicker than the outer, and both are, as a rule, cylindrical. The inner part, moreover, appears granulated. Their outer part, too, is broken up into fine lamellæ when dying or under the influence of chemical agents. Some authors describe it as having a number of longitudinal stripes on its surface.

As stated above, the rods and cones with their fibres and granules, have a sheath (*Merkel*). The sheaths of the cone-fibres end in the outer molecular layer, and their bases there form the broken line, above referred to. The longitudinal stripes often seen on the surface of the inner parts of the rods and cones, is explained by folds in these sheaths. According to *Krause* and *Schultze*, small fibrillæ start from the limitans externa, and surround the basis of the inner parts of the rods and cones, forming the so-called fibre-baskets (Faserkœrbe).

In plain views of the external surface of the retina, the

optical transverse sections of the rods and cones, form a regular mosaic. This shows, however, a different arrangement according to the region from which the specimen is taken. While in the region of the macula lutea every cone appears to be surrounded by a single ring of rods, the latter are more and more numerous and the cones farther apart from each other, the nearer they approach the periphery of the retina.

Kuchne, Boll and others have recently found that during life the outer part of the rods has a purple hue, being saturated with the so-called retinal purple which is secreted from the pigmented epithelial layer.

From the description given in the foregoing, the way in which the connection between the optic nerve and the rods and cones is established, is the following: The opticus fibres enter the ganglionic cells which send one or two peripheral offsets into the inner molecular layer, where they anastomose with the central offsets of the nuclei of the inner granular layer. The peripheral offsets of these enter the outer molecular layer from which the central offsets of the rods and cones (the rod-fibres and cone-fibres) are seen to emerge. As *Merkel* has proven, the peripheral fibres of the inner granules are in direct connection with the central offsets of the cone-granules; the same has not yet been proven for the rods. We know therefore of a direct communication between the cones and the central organ, while the same is not yet established for the rods.

It is certainly a very remarkable fact, that the so-called "visual purple" which by recent investigations has been accorded so important an influence in the act of vision, does not tint the *cones*, which are undoubtedly percipient organs, but renders the rods, which appear to be at least less important for direct vision, purple. It would therefore appear that the physiological value of the visual purple has been overrated.

The structure of the retina, as we have described it, is very materially altered in its peripheral parts, and in the region of the macula lutea.

Near the ora serrata the nerve fibres, rods and cones gradually disappear, while the supporting tissue becomes more and more prevalent. The rapid attenuation observed in the periphery of the retina is, however, due in a great measure to the abrupt, not gradual disappearance of the inner molecular layer. The granular layers become gradually thinner, and the outer one sooner so than the inner, and finally the one cell layer of the retina, which lies upon the ciliary body is formed. In the parts nearest to the ora serrata, we sometimes find (especially in the eyes of old people) an alteration which *Iwanoff* called, as it seems to me very inappropriately, " œdema " of the retina. In plain views of such a retina, when stained, we see an irregular network of light bands, varying in breadth, and surrounding islets of a darker tint. In transverse sections we see, that these lighter bands are caused by a system of cavities varying in size, which lie in the inner and outer granular layer. These cavities are round or oval, and coalesce with each other, or are separated by pillars, the capitals of which form the darker islets above referred to and seen in the plain views. These pillars consist of fibres with a nucleus and long spindle-shaped cells. Sometimes their transverse septa are formed by trabeculæ running in a transverse direction from one pillar to another. Probably these cavities are filled with a serous fluid during life. (See Fig. 89). This condition of the retina I never found

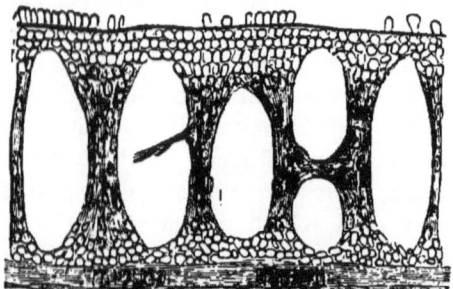

Fig. 89.—Cystoid degeneration of the retina near the ora serrata.

combined with the symptoms of retinal œdema, which are to be detailed farther on, and I therefore think it much more appropriate to call this condition cystoid degeneration of the ora serrata retinæ (*Nettleship*).

The greatest changes in the structure of the retina are

found in the region of the macula lutea, and in the fovea centralis. The macula lutea according to *Koelliker* lies, from forty-two to forty-five mm. distant from the optic nerve entrance, and has a small depression somewhat eccentrically situated, *viz.*, the fovea centralis. The examinations as to the cause of the yellow tint of this part of the retina are not yet concluded. The macula lutea usually forms an oval, the longitudinal axis of which lies in a horizontal direction.

In the fovea centralis, the limitans interna forms a line which is convex towards the choroid. While the whole of the retina must therefore be thinner in this place, its layers (except the nerve fibre layer) are considerably thickened in the parts surrounding the fovea centralis. All of the layers, however, are not of equal thickness, and the nerve fibre layer becomes gradually thinner, so much so that we find the ganglionic cells near the fovea centralis lying directly under the limitans interna. The ganglionic cell layer is here found to be six or eight times thicker, than in other parts of the retina, and its cells in this region are said always to be of an oval shape and bipolar.

The inner granular and inner molecular layer are comparatively but little thickened. The molecular substance of the outer molecular layer is totally wanting in the fovea centralis. Its fibres are, however, strongly developed, and while in other parts of the retina they run mainly in a vertical direction, they are here all bent like a bayonet, so, that the horizontal part is longer than the others, and grows more so the nearer the fovea centralis. The outer granular layer in this region is also somewhat thinner. The rods are as already stated, very much less numerous, and the number of the cones is considerably increased, the latter are thinner and considerably longer, than in other regions of the retina. Right in the fovea centralis all the layers of the retina are so close to each other and so much thinner, that it is very difficult to distinguish them from each other. It seems, however, that none of the cellular layers disappear entirely. The supporting fibres are very much thinner in the region of the mucula lutea, and in the fovea centralis itself, they are altogether wanting. The fovea centralis has, furthermore, no rods. *Schwalbe* states that the basis of the cells of the pigmented epithelial layer is much smaller in this region, but that they are much higher.

At the papilla the retina (except its nerve fibre layer) terminates, as *Schwalbe* first stated, on the lateral side in a vertical line; on the opposite side the end forms an oblique line, and the outer layers reach farther towards the optic nerve than the inner ones. The rod-fibres and cone-fibres . must therefore also here, as in the region of the macula lutea, run in an oblique direction.

2. Pathological Conditions.

A. Œdema Retinæ.

Œdema of the retina may be a purely passive infiltration of this membrane with serous fluid caused by an affection of the choroid, or it may be more or less the result of an inflammatory process in the retina itself.

In the latter case, the affection is always accompanied by hyperæmia of the retinal blood-vessels, while in the former, hyperæmia is usually wanting. In œdema of the retina we find all the elements constituting this membrane saturated with a serous fluid. They consequently appear swollen and somewhat dim. Moreover, there are a small quantity of lymph-cells to be seen in the nerve fibre layer. In consequence of these changes, the whole of the retina is thicker than normal, which is, however, most pronounced in the neighborhood of the optic papilla. Later on small cavities filled with serum may be found in the connective supporting tissue and in the molecular substance, especially in the outer molecular layer. These press the cellular elements aside, and the latter may at a remote period be destroyed in consequence of fatty degeneration, resulting from the undue pressure exerted upon them. In this way the cavities may grow larger, and the serum which fills them will then contain some detritus besides the lymph-cells. The cavities have mostly an oval shape. Capillary hæmorrhages are but rarely observed in the course of such an œdema.

Œdema may be found in all parts of the retina, and is

not, like the cystoid degeneration of the parts near the ora serrata, confined to one region. In the latter affection, moreover, the hyperæmia of the blood-vessels and the serous imbibition of the cellular elements which surround the cavities, are wanting.

A number of larger serous cysts have been described in detached retina. Whether they have originated in such an œdema, I cannot tell.

I have not been able to ascertain what the final changes in retinal œdema are ; but it seems that it may exist as a chronic affection for a very long time, without changing the retinal tissue in any other way than in the manner above described.

B. *Inflammatory Processes in the Retina, and their Results.*

Retinitis like choroiditis, has been clinically divided into a large number of varieties. The histological conditions do not however warrant these clinical distinctions. The nervous elements of the retina, like those of the opticus, are not apt to become independently inflamed. The inflammatory process seems always to originate in the connective-tissue of the retina, and its nervous elements become only secondarily affected. We will speak, 1. of retinitis as we find it as a peculiar symptom in albuminuria, 2. of diffuse atrophic retinitis, and 3. of purulent retinitis.

a. *Retinitis Albuminurica.*

The peculiar form of interstitial retinitis found especially during an inflammatory process in the kidneys, concerns preeminently those regions of the retina in the neighborhood of the optic papilla and the macula lutea. Within these regions all the parts of the retina gradually suffer from the affection and in advanced cases we find not only the blood-vessels and connective-tissue, but also the nerve elements (these only secondarily) altered.

The most visible, microscopical symptom of this affection is the considerable swelling of the involved parts, especially of the optic papilla and its surroundings. Furthermore, the thickened retina around the optic papilla is usually wrinkled and partially detached. The considerable swelling is chiefly due to an inflammatory infiltration and hyperplasia of the connective-tissue and œdema. The connective-tissue fibres are longer and thicker, and have that sclerotic appearance caused by a strong refraction of the light, which we found to be normal to the fibres of the ligamentum pectinatum. The hyperplasia and swelling are most pronounced in the nerve fibre-layer, especially in the papilla. The hyperæmic blood-vessels are usually surrounded by white blood-corpuscles, which lie in the neighboring connective-tissue. The fluid with which all elements of the nerve fibre layer seem to be sodden, is homogenous, in some cases it appears somewhat granular. The swelling of the nerve fibre layer is, furthermore, due to the peculiar club-like swelling of the nerve fibres, already above described, as sclerotic atrophy of these elements. We not unfrequently see such nerve fibres in teased specimens. They are either thickened at one or both ends or altogether, and refract the light strongly. The thickened part is very darkly tinted when carmine has been used. As stated already, I have never found nuclei in these swellings. Nerve-fibres which have been altered in such a way are not only found lying indiscriminately among the others, but sometimes they are seen crowded together in larger quantities. Where this is the case, the nerve fibre layer appears to be more especially swollen, it projects more or less into the vitreous body above the surrounding parts, and crowds the outer layers of the retina close together. (See Fig. 90). Former authors have also mentioned a sclerotic swelling of the ganglionic cells, which by more recent authors is declared to be erroneous. I must, however, state again that besides the sclerotic swelling of the nerve fibres, which as I said contain no nucleus, I frequently found large round and sometimes star-shaped bodies, undoubtedly containing a nucleus, and which I consider to be such sclerosed ganglionic cells.

We find, furthermore, in the nerve fibre layer, and especially in the region of the macula lutea, cells which contain numerous fat-granules. They appear round or semi-lunar, have one or more offsets, and a shining round nucleus. I

think, these cells, too, may be considered as ganglionic ones
undergoing a regressive metamorphosis. I must state,

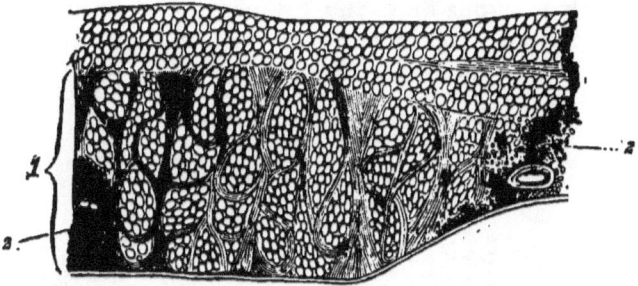

Fig. 90.—Albuminuric retinitis. 1. Nerve fibre layer, considerably thickened through
sclerosed hypertrophic nerve fibres. 2. Hæmorrhage.

however, that the majority of the ganglionic cells appear unaltered, so does the inner molecular layer.

Besides the round-cells which lie around the blood-vessels
and those scattered among the elements of the nerve fibre
layer, I not unfrequently found tubercle-like aggregations of
round-cells in this layer.

The swelling of the nerve fibre layer may, moreover, be
increased by a granular exudation, found under the limitans
interna. This exudation sometimes detaches the inner limiting membrane to some extent, and thus makes it protrude
into the vitreous body.

Further changes characteristic of albuminuric retinitis,
are found in the outer layers of the retina. In these, also,
we find the connective-tissue in a state of hypertrophy
and partly sclerosed, or in a state of fatty infiltration. A
more striking change is, however, the formation of cavities
in the inner and outer granular, and in the outer molecular layer. These cavities are round or oval, and in the
latter case, their longitudinal diameter usually lies at right
angles to the surface of the retina. The cavities found in
the region of the macula lutea generally make an exception
to this rule, and lie parallel with the surface of the retina.
If the cavities are small, they lie either in one of the three
named layers or in two neighboring ones (the inner granular
and outer molecular, or the latter and outer granular layers).
The larger cavities may reach from the inner granular layer

even to the rods and cones. We found similiar cavities in
cases of œdema of the retina. While these, however, are
filled with a serous fluid, the cavities found in albuminuric
retinitis contain threads of fibrine or cellular elements. (See
Fig. 91). The latter are large round cells, filled with fat-

Fig. 91.—*Albuminuric retinitis.* 1. Outer granular layer. 2. Inner granular layer. 3.
Cavity filled with fibrine. 4. Cavity filled with cells containing fat-granules. Both
cavities containing, moreover, peculiar structures of varying size, which coalesce and
refract the light very strongly. Some fat granule cells lie in the outer granular layer.

granules and they have a small shining round nucleus, often
one or more offsets, and are of slightly brownish tint. Between these cells drop-like yellow-brown bodies frequently
lie, varying in size, which may be seen to coalesce. The
hardening fluids seem to cause a shrinking of these bodies,
and their surface consequently may appear wrinkled. Some
of them have a notch, into which one of the fatty cells would
fit. The substance which forms these bodies is too darkly
tinted, and too hard to be considered beyond doubt as a colloid substance, it appears to be more like amyloid substance.
It lacks, however, the concentric structure, and with iodine
does not show the reaction so characteristic of the amyloid
substance. Perhaps, these bodies are the result of a further
regressive metamorphosis of the above-named cells filled with
fat-granules, or they may be simply an exudation coagulated
under the influence of the hardening fluid.

The fibrine seen in such cavities always forms a network of fine threads, similar to those found in the alveoli
of the lungs in croupous pneumonia. Cells and fibrine
are but rarely found together in the same cavity. These

cavities contain either cells or fibrine and seem never to be empty.

A fibrinous exudation frequently lies between the retina and the pigmented epithelial layer, and this seems to be found most frequently in the region of the macula lutea. Wherever it is found, the rods and cones are changed into short club-shaped structures. This change in the shape of the rods and cones is, however, not at all characteristic of albuminuric retinitis. These sometimes may be altered in another manner which I never met with in other diseases of the retina. I am in the possession of specimens where the rods and cones in the neighborhood of the papilla, are two and three times longer than in the normal state. Such elongated (hypertrophied) rods and cones are somewhat granular, and in appearance are similar to the sclerosed nerve fibres and ganglionic cells, that is, they refract the light very strongly and are stained very dark with carmine. It is, furthermore, impossible to distinguish between their outer and inner part, and they are firmly adherent to each other.

The rods and cones may also be broken up into fine lamellæ and myeline-like drops.

Cells containing fat-granules, like those in the cavities, are also seen scattered about in the granular layers.

The blood-vessels show pathological changes which, however, are not characteristic of albuminuric retinitis. We hardly ever examine a retina suffering from the affection under consideration, without finding in it a large number of hæmorrhages. These are either found only in the nerve fibre layer and in the neighborhood of blood-vessels, or they reach through the whole thickness of the retina to the limitans externa, or they may even perforate the outer or inner surface of the retina. Crowded red blood-corpuscles are seen between the elements of the retina in all stages of destruction. They usually undergo fatty degeneration before being absorbed. (*Virchow*). It is a strange fact that we never find either crystals of hæmatoidine or any abnormal pigmentation after such hæmorrhages in a retina suffering from albuminuric retinitis.

These hæmorrhages are undoubtedly caused by some

pathological changes in the walls of the blood-vessels and cannot be explained by the simple process of diapedesis. The existence of such changes is, however, very difficult to prove. I have sometimes found a fatty infiltration of the endothelial cells of blood-vessels. Other changes, found in the walls of the blood-vessels can hardly be the cause of these hæmorrhages, as they are found in other diseases without causing them. I mean the sclerosis of the blood-vessels and a slight degree of perivasculitis. The characteristic features of sclerosis of the blood-vessels are, that their walls become very thick, (and the lumen consequently very narrow), appear hyaline and refract the light strongly. Sometimes the thickening of the walls leads to perfect obliteration of the blood-vessels. This process, which seems to chiefly attack the smaller branches, may, moreover, cause the formation of a thrombus in the blood-vessels.

In cases of perivasculitis, we find the adventitia of the blood-vessels filled with round-cells. This affection is, however, of rare occurrence in albuminuric retinitis.

During this disease of the retina, the optic nerve often shows the symptoms of interstitial neuritis.

b. Retinitis Interstitialis Diffusa (Atrophica).

Diffuse interstitial retinitis is very frequently observed in phthisical eye-balls. It is, moreover, caused by compound injuries to the eye, which do not lead to phthisis, and by such injuries as are inflicted directly upon the retina itself. Detached retinæ also usually show the symptoms of this variety of retinitis, especially when the folds of the detached retina are glued together into one cord. In the so-called pigmentary retinitis, diffuse interstitial retinitis is only a secondary symptom.

The cases which so far have been submitted to anatomical examination, it seems all showed the disease in a too far advanced stage, to allow of determining the original seat of this affection. Diffuse interstitial retinitis, unlike albuminuric retinitis, is not confined to certain regions of the retina, except in staphylomatous and glaucomatous eyes. In the former the process is confined to the staphylomatous portions, in the latter (at least at the beginning of the disease) to the neighborhood of the optic papilla.

In whatever region of the retina the affection begins, it always attacks at first the inner layers of this membrane and, even where the disease is far advanced, the outer layers may yet be found in a comparatively normal condition. The rods and cones make an exception to this rule, especially in cases of detachment of the retina.

According to *Leber*, we find in the first stage of the affection under consideration, the nerve fibre layer thickened in consequence of a round-cell infiltration which is most pronounced along the blood-vessels. This cell-infiltration leads to the new-formation of connective-tissue in the nerve fibre layer and the ganglionic cell layer. We find accordingly at this period in transverse sections, connective-tissue hypertrophy, some of the nerve fibres and ganglionic cells undergoing a regressive metamorphosis, and the remainder of them crowded aside by the connective-tissue. Soon also the supporting (radiating) fibres become thicker, and they frequently assume the sclerosed appearance above referred to. The adventitia of the blood-vessels, which in the beginning appears infiltrated with round-cells, is also thickened by the transformation of these cells into connective-tissue and the lumen of the blood-vessels is accordingly narrow.

When the new-formed connective-tissue begins to shrink, the nerve fibres and ganglionic cells gradually disappear through fatty degeneration. Sometimes we also find ganglionic cells undergoing a colloid metamorphosis. In consequence of these changes, the nerve fibre layer (and by this means the whole of the retina) becomes very much thinner.

The hypertrophy of the radiating fibres is sometimes so considerable, that they perforate the internal limiting membrane, and form little connective-tissue tumors on its inner surface, which may either be flat and have a broad basis, or have a thin pedicle. Moreover, this form of retinitis is very frequently combined with the new-formation of connective-tissue in the peripheral layers of the vitreous body (those touching the inner surface of. the retina). This new-formed connective-tissue, which always firmly adheres to the retina, has generally a lamellar structure, and is often thicker than the retina itself. In other cases we find the connective-tissue of the nerve fibre layer arranged in an arcade-like manner, enclosing smaller and larger spaces and canals, which are usually empty or sometimes contain a few remains of the nerve fibres. These spaces during life are probably filled with serum. The arcade-like arrangement of the connective-tissue seems to be most frequent in the neighborhood of the optic papilla.

While the nerve fibre layer undergoes the changes above detailed, usually the outer layers too, begin to suffer, although in rare cases, as stated, they may remain intact for a much longer period. The inner and outer molecular layers disappear at first, and the two granular layers are thus united into one. Later on also, the cells of these two layers can no longer resist the pressure exerted upon them by the retraction of the new-formed connective-tissue. They become granular and undergo fatty degeneration, and soon the retina consists of almost nothing but connective-tissue and bloodvessels, the walls of which are often enormously thickened. The arrangement of the connective-tissue may, however, for a long time still imitate the normal structure of the retina, and only in the very last stage of this affection, we find the retina replaced by a thin layer of tough connective-tissue containing some blood-pigment, and in no way resembling this membrane. This I saw in a case of traumatic retinitis twelve years after the beginning of the disease.

The rods and cones, as already stated, are usually altered at an early period. They mostly appear as club-shaped structures, as we found them in cases of albuminuric retinitis. According to several authors, hypertrophy of the rods and cones as described above, is also found in diffuse interstitial retinitis (*Leber*).

The blood-vessels of the retina gradually become quite obliterated and transformed into bands of connective-tissue, which at first are easily distinguishable from the surrounding tissue. Later on this distinction becomes impossible, unless their former site can be recognized by some blood pigment embedded in the tissue.

Sometimes also, in this form of retinitis, the pigmented epithelial cells proliferate into the retina. Diffuse retinitis which
is, however, consequent upon the immigration of pigmented
epithelial cells into the retina, and above referred to as pigmentary retinitis, is totally different because a secondary
affection, although histologically the same, changes are observed as in the disease now under consideration.

c. Retinitis Purulenta.

Purulent retinitis is in most cases a part of purulent
panophthalmitis. We furthermore observe it after injuries
which involve the retina directly or in cases of metastatic
choroiditis, which latter disease usually leads to purulent
panophthalmitis.

The first symptom characteristic of this affection, is a very
considerable infiltration of round-cells into the nerve fibre
layer consequent upon hyperæmia of the blood-vessels. On
account of the infiltration, this layer appears much swollen.
Its normal elements are gradually destroyed, and at a later
period it seems to consist solely of round-cells, separated from
the vitreous body, by the internal limiting membrane, which
generally appears wrinkled. Gradually this membrane, too,
is destroyed and the neighboring parts of the vitreous body
which have for some time also been filled with round-cells,
come into direct contact with the altered nerve fibre layer
of the retina. During this process, very numerous hæmorrhages of varying size are observed in the retina. According
to *Leber* and others, these are caused by capillary embolism,
which opinion is as yet not to be considered proven. It is
certain, however, that the walls of the blood-vessels take an
active part in the formation of round-cells, and it appears to
me, that the changes in the structure of the blood-vessels
necessarily caused by this process, very easily explain the
occurrence of the hæmorrhages.

The remainder of the retina is generally invaded by the
disease at a much later period than the nerve fibre layer, and
it is very difficult to distinguish, when the formation of
round-cells in the granular layer really begins, on account of
the similarity of their cellular elements to the round-cells.

It seems, however, that the radiating fibres are the first to suffer, and that the process only later on spreads upon the cellular elements.

In advanced cases, the whole of the retina is replaced by a mass of round-cells leaving no trace whatever of its original structure. Purulent retinitis is generally combined with purulent hyalitis, and it is then impossible to discern which part of the round-cells has taken the place of the retina. The rods and cones are usually changed at an early period. They at first take the club-shaped form above mentioned, and later on are totally destroyed. Frequently we find in their stead a layer of round-cells, (which probably come from the choroid) even before the outer layers of the retina are materially altered.

Circumscribed accumulations of round-cells in the retina have recently been described as tubercles by *Weiss.*

C. *Changes in the Structure of the Retinal Blood-vessels, Hæmorrhages and Detachment of the Retina.*

Besides the alterations which the retinal blood-vessels undergo when this membrane is inflamed, and which have been described above as general ecstasia, fatty degeneration, narrowing of the lumen consequent upon swelling and hyaline degeneration of the walls, thrombosis and perivasculitis, there are a few such alterations which, as it seems, are not necessarily combined with an inflammatory process in the retinal tissue.

Small aneurysms of the retinal arteries are but rarely observed. They appear either as spindle-shaped or diverticlum-like enlargements of the blood-vessels.

In one single case I found an amyloid degeneration of the walls of the retinal blood-vessels in a case of detachment of the retina, caused by a choroidal sarcoma. The walls of some of the blood-vessels appeared perfectly hyaline, the walls of others contained only a number of aggregations of a hyaline substance. The chemical reaction, produced by iodine, was that characteristic of amyloid degeneration.

Hæmorrhages in the tissue of the retina are of very frequent occurrence. We had already several times occasion to mention them. They are found without any inflammatory process in the retinal tissue in the cases which have clinically very inappropriately been called retinitis apoplectica and hæmorrhagica. They result from disease of the heart, thrombosis of the arteria or vena centralis retinæ, from injuries to the eye-ball, hæmorrhagic glaucoma and several constitutional diseases. They are, of course, in no way different'from those caused by the different varieties of retinitis above detailed, and we may frequently find the rupture in the blood-vessel which has caused them. They disappear after having undergone a fatty degeneration by being absorbed.

Sometimes the hæmorrhage destroys the elements of the part of the retina in which it occurs. In these cases, usually a circumscribed retinitis is found to follow, which leads to the formation of a scar, sometimes containing crystals of blood-pigment.

Deposits of lime are but very rarely found in the walls of retinal blood-vessels and chiefly in phthisical eye-balls and detached retinæ. In the earliest period of this pathological process, the walls of the blood-vessels appear infiltrated with minute granules. Later on, larger bodies of amorphous lime are found, and finally entire blood-vessels may be seen changed into cylinders of lime. (See Fig. 92).

The various methods by which the retina may become detached, are not yet definitely ascertained, and it is not the place here to speak more extensively about this subject than has already been done in the foregoing chapters, as we are here only interested in the pathological changes found in the tissue of the detached retina.

As we stated above, the retina can only become detached when the structure of the vitreous body has been materially altered. When detachment has taken place, the blood-vessels of the retina are twisted and bent in many ways so that we may *a priori* assume that the nutrition of the detached membrane must be considerably impaired, even if there are no pathological changes present in the uveal tract. The latter is, however, usually the case.

The result of this impairment of nutrition also undoubtedly of the loss of function, is a regressive metamorphosis of the nervous elements of the retina.   The elements undergo a fatty degeneration, sometimes also a colloid metamorphosis, which may give rise to the formation of larger cystoid structures.   Meanwhile the connective-tissue has become

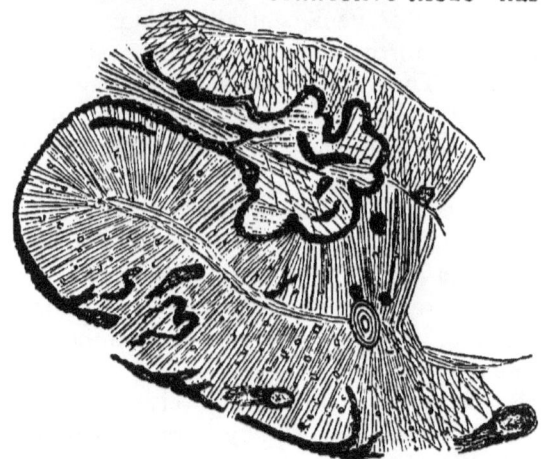

Fɪɢ. 92. -Detached and perfectly atrophied retina. Capillaries changed into cylinders of amorphous lime.

hyperplastic, and later on we find all the symptoms of diffuse interstitial (atrophic) retinitis.   The blood-vessels are transformed into bands of connective-tissue, or sometimes, as stated above, into cylinders of amorphous lime, and often we can recognize their former site, only by the remains of the blood pigment.

While the whole of the structure of the retina is thus perfectly destroyed and replaced by connective-tissue, the limitans interna is always found intact between the folds of this new tissue.   This fact, combined with all the reasons already mentioned, proves the limitans interna to be undoubtedly a separate and independent membrane.

Sometimes we find detached with the retina and lying within this membrane, vitreous bodies from the lamina vitrea of the choroid.   They may contain lime, and lead to ossification in the atrophic retina.

The Results of Retinitis.

In rare cases we may clinically observe that all the symp-

toms of albuminuric retinitis disappear.   It appears doubtful
also whether histologically, a perfect *restitutio ad integrum*,
especially when the disease has reached an advanced state, is
possible.   The final changes caused by albuminuric retinitis
are, it seems not known.   This is easily explained by the
fact that death nearly always results from the primary disease,
while the retinitis is as yet progressing.   If we find in a retina
sclerotic hypertrophy of the nerve fibres, fatty degeneration,
oval cavities filled with fibrine, or the cells containing fat-
granules and above described, sclerosis of the walls of the
blood-vessels and numerous hæmorrhages, we are justified in
making the diagnosis of albuminuric retinitis.   We shall, however, always find that the inflammatory process is not yet at
an end.

The changes which occur after diffuse interstitial retinitis,
are different.   The chief symptom of this disease is the
transformation of the retina into connective-tissue, and partial or total destruction of the nervous elements.

If the process had come to an end during life, we find the
retina replaced by a very thin membrane, consisting of tough
connective-tissue which usually contains some hæmatoidine
crystals and uveal pigment.   This membrane can only be
recognized as the former retina by its position in the eye-
ball.

I frequently found in phthisical eye-balls or eyes which
had been blind for a long period before death occurred, the
nerve fibre layer of the retina abnormally thin, and some
new-formation of connective-tissue going on within it ;
furthermore, some ganglionic cells undergoing fatty or colloid
metamorphosis, and the cells of the granular layers in a state
of molecular infiltration.   I think these alterations are due
to the loss of function, and cannot be considered as the symptoms of a diffuse interstitial retinitis.

In consequence of purulent retinitis, the retina is also
usually entirely destroyed, and we are often unable to find a
trace of it in eyes which have been lost from purulent panophthalmitis.   This is more particularly the case, if the
vitreous body too has been altered into a mass of round-
cells.

D. Injuries to the Retina and their Results.

The position of the retina inside the eye-ball, of course, does not allow of any direct injuries being inflicted upon it, unless other parts have first been perforated. The most frequent and most important combination, is simultaneous injury of retina, choroid and vitreous body. We had already occasion to speak of these injuries when treating upon the conditions found after injuries to the choroid.

Injuries to the retina mostly produce a circumscribed interstitial retinitis. The tissue of the lips of the wound is at first found to be infiltrated with red and white blood-corpuscles, and the wound-canal is filled with a fibrinous coagulum, especially, if the choroid, too, has been wounded. The white blood-corpuscles then increase in number, invade the fibrinous coagulum and gradually lead to the formation of connective-tissue. Such scars seems afterwards always to contain some blood pigment. Sometimes we also find that the pigmented epithelial cells have proliferated into the scar. This is especially the case, when the choroid is injured also. In the neighborhood of the scar the rods and cones are destroyed, and retina and choroid are as a rule firmly adherent to each other. *Berlin* also found sclerosed hypertrophic nerve fibres, like those described above, near such retinal wounds.

We stated already, that granulation tissue may start from the wounded choroid, and grow through the wound canal of the retina into the vitreous body. If the vitreous body has been injured, connective-tissue is formed in it, also near the retinal wound, and thus we find retina and vitreous body firmly united at the site of the wound at a later period.

In rare cases, injuries inflicted upon the retina will cause purulent retinitis, which, as we have stated, may lead to the perfect destruction of this membrane. It is usually accompanied by purulent choroiditis, which finally leads to pan-ophthalmitis.

Although foreign bodies may be retained in the retina, they are but seldom seen to become encapsuled in this membrane, as they mostly cause a purulent retinitis. If, however, they become encapsulated, they are surrounded by a dense connective-tissue, in the formation of which the choroid and vitreous body usually take an active part.

E. TUMORS OF THE RETINA.

a. FIBROMA.

Some authors described small new-formations upon the inner surface of this membrane as fibromatous tumors. These are, however, probably not what we would call a real tumor of the retina, but new-formations of connective-tissue in the outer layers of the vitreous body or hypertrophic radiary fibres which have perforated the inner limiting membrane in the way above referred to and observed in cases of diffuse interstitial retinitis.

The conditions seem to be different, however, in the cases of teleangiectatic fibromatous tumors, which we find drawn in *Pagenstecher's* and *Genth's* atlas. They are small tumors with a broad base or a thin pedicle, and are very vascular.

b. Small-celled Medullary Sarcoma (Glioma).

During the infantile age, the retina is often the seat of a new-formation, which was formerly described as fungus hæmatodes, by *Virchow* and his followers, as glioma. *Virchow* called this new-formation glioma, because it originates in the soft connective-tissue of the retina, which is analogous to the neuroglia of the brain, and because it appears to be identical with the brain tumors described as gliomata. *Virchow* himself stated that it is very difficult to distinguish between glioma and sarcoma, and overcame the difficulty by calling some of these tumors glio-sarcomata. Most of the recent authors have adopted this name for the tumors under consideration. *Delafield* has recently called them sarcomata of the retina, being forced to do so by the result of a number of examinations of such retinal tumors both in a fresh condition, and after being hardened. I too, am convinced that, if we want to call them gliomata still, we cannot consider them as anything else than sarcomata. *Leber*, too, seems to be of this opinion.

All the different authors (*Virchow, Schweigger, Knapp, Hirschberg, Delafield, Leber,* etc.) agree in the description of the structure and elements of these new-formations, and I can add nothing new to their observations. They consist of round-cells, which are sometimes smaller, sometimes larger than white blood-corpuscles, or in other cases are perfectly identical with them. When hardened, they have a large round nucleus. Sometimes these cells have one or more off-sets. It has been stated by some authors, that they are identical with, and derived from the nuclei of the granular layers, which however, is not the case. Between these round-cells we find free nuclei and sometimes very much larger round and even spindle-cells. The tumors in which these spindle-cells have been found, have more especially been called glio-sarcomata.

The cells of the tumor are embedded in a very small quantity of intercellular substance, which when fresh is gran-ular. *Knapp* states that this granular appearance is caused by the hardening fluid.

The tumors under consideration are sometimes very vas-cular. The blood-vessels (mostly of a capillary character), are unusually wide. They take their origin from the retinal blood-vessels.

Sarcomata of the retina are said to originate sometimes from the inner, sometimes from the outer granular layer, in a few cases, also from the nerve fibre layer. *Leber* found primary tumors at the same time in different layers, and *Iwanoff* is of the opinion, in which I concur, that the tumor, being a connective-tissue growth, may spring from the con-nective-tissue elements of all the layers of the retina. It seems, however, that it most frequently starts from the outer layers, and we may sometimes find the inner layer as yet perfectly intact, when the outer ones have already been per-fectly destroyed by the new-formation. In these cases, the retina seems to be always detached, and lying nearer the axis of the eye-ball. There are however, cases in which the retina may remain in contact with the choroid, and the tumor spread inwardly. *Delafield* has, moreover, described a case, in which the tumor originated from the inner granular layer, and had protruded into the vitreous chamber, while the rods and cones were as yet found to be perfectly intact.

During the growth of the tumor, hæmorrhages frequently take place, and as their results, we find smaller and larger patches of blood-pigment. This pigment is either enclosed in cells, or lies between them in the shape of crystals or as an amorphous substance. Fatty infiltration, a complete fatty softening, and the formation of cheesy matter, is not infrequently found in some parts of these tumors, and generally is accompanied by the formation of deposits of lime. We find either minute granules of lime enclosed in the cells, or free larger roundish bodies which may coalesce, and so grow to a considerable size.

The tumor, like all sarcomata, may spread continuously, or produce secondary nodules by infection at some distance from the primary ones. The former seems to be the prevalent manner of their growth in the retina, and the tumor may thus grow all over the retina, spread to the optic nerve and even to the choroid, after an adhesion between retina and choroid has taken place (*Knapp*). The second mode of growth is generally the origin of isolated secondary tumors found in the choroid, the sclerotic and the episcleral tissue. Furthermore, metastatic tumors have been observed in the bones, the lymphatic glands, the liver and other organs.

While the eye-ball is gradually being filled by the new-formation, the intra-ocular pressure becomes increased. This together with the impairment in nutrition of the anterior portions of the eye-ball, causes the formation of abscesses in the cornea, and leads to the total destruction of this membrane, thus opening a channel by which the tumor can spread upon the outer surface of the eye. The tumor but seldom perforates the sclerotic.

When the eye-ball is perfectly filled by the new-formation, the whole of the uveal tract may be destroyed and entirely disappear, leaving only small quantities of pigment behind.

From this description it seems evident, that the so-called glioma of the retina in no way differs histologically from the medullary small-cell sarcomata. I therefore see no reason why we should not call these new-formations by that name.

Some few cases have been described, in which glioma is said to have disappeared by a general shrinking of the eye-ball. From these observations, the new-formation has been thought to be of a fibromatous character. The observations are, however doubtful on the one hand, and on the other a very considerable number of so-called glioma of the retina have up to this date been examined without proving this opinion to be the correct one.

IX.

LENS CRYSTALLINEA.

1. *Normal Conditions.*

THE crystalline lens is fastened to the ciliary body by means of the zonula of *Zinn*, which encloses the *canalis Petitii*, consists of the lens-capsule, the capsular epithelium and the lens-fibres.

The lens-capsule forms a sac in which the remainder of the elements constituting the crystalline lens are enclosed. The clinical distinction between an anterior and a posterior lens-capsule is not histologically justifiable.

The lens-capsule is a perfectly transparent membrane, which is not equal in thickness in all its parts. It is thickest at and around the anterior pole of the crystalline lens, and thinnest upon its posterior surface, especially at the posterior pole. The lens-capsule is generally thicker in advanced age than in youth.

In plain views it appears perfectly homogeneous. A number of authors have seen a fine striation upon its transverse section, which I have never been able to recognize. Such a lamellar structure would, however, be sure proof of the connective-tissue character of the lens-capsule, of which I have no doubt, as it is analogous in every way to *Descemet's* membrane and the lamina vitrea choroideæ.

As has been stated by a great many authors, the lens-capsule is an elastic membrane. If ruptured or partially detached from the lens substance, it will roll itself up. From experiments on the eyes of animals, I had formed the opinion that the lens-capsule would always roll itself up in a centrifugal direction, I have, however, since then seen the human lens-capsule to be rolled up in a centrifugal as well as a centripetal manner. The lens-capsule may furthermore simply retract and thus become wrinkled.

The capsular epithelium is a single layer of epithelial

cells, lying on the inner surface of the anterior lens-capsule, which appear hexagonal in a plain view, similar to the endothelium of *Descemet's* membrane. Each cell has a large round or oval nucleus. *Wedl* and *Hosch* have also described cells with hyaline offsets. These cells are united by a small quantity of cementing substance, which is easily seen when stained with nitrate of silver. At the equator of the lens these epithelial cells grow longer and appear like cylinder cells, and gradually form the so-called lens fibres. The posterior lens-capsule, that is, the portion of the lens-capsule which, beginning at the equator, covers the posterior surface of the lens substance, has no epithelium. Some authors have been misled into the description of such an epithelium by hardened cementing substance, or by the ends of lens fibres attached to it.

The cells of the capsular epithelium are all somewhat granular. According to *J. Arnold*, this granular appearance is more pronounced near the equator, while the outlines of the cells there grow less distinct.

I have never seen any new-formation of cells in the normal capsular epithelium.

The bulk of the crystalline lens is formed of the lens-fibres or lens-bands (*J. Arnold*). Isolated lens-fibres when lying flat, appear as broad bands, and are striated in a longitudinal direction. The transverse striation which has been described by a number of authors, I never found in normal, but sometimes in pathological lenses. When the lens-fibres lie on their edge, they appear much narrower. Their real shape is best seen in transverse sections, and we then find them to be hexagonal prisms. They vary in size, and those taken from the centre of the crystalline lens are usually smaller than those taken from its periphery. The lens-fibres taken from the centre have, moreover, especially at an advanced age, no nucleus, while those from the periphery always have an oval nucleus lying with its long axis in the direction of the lens-fibre. Every such lens-fibre contains only one nucleus, and the statements with regard to fibres with two and more nuclei, do not seem to be correct.

The body of the peripheral lens-fibres seems to consist

of two parts ; a tough peripheral and a softer central part. The latter is formed of myeline, and called liquor *Morgagni* The nearer the centre of the lens-fibres, the more of the harder, tougher substance, and the less liquor *Morgagni* is found. On their narrow sides, the margins of the lens-fibres are indented. This indentation is according to *J. Arnold's* statement, more pronounced in the central fibres, and gradually disappears towards the periphery. The little offsets of the neighboring lens-fibres interlace like those of the bones of the skull. All the fibres are united with each other by a cementing substance, which when fresh is homogeneous or slightly granular, and can be well recognized when stained with nitrate of silver. I never saw as beautiful regular hexagonal figures in a transverse section of the lens-fibres as *J. Arnold* has drawn. The lines produced by the stained cementing substance have always appeared wavy in my specimens. Where the ends of the lens-fibres touch each other upon the anterior and posterior surface of the crystalline lens, they form the so-called lens-stars. In the newly-born, these stars each consist of three lines which lie at angles of about one hundred and twenty degrees to each other, and are united in the anterior and posterior pole. While two of these lines on the anterior surface run upwards and one downwards, the condition is the reverse one upon the posterior surface. These lines never reach the equator, and end in what has been called the " fibre-vortex." In the adult, they branch off into secondary ones. In very old lenses we find these lines changed into fissures filled with liquor *Morgagni.* The lens fibres as they approach these lines, are a little broader and bent.

According to *J. Arnold*, the lens-fibres in a meridional direction, have the shape of a Roman S, from the back towards the front, but they never entirely reach from one pole to the other.

If we divide the lens by cutting through both its poles, and vertically upon the equator, we see that the most peripheral lens-fibres are convex towards the centre ; this convexity is gradually changed into the opposite direction, as the fibres come nearer the centre. The nuclei of the lens-fibres appear in such a section arranged in such a way, as to form a line which is convex towards the anterior surface of the crystalline lens and lies near it.

2. *Pathological Conditions.*

The tissue of the crystalline lens does not become inflamed like other tissues. Although *Iwanoff* and *Becker* have described a hyperplastic process in the capsular epithelium as taking place within the perfectly intact lens-capsule, and called it phakitis, I have never been able to see it. According to *Iwanoff*, the " new-formed cells are much larger and the nucleus easily divides itself into two and more." Furthermore, these cells are said " to be very prone to undergo a colloid or mucoid metamorphosis, and then to form large vesicles, filled with colloid substance, which crowd the nucleus to one side." These vesicles, which *Becker* calls giant-cells, seem to me to be identical with the myeline globules of which we shall speak farther on, and which never contain a nucleus. The pathological changes of the crystalline lens when the capsule is intact, and which are called cataract, are simply regressive metamorphoses of the elements constituting the crystalline lens. We find frequently the anterior capsule of such pathological crystalline lenses very much thickened. Transverse sections of such thickened capsules, show it to be either perfectly homogeneous, or to possess a longitudinal striation (*Babuchin, Becker*).

Atrophy of the lens-capsule, which *H. Mueller* and *Becker* have described, has never come under my own observation, and the thickness of the lens-capsule varies so much in different individuals, that such an atrophy must be very difficult to diagnose.

The deposits upon the outer surface of the anterior and posterior lens-capsule, caused by iritis and cyclitis, do not belong among the pathological changes of the crystalline lens.

A. *Cataract formed within an Intact Lens-capsule.*

It is possible to distinguish both clinically and anatomically between a large number of cataracts, since the dimness

caused by regressive metamorphosis of the lens fibres, may
have a varying shape, and lie in very different regions. The
histological conditions are the same in nearly all of these cases
and we can only distinguish between cataract caused by
physiological progressive sclerosis of the lens fibres, and
that caused by a pathological regressive metamorphosis of
these elements.

As above stated, the central lens fibres when in a normal
condition are harder than the peripheral ones, and have no
nucleus. This central sclerosis, like the formation of horny
scales on the surface of the epithelium of the skin, is progressive, and gradually spreads towards the periphery in such
a way, that more and more lens fibres become sclerosed, until
finally all, or nearly all of them are thus altered. At the
same time, small quantities of liquor *Morgagni* are found to
lie outside the lens fibres. They form round and oval drops
of a varying size, and lie chiefly between the ends of the
lens fibres. The latter elements appear very brittle, no longer
have any nucleus, and in transverse sections we see, that they
have lost their comparatively regular hexagonal shape, are
sometimes perfectly cylindrical, and no longer indented at
their margins. When all the fibres have been thus altered,
we call the condition clinically a mature senile cataract
(cataracta nigra). Frequently, however, we find in these
cataracts a larger quantity of free myeline globules (liquor
Morgagni) and a part of the lens is accordingly more fluid
(especially the peripheral layers).

This hard cataract caused by the physiological progressive
sclerosis is seldom, if ever stationary, and the fibres usually
undergo a further regressive metamorphosis, that is, the cataract becomes what we clinically call hypermature. These
regressive metamorphoses are, however, also found without
preceding sclerosis, and are the histological factors causing
all other kinds of cataract, especially those found congenitally
or in young people.

In such cataracts we find beside the globules of liquor
Morgagni, that the lens fibres are at first granular, which is
the beginning stage of fatty degeneration. Later on, the
molecular granules are changed into larger drops which coa-

lesce. In this way the whole of the lens substance may become fluid, and then consists of liquor *Morgagni* and fat-globules. The existence of the latter is especially proven by the formation of cholestearine crystals, which may be found in such cataracts. Sometimes we also see myeline drops filled with crystals of margaric acid. In other cases, a number of lens fibres which are not yet perfectly broken up, are found to have spindle-shaped enlargements which phenomenon is probably caused by imbibition.

In rare cases (according to *Iwanoff* always) lens fibres, before being broken up, may be found to have a transverse striation. This striation resembles that of the muscular fibres, from which it is, however, distinct, since the striæ do not lie at regular intervals, and do not cross the longitudinal direction of the fibres at right angles.

In most of the cases of soft cataract, we find lens fibres in all stages of destruction. Even where the clinical appearance would seem to justify the idea that all of the lens fibres must be destroyed, we may yet find normal ones and others which, although they are granular, have not yet lost their normal shape.

During the destruction of the lens fibres, lime may be deposited in the lens. *Becker's* statement, however, that lime is only deposited in a place where the lens fibres have been altogether destroyed, is not correct. I have in my possession some specimens of a lens which show only the symptoms of senile sclerosis with a quantity of deposits of lime.

The lime is found in small granules which coalesce and thus form larger bodies. These may also again coalesce, but even very large accumulations of lime retain the granular structure.

During all these changes, the capsular epithelium may either remain unaltered, or it is gradually destroyed by fatty degeneration.

As mentioned above, *Iwanoff, H. Mueller* and *Becker* described a new-formation of cells in the capsular epithelium. *Becker* says that this new-formation may appear later on as a tissue consisting of spindle-shaped cells, and more than ten times as thick as the normal capsular epithelium. I have never seen this tissue or any new-formation of the cells of the capsular epithelium where the lens-capsule was perfectly intact : I shall however, later on have to describe a perfectly similar cell new-formation found when the lens-capsule has been ruptured. Perhaps, this was also the case with the lenses in which *Becker* saw these changes.

Furthermore, he mentions the formation of "giant-cells," and states expressly that they could not possibly be myeline globules, since they have a nucleus. He found them, especially in cases of cortical cataract, in dislocated lenses, in traumatic and secondary cataracts. I must state that I have never seen these cell formations. I have, however, very frequently thought I saw a nucleus in such large myeline-globules and convinced myself only by further examination, that I was deceived by another smaller globule lying above or under- neath the larger one. Sometimes the myeline-globules have also a double contour, and it may thus appear as if we had to do with a cell membrane.

The formation of pus-cells in the lens substance, while the capsule was unruptured, has only once been seen by *Knapp*. *Becker* has never seen it, and I have looked for it in vain, even, in cases of purulent panophthalmitis, and when the lens- capsule was ruptured.

Two varieties of cataract formed inside of a perfectly intact capsule are yet to be mentioned, as showing some peculiar histological conditions ; I mean, cataracta polaris anterior (pyramidalis) and cataracta hæmorrhagica.

Cataracta polaris anterior (pyramidalis) is formed by a cone which lies upon the normal lens substance in the region of the anterior pole. This cone is always covered with lens-capsule, and the latter accordingly has a diverticalum in which the cone lies. The normal capsular epithelium reaches up to the base of this cone. According to *Becker*, the apex of the cone is filled with coagulated fluid, while nearer the base he found a tissue consisting of spindle-shaped cells, very simi- lar to the tissue of the cornea. *H. Mueller* and *Schweigger* found the cone to consist of a fatty cretaceous substance, in which *H. Mueller* could not find any cellular elements. *Hulke* also states that cells are found in this substance. I had occasion to examine one such cataract. The cone was also in this case enclosed in the wrinkled lens-capsule, and two-thirds of it consisted of a lamellar substance without any cellular elements. Its basis was formed by fat-drops and lime granules, and reached below the level of the surrounding normal capsular epithelium. (See Fig. 93).

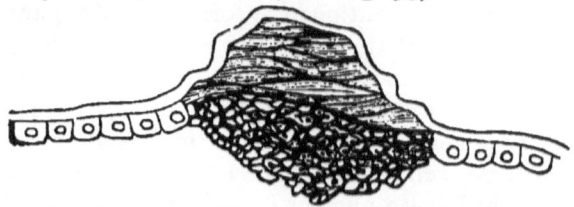

F1G. 93.—Anterior polar cataract. The apex of the cone is formed by a lamellar, dim tissue, without any cellular elements. The basis consists of lime and fat.

Hæmorrhagic cataract has been once examined and de-scribed by *von Græfe*. He found the lens fibres brown, which color was caused by granular and crystallized blood-pigment within them, while their shape was unaltered. The capsular epithelial cells too, were filled with the pigment. It could not be ascertained in this case whether the lens-capsule was intact or ruptured.

Wagner and *Lohmayer* have described the formation of osseous tissue within the lens-capsule. Whether the capsule was ruptured or not, is not stated. More recently *Voorhies* again described such an ossification of the lens substance, but omitted to state anything regarding the state of the lens-cap-sule. *Becker* draws attention to the fact, that ossification in a cyclitic membrane might easily lead to deception, and be taken for ossification of the crystalline lens. I shall later on also have to refer to the formation of osseous tissue within the lens-capsule, which I found, however, always to be ruptured. A direct change of epithelial tissue, like the lens fibres, into osseous tissue has not yet been definitely observed.

B. *Injuries to the Lens-capsule and the Lens-substance and their Results.*

Single small wounds of the lens-capsule can, as it appears from *Ritter's* experimental observations, heal by simple repo-sition of the lips of the wound. *Becker* states, that by seeing specimens of *Leber's*, he came to the conclusion that such small wounds of the capsule may heal with the new-formation of a small amount of vitreous substance, analogous to the capsular substance, and that the capsular epithelial cells do *not* take part in the production of this new-formation. This is a remarkable observation, as we know that similar wounds of *Descemet's* membrane never heal. I am however, not in the position to criticise *Becker's* statement, as I do not possess any similar specimens.

(At the last meeting of oculists at Heidelberg, 1878, *Leber* showed such specimens from the crystalline lens of rabbits. He came to the conclusion, however, that the capsular epithelial cells produced the newly formed glass substance. He stated that these cells proliferate into the wound-canal. Gradually, at first thinner, later thicker layers of an inter-cellular homogeneous substance are formed, and the surrounding lens-capsule grows thicker by the new-formation of vitreous substance on its inner surface).

Larger wounds of the lens-capsule remain permanently open, and this is due to the folds in the capsule which according to *Becker* are observed, or to the rolling up of the lens-capsule, as *Raab* and myself have described. This rolling up, as stated above, takes place mostly in a centrifugal, sometimes in a centripetal direction.

In consequence of these larger wounds of the lens-capsule the lens substance becomes exposed to the influence of the aqueous humor or vitreous body, and the result of this exposure is the formation of a traumatic cataract. In the simplest form of these cataracts, we find the lens fibres near the capsular wound swollen (by imbibition) and granular. Gradually these lens fibres are broken up, and the myeline becomes free and can be absorbed. The capsular epithelial cells may by imbibition swell too, and appear as large vesicle-like cells. *Becker* speaks also in these cases of an inflammatory new formation of cells and "giant-cells." My own examinations have not enabled me to agree with this statement.

In this way the whole of the lens substance may be broken up and absorbed, and the anterior and posterior halves of the inner surfaces of the lens-capsule may become adherent to each other.

Ruptures of the posterior lens capsule cause the same conditions, although the progress seems to be a slower one, and we frequently then find particles of the broken lens fibres suspended in the vitreous body.

If, in consequence of the injury, the iris and ciliary body, or the whole of the uveal tract become inflamed, the conditions inside the ruptured lens-capsule may appear very different. The fibrino-plastic exudation, caused by these inflammations, can enter the wound in the lens-capsule, and here also be transformed into connective-tissue, which gradually leads to destruction of the lens fibres. The new formed tissue consisting of round-cells and spindle-cells lies close to the lens-capsule, and fills all its folds and wrinkles. Frequently it is seen to contain new formed blood-vessels which are some-

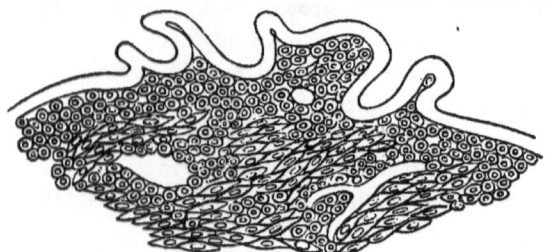

FIG. 94.—Connective-tissue within the ruptured lens-capsule.

times of comparatively large calibre. (See Fig. 94). This tissue is exactly the same which *Becker* has described as formed within the intact lens-capsule. How far the capsular epithelial cells help to form this tissue, I have not been able to ascertain, as they were always wanting in my specimens.

I once found the same tissue inside the ruptured capsule of a crystalline lens, which had been dislocated under the conjunctiva.

The remainder of the lens fibres in these cases were always granular or broken up.

This new-formed tissue sometimes glues the crystalline-lens to the cornea, and probably always to the iris, except where it is found in dislocated lenses, and the conditions are changed accordingly. Synechiæ between the usually cataractous crystalline lens and the cornea may, as we have seen, also happen when the capsule is perfectly intact.

The osseous tissue sometimes found within the lens-capsule probably always takes its origin from such new-formed connective-tissue. Possibly the deposits of lime, usually found in such lenses, have a direct influence upon the formation of osseous tissue. I am in the possession of an eye with general ossification of the choroid, in which the folded lens-capsule, which lies embedded in a cyclitic membrane, is perfectly filled with osseous tissue. The origin of the affection was an injury. (See Fig. 95.) I have, however, not yet

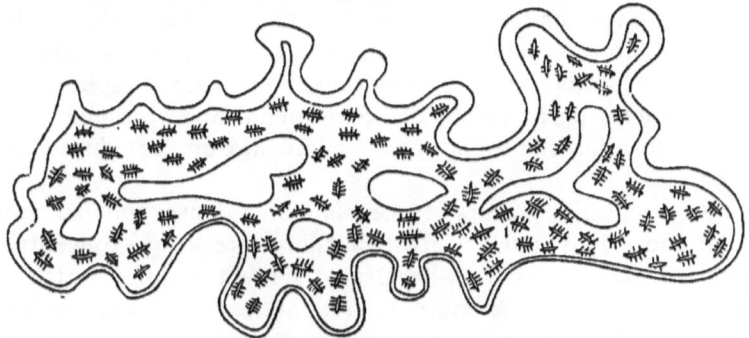

FIG. 95.—Osseous-tissue formed within the ruptured lens-capsule.

seen a specimen, where the whole of the lens substance was changed into the spindle cell tissue, above described.

Foreign bodies are sometimes retained in the lens substance. *Iwanoff* states that they are then found to be surrounded with pus cells, and *Becker* adds that these pus cells come from tissues outside the lens-capsule.

X.

VITREOUS BODY AND ZONULA ZINNII.

1. *Normal Conditions of the Vitreous Body.*

THE vitreous humour consists of a jelly-like substance, in which cells are suspended.

A number of authors are of the opinion that the vitreous body is inclosed in a membrane, the so-called membrana hyaloidea, and *Schwalbe* has recently joined in this view. I cannot, however, agree with this opinion. According to my examinations, no such limiting membrane belongs to the vitreous body, and it is separated from the retina only by the limitans interna of that membrane. The jelly-like substance of the vitreous body is, however, somewhat tougher and denser in its periphery. The endothelial and epithelial cells described upon the membrana hyaloidea, I am convinced, do not exist.

The jelly-like substance consists of a denser mucoid and a thinner fluid part. Most authors speak of concentric layers in the denser peripheral part, while the inner part, the nucleus, is said to be more homogeneous. *Schwalbe*, moreover, found septa in the vitreous body running in a radiary direction, and one septum running concentrically with the surface of the vitreous body. After having hardened the vitreous body in a dilute solution of chromic acid, I have seen similar conditions, and it seems therefore that we have concentric layers in the periphery, and radius-like septa between which the thin fluid part of the vitreous body is lying.

A canal is found beginning at the optic papilla and running through the vitreous body to the fossa patellaris (into which latter the crystalline lens fits), which is filled with fluid, the so-called canalis hyaloideus. During fœtal life this canal encloses the arteria hyaloidea. By injecting a stained fluid into the intervaginal space of the optic nerve, this canal may be filled, and we must therefore consider it to be a lymphatic channel, in direct communication with those of the optic nerve and retina. According to *Schwalbe*, this canal is surrounded by a vitreous membrane to which some cells are often attached. They form, however, no endothelial coating of this canal, but are the cells of the vitreous body, to be spoken of directly.

A number of authors have found fibrillæ in the vitreous body. I have never been able to find them in the normal condition.

The vitreous body always, however, contains cellular elements. They appear to be more numerous in its outer than its central parts, and *Schwalbe* calls some of them directly subhyaloid cells. The same cells are, however, found in other parts of the vitreous body, and this name appears therefore inappropriate.

Iwanoff makes a distinction between three separate kinds of cells in the vitreous body. Although they may be here referred to as different types, I must state that these cells are very variable in shape, and the different kinds are seen to merge into each other. We find round-cells with one or more nuclei, some of which are seen to contain smaller and larger vacuolæ, by which the nucleus is crowded to one side, and which appear like seal rings. Then we find cells with one or more offsets, and of an accordingly varying aspect. The third kind of cells described by *Iwanoff* contain light vesicles, which are said to be filled with a fluid, and are perhaps, identical with those containing vacuolæ. *Lieber* and *Kuehn* saw minute granules taken up by these cells, in molecular motion. These cells, furthermore, have been considered as producing the mucoid tissue of the vitreous body, and have accordingly been called physaliphora.

With regard to the nature of all these cell forms, I must agree with *Schwalbe*, who declares them to be lymph cells, that is, wandering cells coming from the membranes surrounding the vitreous body.

2. *Pathological Conditions.*

The question whether the vitreous body can become inflamed, independent of an inflammatory process in any of the surrounding membranes, has of late been frequently discussed. Since the vitreous body has neither blood-vessels nor cells of its own, we are justified, it seems, in denying *a priori*, the possibility of such an independent inflammation. Experiments made in order to solve the question, have led to the same result, since it is simply impossible to bring a foreign substance into the vitreous body with the intention of there creating an inflammation, without piercing other membranes of the eye ball, which can thus become inflamed. The best conditions for such experiments would be found in an eye, from which the crystalline lens had been removed, while the posterior lens-capsule remained intact, by bringing the foreign substance into the eye ball through cornea and lens-capsule. *Schmitt-Rimpler* has used such eyes for his experiments. But even in these eyes the hyalitis, caused by the experiment, does not prove the possibility of an independent inflammation of the vitreous body. *Pagenstecher* has, furthermore, directly observed by experiments, that the cells found in the vitreous body thus artificially irritated, come from the surrounding membranes.

I agree therefore with those authors, who deny the possibility of an independent inflammation of the vitreous body, and can only acknowledge the existence of secondary hyalitis. As we find in the contents of the synovia of a joint the results of a serous, fibrinous or purulent inflammation of this membrane, so we find in the vitreous body the products of the inflammatory processes of the surrounding membranes. These latter may, however, show a different form of inflammation from the one found in the vitreous body, as the cells when once exuded into the latter have ample space for further changes.

A. Liquefaction of the Vitreous Body (Synchisis).

Chronic affections of the uveal tract may produce a change in the consistency of the vitreous body, which finally leads to its complete liquefaction.

Von Wecker states that this liquefaction is caused by a large number of cells which immigrate into the vitreous body. This appears, however, not to be the case, as the immense number of cells found in the vitreous body in a case of purulent hyalitis do not cause synchisis. Moreover, he explains the opacities, clinically observed in such a liquefied vitreous body, by these cells.

We sometimes find in the liquefied vitreous crystals of cholesterine, and then the disease is clinically styled synechisis scintillans. Recently *Poncet* also found crystals of tyrosine and phosphates in a case of synchisis scintillans.

B. Plastic Hyalitis.

When describing the conditions which exist during the inflammation of the ciliary body and especially the formation of cyclitic membranes, we had to mention plastic hyalitis in the fossa patellaris which helps considerably in the formation of these structures.

We find at first a larger number of round-cells immigrating into the vitreous body which then appear to lie chiefly behind the lens, often embedded in a fibrinous coagulum, which gradually go over into spindle-cells and lead to the formation of a tough connective-tissue with new-formed blood-vessels.

The same process is observed, if a foreign body has pierced the vitreous. The immigrated cells then chiefly lie along the wound canal, and again are transformed into connective-tissue. I possess a specimen of an eye, injured by a piece of a gun cap which perforated the cornea, iris, lens and vitreous body before becoming retained in the sclerotic, choroid and retina at the opposite side of the eye ball. In spite of the ensuing purulent iritis and cyclitis, the inflammation in the vitreous body remained confined to the wound canal, and led to the formation of a band of tough connective-tissue running from the place of its entrance to the place where the foreign body became embedded in the sclerotic.

Such a new-formation of connective-tissue in the vitreous body is also seen after hæmorrhages into its structure. We then generally find a small amount of fibrine filled with round-cells and surrounded by the red blood-corpuscles. Gradually this fibrine is changed into connective-tissue, in the formation of which the red blood-corpuscles also seem to take an active part as they entirely disappear.

We had, furthermore, occasion to mention plastic hyalitis, occasioned by affections of the retina and optic nerve. I mean here the new-formation of connective-tissue in the excavated optic papilla, and the membrane like new-formations upon the inner surface of the inflamed retina. In these cases the plastic hyalitis only concerns the outer layers of the vitreous body.

If such membranous new-formations do not adhere to the retina, they may by their retraction lead to detachment of the vitreous body, in which the substance of the latter becomes naturally condensed. We find this detachment, as has first been made known by *Iwanoff*, in a number of pathological, especially injured eye balls, and most frequently when a foreign body has become encapsuled in the vitreous.

Von Wecker mentions an observation made by *Poncet*, which proves that the connective-tissue in the posterior parts of the vitreous body too, can be ossified. The formation of osseous tissue in cyclitic membranes has been mentioned above.

The blood-vessels found in the connective-tissue which is formed in the vitreous body, come from the ciliary body, the retina or the optic nerve.

The vitreous body may also become detached by fluids which are found to lie between it and the retina, and this mode of detachment seems to be caused more by chemical than by mechanical influences. If this were not the case, the fluid would certainly be taken up by the vitreous body, and the detachment thus heal.

C. Purulent Hyalitis.

After injuries, and in the course of a purulent inflammation of the uveal tract or during purulent panophthalmitis we may find purulent hyalitis, which is characterized by the presence of an immense number of cells in the vitreous body. Their number may be so large that it is hardly possible to see anything but cells. The latter have all sorts of shapes, and frequently two or more nuclei. They have sometimes very long thin offsets, which appear like a network of fibrillæ.

This condition may lead to perforation of the eye ball or it may become chronic and lead to the formation of connective-tissue, which is one of the chief factors from which the shrinking of the eye ball, clinically called phthisis bulbi results.

In rare cases this formation of connective-tissue is very quickly accomplished, and concerns the whole of the vitreous body and may lead to the incorrect diagnosis of introcular tumor. It may furthermore make the eye ball as hard as in glaucoma, and when shrinking produce again phthisis bulbi.

Anatomically we can speak of phthisis bulbi only, when the vitreous body has thus been changed, and we must make a more distinct separation between anterior phthisis and phthisis bulbi, than this is usually done by clinicists.

The Zonula Zinnii.

1. *Normal Conditions.*

In the region of the ora serrata, a number of well contoured, light and tough fibres are seen to spring from the vitreous body, of which they are a part, as *J. Arnold* has proven. They lie at first upon the retinal layer of the ciliary body, and follow all its windings up to the most anterior portion of that body, From there they are bent inward and pass on to the anterior and posterior lens-capsule ; some of them return to the vitreous body. They have therefore like the ciliary body a *pars plicata* and a *pars non-plicata.* These fibres which hold the crystalline-lens in position are called zonula zinnii (ligamentum suspensorium lentis, zonula ciliaris). They are arranged in bundles by a very fine and easily destroyed homogeneous substance, after they have bent inward from the ciliary body. According to *J. Arnold*, we find besides these fibres, which run in a meridional direction, a number which after having run a short time in this direction, go over into an equatorial one.

Some authors have seen a transverse striation on these fibres, and therefore considered them to be of a character muscular Cells sometimes found between them, are wandering (lymphatic) cells.

Where the zonula fibres are merged into the lens-capsule, this latter appears thickened.

2. *Pathological Conditions.*

Pathological changes in the tissue of the vitreous body must needs influence the condition of the fibres of the zonula *Zinnii.* There have, however, but few pathological changes of these fibres been observed. *Becker* states that they may become thin and atrophic, or thickened and granular.

When the fibres of the zonula have been severed, they appear wavy like elastic fibres.

THE END.

INDEX.